Rhianna

Amanda L.V. Shalaby

CRIMSON
ROMANCE
Avon, Massachusetts

This edition published by
Crimson Romance
an imprint of F+W Media, Inc.
10151 Carver Road, Suite 200
Blue Ash, Ohio 45242

www.crimsonromance.com

ISBN 10: 1-4405-5153-7
ISBN 13: 978-1-4405-5153-6
eISBN 10: 1-4405-5133-2
eISBN 13: 978-1-4405-5133-8

Dedication

FOR MY GRANDMOTHER, CATHERINE M. FISHER, WITHOUT WHOSE VISION OF A RED-HEADED ENGLISH GIRL STANDING BEFORE A FIREPLACE IN A WHITE, SATIN GOWN AND SATIN SLIPPERS THIS STORY WOULD NOT EXIST.

FOR MY MOTHER, DEBORAH L. VAIDEN, WHOSE WEALTH OF KNOWLEDGE OF ALL THINGS ENGLISH AND LOVE OF READING PROVED INVALUABLE.

FOR BERRY, WHO SAT DEVOTEDLY AT MY SIDE.

Prologue

The sound of pounding horse hooves brought Mauvreen from her midwife duties, down to the first floor of the hunting lodge. She quickly answered a frantic knock at the door, where she met familiar, anxious eyes.

"Where is she?"

"Upstairs," Mauvreen said, urging him inside and closing the door behind him.

"I got here as fast as I could from London. How—?"

"She has been thirty-eight hours in labor."

His hurried breathing stopped. *Thirty-eight?*

"And?"

Mauvreen shook her head. "Soon. Come with me."

She led him quickly up the wooden stairs and down the hall that led to Hallie's bedroom. Mauvreen clutched her chest as a scream echoed through the cabin—the bone-piercing cry of a woman in the final stages of a difficult childbirth.

"My God, *Hallie* . . ."

Pushing past Mauvreen, the father-to-be bounded toward the bedroom. He was on his knees beside the bed before Mauvreen reached the threshold, one hand cupping the crown of Hallie's head, the other clutching her hand. He appeared oblivious—or willfully blind—to the blood-soaked sheets beneath her.

Hallie turned her face to him and attempted a smile through the pain. She was too drained.

"My love."

"I'm here."

She drew a shallow breath. "It won't be long now. I can feel it."

Brushing away the sweat of her forehead, he nodded reassuringly.

"Yes, it shall all be over soon, darling." Turning abruptly to Mauvreen, he asked, "Do we not have forceps?"

Mauvreen, fighting her greatest fears to remain outwardly calm, examined Hallie's progress with steady hands.

"No, but we are close. Focus, Hallie."

The lovers' eyes met again.

"I wanted to be here sooner. There was no carriage or beast that could move quickly enough."

"Hush, my love," she said. "The baby has waited for you."

Another contraction brought a powerful cry. Hallie threw her head back into her pillow as she arched her spine. Her fingers turned white around her lover's hand, matching the shade of her cheeks, the color drained from her sweet, young face many hours since.

"Push, Hallie."

The contraction passed. Mauvreen ran a wet cloth along the insides of Hallie's legs. It was a fruitless effort. The blood continued all the more as the baby drew closer.

"Come along now, little one," Mauvreen said, as another contraction kicked in. "Ah! There you are."

A head appeared. A continuous, blood-curdling scream sounded. And then, moments later, the softer cry of a newborn infant filled the air.

"A girl," Mauvreen announced.

Hallie, who had fallen limp into the folds of bedsheets around her, forced her eyes open at this announcement and locked them on the baby as she caught her breath. Even as her lover kept his eyes on *her*, from that moment on it was clear Hallie saw only her daughter.

Mauvreen worked furiously to cut the cord, rinse the baby, and hand her to her mother. Wrapped in a blanket crocheted for her by Hallie, the little girl was placed swiftly beside her.

"Oh! She's lovely," Hallie said, her voice barely a whisper. "The most beautiful thing I've ever beheld."

Her lover helped position the baby more securely in her exhausted arms.

"Beautiful," he said, "like her mother."

Meanwhile, Mauvreen collapsed into a scroll-backed leather chair in the corner of the room. Its angle was blessedly away from Hallie's line of vision and it was there Mauvreen fought her tears.

She allowed the small family a quiet moment together before catching the father's eyes. "May I see you a moment?"

Her look conveyed the urgency of this request. Kissing both his girls on their foreheads, he prepared to oblige.

"I'll be right back," he said, and rose to follow Mauvreen into the hallway.

Hallie seemed hardly to notice. She never lifted her gaze from the new life she held beside her.

Closing the door softly behind them, Mauvreen rested her hand on the father's arm. "Do you understand," she began gently, "Hallie is hemorrhaging?"

He met her gaze with a blank stare, followed by a look of sudden understanding. "Dear God—what are you saying?"

Mauvreen spoke slowly and deliberately. "There isn't much time left."

She worked hard to compose herself, wiping away tears and resisting their multiplication, while he braced himself against the wall with an extended hand.

"How much?" he pressed.

"There is no saying." She added delicately, "Make the most of what you have."

He raised his fingers to his temple, as if it would force her words to sink in. "I should not have left her during this time."

She tightened her grip on him. "Whether you were here or there would not have made any difference."

"I doubt I'll ever accept that." His eyes widened suddenly. "And the child?"

"She will be fine, I'm certain of it."

The shadows that fell over his face could not hide its severe expression. "She can never know the truth—it would ruin her. I need to know I can trust you on that."

"Hallie is as much family to me as she is to you. Whatever you decide to do with the baby, you can trust me to help in any way I can. You have my word."

Taking a deep breath, he attempted to collect himself. As he prepared to reenter the bedroom, he took her hand in his. "Mauvreen, I know you have done more for Hallie than any doctor ever could. And I thank you."

Mauvreen shot him an appreciative gaze before he returned to his place beside the bed. She followed silently behind him, pulling fresh bedsheets and blankets from a corner dresser and placing them beside the bed.

The new mother appeared deliriously happy, her eyes and her smile bright as he leaned over her.

"Hallie."

"My love," she said, her daughter grasping her forefinger with all five of her own.

"I love you."

Her eyes flickered to his. It was clear that there was nothing he knew that she did not.

"And I you." Resting her hand on his, she said, "You must do something for me."

Holding a damp cloth to her forehead and wiping away a few stray hairs, he promised, "Anything."

Her smile widened. "I have a name for her."

Chapter One

Manoir Vallière, France, 1832

Ordinarily, it would have been a predictable morning at the estate. The autumn air was crisp and the sky cloudless as the girls and their horses enjoyed an early trot along the property's meadows and grassland. Neither could have had any knowledge of the peculiar guest who was shortly to arrive at the *manoir*, nor of the events that his visit would inspire.

On this morning, Rhianna Braden reflected on her life as she rode through the fields alongside her companion, Soleil Vallière. Perhaps it was the want of conversation between them that led to this rapt musing, though such thoughts had been a frequent pastime as of late. Still, she was surprised when a vivid girlhood memory came suddenly upon her.

"They mean to send me away!" she heard her young voice exclaim.

It was now ten years since she had been sent to Madame Chandelle's School for Girls at the tender age of nine, but she recalled her cries as clearly as when she first spoke them.

"Who means to send you away?"

The voice was soothing, its owner affectionate. Rhianna often still thought of her—her only friend in England. The person whose acquaintance she could never admit to having, their precious few visits shrouded in secrecy. Worst of all, it was impossible to write to this person, hence, all communication had long since been cut off.

"Father and mother."

The words still stung after all these years. At the time she spoke them, her cheeks were moist and her eyes misty—Rhianna could almost feel the dampness on her skin now, before she pushed the memory away.

Of course, if she had only known then what a positive change her move to France would be, she would have spared herself the hot tears that soaked her childhood pillow. Now, skilled in all the accomplishments of young womanhood and residing in the Vallière home as one of the family, Rhianna wondered at this decade of transition from an English curate's daughter to a teacher at Madame Chandelle's to working as a companion to Soleil.

Indeed, at nineteen, her days were consumed with the Vallières and their activities. The bond that developed among them was, from the beginning, immediate and mutual—a bond Rhianna did not think possible to exist in a family. She recalled the first time her own parents had rejected a visit from her how the Vallières demonstrated their kindness by taking her into their home; Rhianna hoped always to reflect the generosity they continued to show throughout her years of acquaintance with them.

Their silence continued until the girls reached the easternmost plateau of the grounds. It was a favorite lookout place of theirs and, as on all mornings in this particular spot, a breathtaking scene lay before them. All the valleys of the neighboring properties came into view, draped in golden sunlight. Acres upon acres of flourishing, untamed land met them, accented in beaming rays of early morning light and outlined by sharply peaked mountains against the distant horizon. Never was there a more splendid place to fully immerse oneself in the deepest of contemplation, and it was here that the two girls reined in their horses.

After a moment's pause, Soleil's meditations were broken and she turned to Rhianna with an anxious look.

"What were your impressions of Count Armand Deveraux last night, Rhianna? You know how I trust your judgment and I am positively desperate for your opinion. I seem to be remarkably well aware of what my own is, but I fear my mind is clouded."

Rhianna tugged on the reins to ease her steed that, at the sight of a rabbit, had become restless. She could not suppress a smile.

"Certainly, his good qualities cannot be doubted," Rhianna observed. "From what time we spent with him—though not opportunity enough to perceive the most intimate details of his character—I managed to form a very high opinion of him. And he seemed very much to fancy you."

Soleil's dimples deepened in her cheeks. "We may have an opportunity of being in his acquaintance again in a few days' time. Will you do me the favor of paying particular attention to his disposition? I am certain to be blinded the moment I am in his presence!"

Rhianna promised to do as much, and added, "From his sweetness alone, one would imagine his person could only improve upon further acquaintance." Brushing the horse's mane with her fingers to further calm him, Rhianna concluded, "I confess, too, his appearance was very agreeable, very striking. His voice, expression, countenance—I cannot say I have before met a man whom I would deem so worthy of consideration for my dearest friend." Soleil smiled broadly, and Rhianna added, "Of course, if you were to marry, I don't know what I would do with myself!"

"Rhianna," Soleil quickly reflected, "you must know I am not the only one with such possibilities in my future. Each passing day I anticipate a confession from you." When Rhianna offered a perplexed look, Soleil more daringly questioned, "Has he not *yet* expressed his feelings?"

Rhianna was left no choice but to affirm her puzzlement. "I cannot think who you mean, Soleil."

Leaning closer, as though she might be overheard, Soleil hinted, "Someone with whom we are both most intimately acquainted."

Rhianna spoke the thoughts that came to her mind. "Surely, you cannot mean Philippe."

Her friend's sudden blush betrayed her thoughts.

"Soleil, you are quite imaginative, I declare!" Rhianna cried. "He views me in the same manner in which he views you, as his sister. There can be no deeper feelings on his account."

Soleil insisted otherwise. "On my word, Rhianna, Philippe is quite in love with you and has been, you may be assured, since the day you entered into our very house."

"I cannot believe so positively absurd a notion!"

"And, pray, where is the absurdity in it? Do you find my brother so lacking in sense as to *not* fall in love with a girl so learned and handsome as the one I see before me?"

Rhianna could barely find words, as Soleil insisted her red curls and green eyes had quite done him in.

"In all seriousness, Soleil, why would a man who could have his pick of all the loveliest and wealthiest women in France ever consider the daughter of an English *curate*? It's preposterous!"

"Did you not see his expression as he danced with you last night? Mind you, it is the same expression he always has when he dances with you. You put him into quite a stupor!"

"If Philippe had any such expression, it was most certainly due to the wine," she returned, with a laugh.

Thus, Rhianna made it apparent that no persuasion, no matter how convincing, could influence her to believe that Philippe Vallière was in love with her and Soleil pursued it little further.

With these final reflections, the girls returned their attention to the landscape before making their way back toward the stables.

*

Had Soleil not been so excessively tired from the previous night's dance—not to mention the sleeplessness that resulted from meeting a handsome gentleman—she would have accompanied Rhianna on her walk through the garden. As it was, Soleil bid *adieu* to her companion at the stables and entered the manor house.

Rhianna, resolved to enjoy the morning air a while longer, wandered along under sapphire skies in peaceful intimacy with the nature surrounding her. Leisurely, she strolled among the flowers, breathing in their pleasant fragrances. There was evidence of perfection in every turn and Rhianna felt, as she often did, that walking through this garden was much like walking through a painting—a painting where no leaf had gone astray and no flower wanted a petal. Perhaps, she mused, the gardens of Kingsley Manor imitated a similar design . . .

As she twirled the leaf of a rhododendron bush between her fingers, a mental image of the house brought a smile to her face. Kingsley Manor, the great manor house that sat atop the hill beside her old English cottage, the very staple of her girlhood dreams of petticoats and pearls. She had dreams of it still.

Thus transported, Rhianna recalled a girlhood conversation with a young neighbor, Brenna:

"Just once, Brenna, I would like to walk up a Kingsley Manor staircase or to dance in its ballroom. Just once, I would like to have a necklace with matching earrings and gloves for my gown."

"That would be lovely," Brenna replied, wistfully. *"And perhaps, too, some handsome fellow would ask you to dance."*

When she caught sight of Philippe Vallière entering the garden from the opposite side, her reminiscences came to an end.

"Philippe." She smiled widely at the sight of him. "What brings you to the garden this morning?"

His lips curled in response. "I cannot see how it was to be avoided, on such a day."

"Well, you must have read my thoughts," she declared, as Philippe approached her. "I was only just this moment feeling the ache of having no one to share this inspiration with. The garden is so enchanting."

"Unquestionably, it is that," he asserted, his manner distracted. "There is something about it today that makes it more so than usual."

Unaware of any hidden implications, Rhianna readily agreed.

Seeming at once to forget the garden, Philippe went on, "I am glad of finding you. Indeed, I have searched for you all morning."

"Have you?"

"Yes. Rhianna, I must speak with you on a subject that has consumed me as of late."

Not his words only, but also the manner in which he spoke them caught her attention acutely. All fascination with the garden was lost as her eyes met his and she beheld in them the agitation of his emotions. Philippe appeared to be in a state so ill at ease that she was certain she had never seen him thus in their ten years' acquaintance.

"It is of the utmost importance," he added.

Rhianna recalled her earlier conversation with Soleil, but dismissed it at once, unable to conceive he was, in fact, or would ever, head toward the delicate subject of love.

"I can see that it is," she replied with care. "Philippe, I have not before seen you so distressed. Pray, do not leave me in wonder."

"You must not, Rhianna, mistake my anxiousness for distress. My affliction is one of joyful anticipation. And you alone can relieve me of my restlessness, allay me from this malady."

Rhianna was earnest in her concern. "Philippe, I have not the privilege of understanding you . . ."

"No, indeed, you do not, for I have been too concealing in my behavior. Repeatedly have I asked wherefore? To what end should I suppress it? For years have I kept silent, my soul restrained and inwardly anguished while awaiting the sensible and perfect moment—but no more! My secret shall be masked no longer. For my own sanity it cannot!"

His meaning could no longer be mistaken. These opening words produced a shock in Rhianna, for they were beyond everything she could have supposed. She stood silent as he took her hands in his and continued with his declaration, his unrestrained passion in presenting it rendering her wordless.

"It has been said the gift of a rosebud is considered a confession of love. I should like to give to you all the rosebuds of this garden—nay, those of all the gardens in France! Tell me your heart does share mine's affections, that your soul shares mine's desires. I treasure you, my dear Rhianna, and I want to treasure you always. Grant me the permission to do so and cease this torment!"

No sooner had he avowed this last to her than a servant came racing toward them from the house. Once within audible distance, the servant exclaimed his winded announcement.

"Count Vallière, Miss Braden! I beg your pardon, but there is a guest arrived only a few moments ago. He comes from England for you, Miss Braden, and requests to speak with you on a matter of great importance! Marquis Vallière is with him and begs you to come directly."

The awkward interruption drained all color from Philippe's complexion, while Rhianna's cheeks flushed pink with embarrassment. After a weak recovery, Philippe recognized the need to put aside his proposal.

"Where are they?" he called out to the servant.

Rhianna was grateful for his response, for she was not yet lucid enough to form words of any audible quality. First, Philippe's declarations and, now, a mysterious visitor from England! She decided it imperative that she focus only on taking in each breath.

"The drawing room," the servant responded, with his first look of curiosity at the scene before him.

Philippe lowered his eyes to the hands he yet held and seemed unwilling to release them.

"You must go," he stated with chagrin.

Feeling severely for him and how his proposal had been so critically disrupted, she hardly knew how to respond, either to him or to the servant.

"Philippe . . ." His name was all she could manage and, yet, it said everything to him.

"Come," said he, with grand composure, "we shall *both* go."

There could be no other option. They withdrew from the garden and hastened toward the house.

*

His arrival was early in the day and unannounced, but Guilford, Lord Kingsley, received a warm reception to the Vallière home. A strikingly tall man, with a broad stature and a generally pleasing appearance, he entered the Vallières' drawing room with little time for social graces. With a brief introduction and hurried civilities, he explained his visit from England to Marquis and Marquise Vallière.

"I hope you will forgive the discourtesy," he expressed. "It is unfortunate that we must meet in this manner, but the tidings I bring are rather urgent."

Even under such circumstances, Lord Kingsley had a composed way about him. His calm, gentle manner recommended him to Marquis Vallière who, although characteristically cautious and fittingly concerned, felt quickly at ease with this unknown traveler.

"Please, will you not have a seat?" insisted the somewhat rounder, though in no way displeasingly shaped Marquis Vallière. Turning to his butler, he instructed, "Belmont, do bring our guest some refreshments."

"I thank you for your kind hospitality, Marquis Vallière," Lord Kingsley replied somberly. "However, I feel I cannot rest until I have carried out the purpose of my visit. I bring a message to Miss Rhianna Braden. It is my understanding that it is here, in your excellent care, that I may find her."

Marquis Vallière was excessively protective of his children and, as he had for the last decade considered Rhianna as one of them, his first reaction to this comment was guarded.

"Of course," he responded, with a thoughtful nod. "I imagine this message is from someone of close connection to her."

"It is. I have personally been well acquainted with Miss Braden's father for many years and, in fact, bestowed him with the benefice at Thornton Church where Miss Braden lived prior to her schooling at Madame Chandelle's School for Girls."

"Ah! I see," he declared, his investigation nearly complete and his inquiring mind all but satisfied. "And I trust her father is well?"

Lord Kingsley hesitated before answering, "It is of Mr. and Mrs. Braden that my message refers. I am afraid it is not good news and, if it is not an unreasonable request, it is my hope that it be related first to Miss Braden."

"Oh dear," Marquise Vallière declared, speaking for the first time since their introduction. She wrung her hands together.

Marquise Vallière was a petite, slender woman whose exquisite fashion and irreproachable character were eclipsed only by her common sense.

"I do not believe Rhianna and Soleil have returned yet from their riding," she told her husband.

As she spoke her words, Soleil entered the room. Belmont closed the double doors behind her.

"What is it, Mother? You look troubled."

Soleil, noting the intensity in the air, turned to the unacknowledged guest. Marquis Vallière hurriedly introduced him.

"My dear, this is Lord Kingsley of Thornton, England. He is the friend and patron of Rhianna's father and wishes to speak with her *tout de suite.*"

Stationed beside her mother, and at once afflicted, she offered, "Rhianna had mentioned going for a walk in the garden. To my knowledge, she is yet there."

A servant was dispatched to find her at once.

*

Neither Rhianna nor Philippe wasted a moment. As the doors were opened and the two entered the drawing room, Rhianna moved instinctively toward Marquis Vallière, a man she had for many years viewed with a deep, fatherly regard.

"What has happened?" she implored him.

"There you are, child," he received her. "Rhianna, we have a Lord Kingsley to see you."

At the mention of this name, Rhianna's heart fluttered so intensely that she was certain it could not endure another surprise in the same day. Could she have heard him correctly? Lord Kingsley, owner of her most beloved Thornton, England manor house?

"I beg your pardon?" she replied.

The tall man beside her bowed—the most graceful bow she had ever witnessed—and she pressed her hand to her chest as if to ease the palpitations. When his posture straightened, she curtseyed with equal elegance and he took a step toward her.

"It is a pleasure to make your acquaintance, Miss Braden," he began, his voice kind and mild. "My only wish is that it would have been under happier circumstances."

Rhianna wondered only briefly if her outward appearance revealed the fusion of emotions within. This was the man, the *face* of the man, who inhabited so many of her dreams that even ten years in France could not allay, the man who invited her to balls and greeted her at the gates on many a wakeful night, *the man who lived in Kingsley Manor.*

"I come to inform you of an occurrence which brings me great pain to relay. Forgive me, for I know I shall never find the appropriate manner with which to report it."

Marquis Vallière stepped forward. "Perhaps we should excuse ourselves."

He motioned to his wife and children to leave so that Lord Kingsley might carry out his obligation with confidentiality, but Rhianna awoke from her reflections in time to intercede.

"No, pray, do not leave. Whatever Lord Kingsley has to say, he may say it before us all. Indeed, I prefer you stay," she said, turning to Lord Kingsley, "if it is not objectionable to you, my lord."

Guilford Kingsley showed no disapproval. "If that is your wish, it is entirely at your discretion."

"Thank you. Please, proceed."

He nodded in accord, and said, "Though we have never had the privilege of meeting, Miss Braden, I have been a friend of your father for a great many years. Therefore, I have taken it upon myself to personally bring you a message which, in my opinion, cannot be given by way of written word."

For the second time this day, Rhianna received a shocking announcement: a carriage accident, which Mr. and Mrs. Braden had not survived.

"When did it happen?" Marquis Vallière delicately questioned, as Philippe and Soleil assisted Rhianna to the nearest seat.

"Three weeks past," Lord Kingsley declared. "I left almost as soon as it was made known to me. Miss Braden, allow me to be among the first to offer my deepest of sympathies."

"Thank you," she responded, her voice barely above a whisper.

"Belmont, please, some water," Marquise Vallière requested, as she and her two children surrounded Rhianna.

Condolences were offered by the others, but she hardly heard them. Water was soon given her, but she was hardly aware as she sipped from her glass. Philippe's hands held one of her own, but little did she feel it. Her mind accepted the knowledge imparted by Lord Kingsley that funeral services had been carried out, but beyond this her mind could not process.

Emotionally fatigued, Rhianna soon retired to her room, not to emerge for the rest of the day and night. There seclusion afforded her a chance to reflect, however deliriously, on the day's events.

*

The horses moved gracefully through tall, wrought-iron gates, blithely pulling their two-wheeled *barouche* toward the manor. Bathed in the light of a beaming, springtime sun, they danced past the hedgerows that grew along the property's enclosing stone wall and up the familiar cobblestone approach.

Breathlessly, their passenger gazed from her window, clinging to her reticule. The landscape was vast and impressive, populated with meticulously placed shrubbery, spring flowers in full bloom and, in the center of the lawn, an ornate, Grecian fountain spurting forth its sparkling waters. It was just enough to distract her until the *barouche* pulled up to the front of the great Kingsley Manor.

At long last, the horses pulled to a stop. The driver stepped down and opened the carriage door, offering his hand to assist her. Accepting it with one slender, lace-gloved hand, she, too, stepped down, lifting her parasol high above her red curls and porcelain skin. After smoothing out her muslin gown, she raised her eyes toward the portico before her. She blushed, as the enchanting lord of the manor himself appeared to greet her.

Removing his top hat, he approached with a bow, and said . . .

"I regret to inform you Mr. and Mrs. Braden did not survive."

Rhianna jerked upright to a sitting position, her heart racing and her palms sweaty. A glance to the far wall revealed the tracing of a moonlit *escritoire* that reminded her of where she was. The familiar dream had taken a turn for the worse.

Gradually she took control of her erratic breathing, as the bedroom that had become home the last few years seemed to wrap its arms around her. Some hours yet remained before the sun would rise, but though she was inclined to fall back into her bedcovers and pull the white linens up under her chin, she feared what surrendering to sleep would bring.

She decided to seek comfort from the one object that, as a child, brought her peace in a foreign land—the only piece of England she still had. With the house and those in it sleeping soundly around her, Rhianna swung her feet over the side of the bed, lit a taper, and carried it to her dressing table.

Taking a seat on the ivory, embroidered cushion mounted on a mahogany frame, she placed the taper before the mirror and opened one of the small drawers. Lifting the brooch in her fingers, she examined the gold trinket from all angles as she had many times before.

Of course, it was more than a familiar ornament. Rhianna was wholly intimate with it, knew every stone, every change of hue in each of the pearls, its oval center a window to the past. Indeed, as she examined the object—a going away present from her dear, mysterious English friend—she could still hear the sound of the impending carriage coming to take her away from the only world she had ever known.

Memories of the past held her captive for a time, but she at last returned the brooch to the drawer. Her home was here now, and despite the sadness that had loomed over Rhianna's young life, her broken heart had healed by rooting itself, not in England, but in France.

Suddenly, raising her eyes to her reflection in the mirror, she was at once startled to see the likeness of her nine-year-old self looking back at her. Rhianna leapt to her feet as the same fair skin, red curls, and green eyes met her, but with the appearance and innocence of her younger years.

And with a blink, that young girl's image was gone.

*

Lord Kingsley's intention to reserve a room at a nearby inn was at once overthrown by the Vallières. It was quickly settled that the two weeks he intended to remain in France would be spent with them at the *manoir*.

During the course of the next several days, Rhianna recovered enough to speak with Lord Kingsley at length about the accident. She was glad when, finally, she could express her appreciation for his coming to France. To her consternation, however, as the shock of her parents' death wore off, Rhianna discovered an unsettling truth: that other than said initial shock, she felt very little. This troubling find left her questioning her very humanness, and even many hours of meditation could not open her to forgive the coldness of her heart.

Despite a dark cloud of self-condemnation looming over her, Rhianna found speaking with Lord Kingsley a welcome respite. Always interested in the lives of those who resided in Kingsley Manor, she was eager to hear him speak of its mistress, Lydia—Lady Kingsley—and of their two children, Desmond and Audra. As the days continued to pass, Lord Kingsley transformed from the fictitious creature of her imagination to a real person—and a good-natured, sympathetic one at that. Rhianna soon hoped to learn from him, indeed, to emulate the apparent goodness in this man, who showed gracious attentiveness even to her own inconsequential account of life in France.

At dinner one evening, shortly after his arrival, Lord Kingsley made Rhianna an offer she could hardly refuse. Indeed, he told her it was an offer he always intended to make, but had hesitated for fear of overburdening her: If she wished, he would be glad to personally escort her back to Thornton, England. More than that, Guilford Kingsley completed his invitation by including a place to stay at his own Kingsley Manor.

"Kingsley Manor! Do I understand you correctly?" she asked across the table.

"For as long as you wish," he told her, as a servant offered Philippe a clean fork to replace the one he had dropped to the floor.

Rhianna had not been to Thornton since she was a nine-year-old girl. Moreover, she was not devoid of a desire to return once again, though she quickly reproached herself for having such narrow-minded reasons as seeing her place of birth and staying at Kingsley Manor. After all, there was the matter of cleaning out her parents' cottage to consider, though she was certain there would be nothing of sentimental value within. And, of course, as Lord Kingsley suggested, she may wish to pay her respects to the deceased.

"That is very generous," Marquis Vallière said, followed by his wife's echoing sentiments.

Soleil, the only one at the table who knew just how large an offer this was to Rhianna, mirrored her mother's feelings and caught her friend's hand under the table with an excited squeeze.

"Lord Kingsley, I hardly know what to say," Rhianna replied, setting her wineglass down on the table without taking a sip.

"You should seriously consider it," Marquis Vallière encouraged. "After all, we are not going anywhere."

"No, we are not," Philippe said.

Rhianna understood *his* meaning at once, and was, in fact, the only one to understand him. Neither she nor Philippe had discussed his interrupted proposal from that fateful morning with anyone, nor had he broached the subject again with her.

Collecting herself, Rhianna tried not to be dazzled by the idea of living at Kingsley Manor and considered her life in France. Here was her home, and besides the lure of the manor, what did Thornton hold for her?

"Lord Kingsley, I do hope you will give me some time to think it over," she said.

"Take all the time you need," he answered. "The option is there, if you wish to accept."

As the night wore on, Rhianna became increasingly aware that a fascination with returning to England was strong within her—not to mention the prospect of fulfilling her childhood dream of not only stepping foot in Kingsley Manor, but *living there.* Nevertheless, the notion of leaving France, where she had made both a home and a family, was a melancholy one. Moreover, there was Philippe's confession of love to consider . . .

But the prospect of marrying Philippe frightened her terribly—and is that what one ought to feel after receiving a proposal from an agreeable gentleman? Rhianna suspected not, and her suspicions grew stronger as Soleil's fascination with Armand grew daily. Of course, if she rejected Philippe, Rhianna could not help but wonder what she would do if Soleil were to marry. Under such circumstances, would she find reason to remain in France? Or, was marrying Philippe the only sensible option for a woman in her position? The Marquis and Marquise seemed to be very happy together; perhaps she could have something similar with Philippe. On the other hand, what could England possibly hold for her? And would she ever forgive herself if she did not go?

*

Marquise Vallière and Soleil had immediately seen to it that their dressmaker prepare the necessary mourning wardrobe for Rhianna, and on the day following Lord Kingsley's offer to accompany Rhianna to England, the first of three outfits was completed. Thus smothered in layers of black *crêpe*, Rhianna decided to debut her dreary new costume with a turn through the garden.

She was not there long when Lord Kingsley appeared. "Miss Braden, may I have a word?"

Always pleased to see him, the somber mood her clothing inspired quickly lifted at his arrival. "Good day, Lord Kingsley. Of course."

Guilford held his hands behind his back as he walked with her. The day was fine, as it had been the day Philippe professed his love. Rhianna was at once grateful that it was Lord Kingsley, and not Philippe, who accompanied her on her stroll.

"I believe you are aware that I bestowed Mr. Braden with the benefice at Thornton Church," he said to her.

To this common knowledge, Rhianna replied in the affirmative. "I am."

He paused before his next statement, but his countenance gave off a serious air. Rhianna got the distinct impression there was something more. As, in fact, there was.

"What you are no doubt unaware of," he said at last, clearing his throat, "is that I deeded it to him many years ago."

Rhianna stopped and turned to him. As she did so, her arms fell to her sides and her hands closed over folds of ebony fabric.

"I beg your pardon?"

Lord Kingsley supported his statement with a nod. "You are the sole heir, Miss Braden. The benefice is now under your control."

Rhianna realized suddenly that she was staring. Quickly returning her eyes to the path, she began to place one foot carefully in front of the other. He followed her.

"I hardly know what to say, Lord Kingsley."

"Then you have already fulfilled my request." As she turned to him yet again, he continued, "It is not public knowledge that such is the case. In fact, at the time the matter transpired, it was under the stipulation that it remain, for all intents and purposes, a private transaction. I had my own reasons for doing so, and I'm sure you will understand I cannot elaborate."

Rhianna mumbled something in agreement, though she hardly knew what.

"Miss Braden," Lord Kingsley went on, "obviously, no one could foresee the sad situation that has now befallen us. I must admit to you, though, I did not anticipate the matter of the benefice coming to light at this time."

He paused, and Rhianna felt the necessity of a response.

"I'm not entirely sure I comprehend you," she admitted.

"It is my wish," he told her, discreetly scanning the garden around them, "for the time being, that the general understanding continue to be that the benefice is Kingsley property. I am hoping that in placing this delicate situation in your confidence you might be willing to work with me." Lord Kingsley drew a long breath, and added, "I realize you would have no reason to grant this peculiar request of mine. Furthermore, you have not been of my acquaintance for more than a week . . ."

"Lord Kingsley," Rhianna said, incited by her clearer understanding, "please, say no more. We may not have known each other for very long, but I am forever indebted to you for overseeing my parents' funeral arrangements. Not only that, but your kindness in traveling to deliver the tragic news of their passing to me personally will not be forgotten. Whatever your reasons, it would seem to me the least I could do. In fact, I would be happy to oblige."

Rhianna saw him suddenly release the tension that had been in his shoulders and his arms relaxed at his sides. He smiled at her.

"Thank you, Miss Braden. It is . . . of great relief to me."

They walked on in silence as Rhianna considered the impact this would have on her decision of whether or not to leave France.

"I imagine, then," Rhianna said, as if thinking aloud, "I have no choice but to go to England."

"Well, that all depends," Lord Kingsley said, "on how involved you wish to be in selecting a new clergyman. The extent of your participation, of course, is entirely up to you."

"Lord Kingsley," Rhianna confessed, "I do not pretend to know the first thing about choosing an appropriate clergyman."

"I will be happy to make my recommendations to you, either in person or by post."

Rhianna's head swirled. This added an entirely new element to her situation, and not one that in any way simplified matters.

"Well, Lord Kingsley, it would seem I have quite a lot to think about and I suspect a bit of tea is in order."

"May I accompany you back to the house?"

Feeling a bit overcome by her thoughts, Rhianna was glad to take his arm and make her way with him back to the *manoir*. That she would have control over the benefice was of itself enough to fuel her recent insomnia, but Lord Kingsley's request for silence even more so. After all, what reasons could a man have to deed away property and then fear its discovery?

It would be difficult, but she resolved to curtail her mind's wandering until she was out of his presence.

*

Near the end of Lord Kingsley's two-week visit, the choice of whether to remain in France or return to England was still not made. The evening before Rhianna had to decide, she and Soleil politely stayed with the party after dinner for only as long as was socially necessary before excusing themselves to escape upstairs.

Soleil privately hoped she might persuade Rhianna to go to bed early. The latter had been up nearly every night since Lord Kingsley came and Soleil began to fear for her friend's health. But, as with all previous nights, she was unsuccessful. When it had grown late, Rhianna protested against Soleil's continued companionship, declaring it was unnecessary for both of them to lose sleep.

"As if I could go to my room and get a moment's sleep," Soleil professed. "I could hardly think of leaving your side while you are in this weakened state."

"I will be fine, Soleil, you really mustn't stay."

"You know the depth of my affection for you, Rhianna. I am going to stay in this room tonight and do not expect me to change my mind."

Soleil knew Rhianna had no energy to persist in urging her, and clearly it would be a fruitless venture. She smiled as Rhianna accepted with a sigh.

"I do not know how I am supposed to feel, Soleil," Rhianna declared, at length. "You know better than most that I never was close to my mother and father. If I return to England and visit their graves, it will be out of a sense of obligation only, to do what is right and honorable."

"Of course, we support any such endeavor."

"But I have no *attachment* to them, Soleil. That is the difficult thing. Of course, news such as this is shocking, and I still hardly believe it, but they did not love me, as you and your family have."

"You must not say such things," Soleil told her delicately. "I have no doubt they cared for you very much."

"If such was the case," Rhianna declared, with only a trace of the inner regret and heartache she had long suppressed, "they neither demonstrated it nor declared it."

To this, there was nothing to be said, for her words had been proven true in the many years of little correspondence. The few letters sent, always in her father's hand, bore no measure of feeling and, in ten years, not one visit was requested of her, nor performed on their part.

Soleil fell to the seat of the rosewood vanity, her body facing away from the mirror, her arms draped across the back of the chair. Without any convincingly positive response, she remained silent and watched with uneasiness as Rhianna sat curled before the great bay window of the room, gazing blankly into the moonlit countryside.

The hours passed and fatigue set in. With so much to meditate on, conversation continued intermittently. Soleil was glad amidst the tragedy to observe Rhianna's emotions had not crumbled beneath her. Rather, her demeanor was merely solemn, reflective.

But Soleil was yet unaware of a matter of particular significance.

The words that caused Soleil suspicion did not come until nearly twelve o'clock. They came subtly and were peculiar enough in character that one would naturally be inclined to reflect on them for meaning. Rhianna, drowsy and incoherent, spoke them aloud unwittingly, saying, "He would not wait for me."

All at once, Soleil had a sense that there was something more—an underlying element troubling her friend. She could not seem to place Rhianna's words in accordance with any subject that had distressed them as of late. After some time pondering this sentiment, she came to no sensible explanation.

"You must forgive my presumptuousness, Rhianna, but I must know," said Soleil, "is there something you have not told me? Indeed, I know you too well not to discern you have something else vexing your thoughts."

Rhianna turned to her somnolently. Soleil moved toward her and seated herself beside her friend on the sill. She said nothing, so as to allow her sisterly companion a moment to collect her thoughts.

"My dear Soleil," she began, "I should never have imagined you *not* to discern as much, and I confess I am grateful for it. I so wanted to tell you, yet I could not seem to find the words on my own. Even now, I can hardly begin."

Soleil, though anxious, refrained from interrupting and gave her a moment to continue with her delirious reflection.

"But I suppose it no longer matters," Rhianna sighed, "for I am to be in mourning for a whole *year.*"

Soleil held her breath, wondering at the implications, while Rhianna faded in and out of aberration.

"What no longer matters, Rhianna?" she implored.

"Why would Philippe ever want to wait an entire twelvemonth?"

The mention of her brother's name all but confirmed her suspicions.

"Do you mean to tell me," Soleil cried, with a start, "that *Philippe has proposed?*"

Her last words were uttered an octave higher than those at the start of her question and Soleil covered her own mouth at the realization of it. Simultaneously, Rhianna's full mental powers appeared to return and both women listened intently to the silence around them. Fortunately, the house remained silent.

"Yes," Rhianna replied at first. "No," she retracted suddenly. "That is, he *attempted* to before he was interrupted."

"Gracious God, when?"

"The morning after the dance, after you and I parted at the stables, Philippe met with me in the garden. It happened moments before Lord Kingsley's arrival."

Soleil was quite struck by this and considered Rhianna with great admiration for speaking of it with such fortitude.

"What awful timing, Philippe! Oh, Rhianna!"

"You were right all along! How could I not have known? It was all so obvious, you must wonder at my naïveté." Rhianna continued, "I can only imagine that he will now withdraw his offer."

"Oh, for shame, Rhianna! There is nothing to reconsider as far as *you* are concerned. I congratulate him on choosing so amiable a girl! As to withdrawing his offer, you misjudge him severely. I know my brother very well. He would not wish to detach himself because of your changed situation. Philippe is far too loyal. He will wait."

Another silent pause ensued, this one being longer than the last. Finally, Soleil asked the question which was to complete her understanding of the situation.

"Rhianna, forgive me," she began delicately, "but there is one more thing yet to ask, and do tell me, please, if I am being too curious." Rhianna gave her full attention, and Soleil inquired, "As to *your* feelings . . . regarding Philippe?"

She stopped, but that Rhianna understood her meaning was clear as her cheeks flushed with color.

"I do care for him, Soleil," she confessed, at length, "though I always felt my affection was of the most sisterly kind. But he is so good-hearted and generous to all, and he cares so strongly for the welfare of those dear to him. It is so contrary a demeanor to that of any I have come across in all my male acquaintances." She paused, before adding, "I think I do not deserve him."

"*That* is not true. But, do not imagine me to be excessively partial toward him," Soleil expressed with all honesty. "*We* shall be sisters with or without him, so if you do not share his feelings, do not hesitate to say so. I shall not be offended."

With a moment's further reflection, Rhianna said, "Although I have confessed nothing to him, Soleil, I believe I could very well love Philippe."

*

The following morning, despite much tossing and turning, and little sleep, Rhianna arose early, her decision made at last. Below, she could hear a stir in the morning room. The others, too, it seemed, had arisen early and were already downstairs. Dressing quietly, so as not to wake Soleil, she hurried to greet them.

As she entered the room, she was surprised to find that everyone was *not* already gathered there. Instead, she found only Philippe was up and about.

"Oh! Philippe," she declared, startled to find him standing by the window. He turned immediately toward the sound of her voice, as she said, "I have intruded on your solitude, forgive me."

She turned to withdraw from the room, but he stopped her.

"Not at all," he quickly returned. "Pray, do not leave. My solitude has, in fact, been dragging for some time now and I would be glad of your company."

Rhianna was certain it to be the most uncomfortable moment she had ever known. Ordinarily, she was never timid before Philippe. Indeed, she had always felt a sense of ease in his presence. But this morning was different. After all that had passed, she knew not how to conduct herself.

"Please, I beg you," he further entreated, taking some few steps in hesitant advancement toward her. "Stay."

At last, she moved to the window and stood beside him, as she would normally have done in this same circumstance, but resolved to keep her face inclined toward the window, her only retreat from the uneasy situation.

After a long moment overlooking the estate grounds where she and Soleil had last ridden two weeks prior, she commented, "While I am away, I shall remember the *manoir* just as it is today, the house and everything surrounding it bright and sunny."

With this confirmation of her decision to go to England, she felt Philippe's eyes upon her.

"Strange," he replied somberly, "how the most bright, sunny day could be so hideously drear."

A great sadness fell over her and her gaze blurred. As she allowed her fingers to play languidly with the curtain, a single tear slid down her cheek. Anxious to hide her emotion, she raised her hand to remove it, but Philippe interceded. Enclosing her fair hand in his, he eased her toward him and kissed the small tear away.

"I never expected that such a day would come when you would leave us," he told her, regaining control over his own emotions and shifting to his proper distance from her. "Nor did I imagine how intolerable it would be for me if you went away."

"Philippe, please, you must not say such things," she struggled. "It will make it more difficult for me to go." As she spoke, she could not raise her eyes to his.

"And what of me? Am I doomed to return to that cursed silence which has anguished me all these years?" He pleaded, "Let me speak, and find forgiveness in your soul, indeed, pity me, for if I do *not* speak, I will die within, broken of spirit and broken of heart. Rhianna, can you not feel how this house is already in despair with the pains of its loss?"

His words pained her deeply, as another tear fell, and then, another.

Philippe concluded his plea, saying, "My selfishness is overtaking me on this matter, but I know not how to hide my distress at your leaving. We need you here, Rhianna. Soleil needs you here. *I* need you here."

His straightforward manner, his unswerving resolve to discuss the only subject she was ill prepared to reflect on, caused Rhianna the greatest of consternation.

With effort, she declared, "You speak as though I am never to return."

Its effect was hardly that for which she hoped, as he replied, "And I venture to say you will not. As I stand here before you, I can see the future. You will go, and you will meet an Englishman, and you will fall in love . . ."

"Philippe!"

"Since we were children together," he continued, with vehemence, "I have had it in my heart that you would be my wife. Will you deny me of all hope? Deny me my only meaningful wish?"

Rhianna took a moment to collect her thoughts and emotions. "Surely, I need not remind you of my situation, Philippe. My connections are poor . . ."

"Your connections mean nothing," he cried, his own emotions overtaking him. "It would not change my feelings if you sold flowers on the streets of Paris. *Nothing* could ever change my feelings."

The two stood for a few moments in agonizing silence. Wishing only to escape from the morning room, Rhianna prayed there might appear an opportunity for release.

"Philippe," she told him, at last, "I dread to think of how I will get on without you all. But I feel it is my duty to pay my respects to my parents. Surely, you understand."

Philippe nodded. "Rhianna," he gently responded, a choking sound in his throat, "if that were all, then you not being a part of our lives for a time would be far more bearable. But I fear we are in danger of losing you for good."

This concept brought animation to Rhianna's person and she found courage enough to raise her eyes to meet his.

"What a notion! What reason could I possibly have to remain in Thornton once my obligation is finished? I have nothing holding me there, Philippe."

"What is it that holds you here, Rhianna?" he asked, his hand still wrapped around hers.

With this, she knew Philippe was hoping for some small confession on her part, but something held her back. She *did* love Philippe, she always had, but love has many forms. And, deep within her heart, did she not feel he deserved better than a curate's daughter? Though he would not admit it, as far as Philippe was concerned, it would be a poor match. Rhianna suspected that some time away from Manoir Vallière to think might be beneficial for them both. In the meantime, she resolved not to allow him the opportunity for his affections to be alleged further.

"*Everything* holds me here. France is my home," she declared. "It grieves me very much to go; it shall be sorely missed."

Philippe raised the back of her hand to his lips before releasing it.

"And you, my dear Rhianna, will be painfully missed in return."
He concluded, "You must come back to France. I will not hear of
it otherwise."

Voices were soon heard descending from the upstairs chambers.
To Rhianna's great relief, it was only moments before Marquis
Vallière, his wife, Soleil, and Lord Kingsley were all assembled
together with them, ending what was to be her last private
conversation with Philippe before her departure.

*

It was soon settled. Rhianna Braden would return to Thornton,
England and reside as a guest at Kingsley Manor. With her bags
quickly packed, everyone gathered together in front of the Vallière
home to see her off the very next morning.

Still overwhelmed with the developments of the last fortnight,
Rhianna, dressed in black bombazine, bid dreamlike farewells to her
surrogate family. The picture seemed an illusion as she took trancelike
steps toward a halted *barouche*, the door opened for her entry.

As the coachman pulled away, Soleil and Philippe were the last
to return to the house. In fact, Rhianna did not see them return,
for a hill obstructed her vision. But Philippe stood outside that
sad home long after Rhianna's carriage disappeared from sight.

Chapter Two

Guilford Kingsley was notably devoted to her comfort the whole of the trip, but it was a long, exhausting journey. Rhianna was glad for the quiet hours when she could reflect on recent events, though, at first, thoughts of Philippe and their last conversation tormented her with some regularity. As they drew closer to their destination, however, her musings shifted to that of her life before France, her childhood memories of England. Indeed, as their *barouche* traveled beneath a hazy English sky, farmers plowing their hawthorn-enveloped fields along the roads between the scattered towns of Essex, Rhianna had a strong sensation of being exactly where she ought to be.

As they neared the final stretch, both travelers were equally fatigued and eager to bid the carriage *adieu* in exchange for the amenity of a fireside. At last, the carriage turned onto a road that Rhianna knew well. She moved closer to the window as they drove past the old stone church and the little cottage where she had spent the first nine years of her life.

To her surprise, little had changed. The same cold stones decorated its outer walls and the same thin branches of an apple tree rattled against the glass of the cottage's southern windows. It only seemed smaller to her now, seen through the eyes of a grown woman.

At last, the horses picked up their pace and began their assent up the very hill which held at its peak, the house—Kingsley Manor—that inspired many a pleasant daydream to a child and, now also, to a young woman, who was never meant to experience the luxuries of aristocratic life.

The horses moved gracefully through tall, wrought-iron gates, blithely carrying their two-wheeled barouche toward the manor.

Bathed in the light of a beaming, springtime sun, they danced past the hedgerows that grew along the property's enclosing stone wall and up the familiar cobblestone approach.

Rhianna's dream came back to her, as colorful and vivid as ever. She could see herself, seated on the cottage stoop beside her friend, Brenna, gazing upward at Kingsley Manor, her imagination having run away with her.

Breathlessly, their passenger gazed from her window, clinging to her reticule. The landscape was vast and impressive, populated with meticulously placed shrubbery, spring flowers in full bloom and, in the center of the lawn, an ornate, Grecian fountain spurting forth its sparkling waters. It was just enough to distract her until the barouche pulled up to the front of the great Kingsley Manor.

At long last, the horses pulled to a stop. The driver stepped down and opened the carriage door, offering his hand to assist her. Accepting it with one slender, lace-gloved hand, she, too, stepped down, lifting her parasol high above her red curls and porcelain skin. After smoothing her muslin gown, she raised her eyes toward the portico before her. She blushed, as the enchanting lord of the manor himself appeared to greet her.

Of course, the experience did not perfectly resemble her dream. When she awoke from recalling it, she saw that the flowers were not in season and the dry fountains were not emitting any sparkling waters. Neither did the lord of the manor come out of the house to greet her—this last, however, was understandable, as he needed first to exit the *barouche*—and, though Rhianna was not so well-dressed as she would have liked and there was no lace-gloved hand to offer Lord Kingsley as she alighted the vehicle, the event itself was every bit as splendid as her heart could wish.

Situated in the middle of a monumental landscape of almost two thousand acres of park and woodland, Kingsley Manor stood with its more than one hundred rooms, hallways, and corridors. With an exterior constructed in the dramatic Baroque style, Kingsley Manor faced south, with two symmetrical wings on either side, everywhere exploding with fanciful shapes, pediments, and opulent decoration. As Rhianna stood before the center block portico, fatigue wrestled with her as she attempted to engage the finer details, but it could not best her resolve to soon know every brick, statue, and stone.

Their baggage was scarcely unloaded from the carriage when, from atop the portico, the front doors of the manor flung open and a girl of about twelve hastened down the stairs.

"Papa!" she cried, with open arms.

"Audra!" Lord Kingsley called, as he knelt and embraced her.

Felicity beaming from her expressive eyes, she explained, "I saw you from the window of the drawing room. Desmond and Mama are there."

"Are they?" he said, delighting in her youthful animation.

"Yes," she affirmed. "And you will never guess! Cousin Pierson also is with them."

This piece of news, he was clearly unprepared for. The change in Lord Kingsley's air was dramatic. His shoulders stiffened visibly and his expression hardened. He shot a glance toward Kingsley Manor that Rhianna imagined could turn the sky black.

Audra was not unaware of this and looked at him questioningly. "Papa?"

Her observation seemed to recover him, enough, at least, to better conceal his emotions.

"Well, we mustn't keep them waiting, shall we?" he replied. "Audra, I would like to introduce you to Miss Rhianna Braden." A synchronous curtsey followed, before he added, "You remember her father, Mr. Braden, who visited me while I was sick."

"I do remember him," Audra confirmed to her father. "He was a very dull man."

"Audra!" her father reprimanded. "Do you not know Mr. Braden passed away not two months ago?"

At this, she lowered her chin and looked up with a remorseful gaze.

"Forgive me, Miss Braden. Please accept my condolences." Rhianna nodded her acceptance of this apology, and Audra, addressing her further, added, "You seem nothing like him. I like *you* exceedingly well."

Rhianna could not help but be drawn to Audra's unaffected personality, despite her candid comments.

"You should know," Rhianna replied, with a grin, "I like *you* exceedingly well, also."

Audra curtseyed again with a wide smile. "I think we shall become the best of friends."

"Come," Lord Kingsley announced, as the servants gathered their bags, "it has been a long journey. Audra, why not lead the way inside?"

*

She dared not breathe. Everything about the entrance hall, from the white marble floor to the winding staircase, from the crystal chandelier to the various classical artifacts and columns was just as she had imagined it should be.

"Thank you, Henry," said Lord Kingsley to the doorman, his resounding voice awakening Rhianna with a start. "See to it that Miss Braden's things are placed in the lavender guest room."

These orders were immediately carried out. Meanwhile, Audra grasped Rhianna's hand in hers and led her eagerly to a set of double doors.

Another servant approached and addressed Lord Kingsley. "Whom may I say is arrived?"

"Miss Rhianna Braden, Alfred."

"Very good, sir."

His gloved hands reached for the doorknob, whose door Rhianna supposed led to the drawing room. Before she took her first steps inside, laughter issued forth from behind the doors and, to her surprise, it sounded as if there were only two persons, although she imagined there would be three. A man's laughter, in particular, stood out as an intimidating sort of roar and she wondered if this laugh belonged to the "Cousin Pierson" whose visit, from Lord Kingsley's reaction, was so unwelcomed. Rhianna drew a defensive breath as they prepared to meet with those inside.

Alfred entered and Audra followed with a bounce in her step, pulling Rhianna along with her into the drawing room. Her eyes quickly scanned the four walls, absorbing as much as possible of the feminine decor, French windows, built-in bookshelves, and relaxed, informal arrangement of furniture.

"Lord Kingsley, Miss Kingsley, and Miss Rhianna Braden," Alfred announced.

The party of two in the gold-and-blue-themed drawing room did little to ease Rhianna's discomfort, as it seemed the addition of the announced three brought their pleasures to a cease. Both the woman and the man seated before them appeared ill at ease, and they did not, at first, hide their sentiments well. Rhianna had the feeling of having intruded on their good time.

"Darling . . ."

The woman placed her drink on a table beside her and rose from her seat beside the fireplace, whose surround and central plaque were of a neoclassical design with fluted pilasters and marble inserts. The Kingsley coat of arms, featuring a white rose— the symbol of love and faith—was portrayed on the overmantel.

"Welcome home," she continued. "I see you have brought back with you a guest."

"I have." Without expression, Lord Kingsley added, "I confess, I was surprised to hear she is not the only one."

This last comment, in direct reference to Cousin Pierson, did much to cause uneasiness to the entire company.

"Well," the woman replied, "as you see, it is only Desmond and me."

Had Rhianna not been so conscious of the tension in the air, she might have imagined the woman's response rather smooth.

Introductions followed. The woman was presented as Lord Kingsley's wife, Lydia, and the man as the Kingsleys' only son, Desmond. Only Audra seemed sorry to see that Cousin Pierson had left, whereas Lydia and Desmond appeared indifferent and Lord Kingsley seemed irritated, as before.

Rhianna continued to feel intrusive, but her reception was one of graciousness. Despite the initial awkwardness, Lady Kingsley and Desmond recovered enough to prove even friendly. Sympathies for her losses were bestowed, refreshments offered, and attention was given to her comfort. Their meeting was not long, for the hour was late, and Rhianna was soon persuaded by Lord Kingsley to retire for the evening.

Even exhausted as she was, sleep, for a time, was out of the question. A friendly, young servant named Katie settled her into the so-called "lavender room," tended to the coal fire, and left before Rhianna could wrap her mind around where she was. But the following few hours of quiet and uninterrupted contemplation and exploration were not sufficient to allow the reality of her situation to sink in. The clock chimed two when, after thoroughly inspecting the bedchamber, from the canopied bed and mahogany storage pieces to the lavender wall tapestry and settees upholstered in silk-embroidered wool, Rhianna concluded that several weeks would not be enough to convince her of where she was, and she at last went to bed.

*

Rhianna had not been asleep long when she awoke to the sound of galloping horse hooves and rolling carriage wheels. With a glance toward the window, she wondered that anyone would be out in the dark of the early morning. Indeed, for what reason would someone be traveling during the predawn hours in what sounded like a panicked hurry?

Far too curious not to investigate, she arose from her bed and crossed the Persian rug to the windowsill. Pushing aside heavy, lavender drapes just enough to peek through, Rhianna could see the dim-glowing, swinging lanterns of a carriage as it raced away from the manor. Whoever its passenger was clearly had reason to be quick and was already some ways down the approach. Had Rhianna waited a moment longer, she would have missed the scene altogether.

Apparently, *someone* had reason to be out before daybreak. Her mind was at once awake and formulating theories. Her first thought was that there was some sort of emergency and Rhianna hoped no one was ill or worse. Tragedy had been no stranger to Rhianna as of late. Yet, something gave the impression that this was not an emergency, at least, not of that particular sort. Something about this event seemed . . . darker. She told herself it was the dead of night—not to mention her first night in a new place—that inclined her to think the occurrence more mysterious than it was in reality. But her attempts to be sensible failed and she returned to thoughts of schemes and intrigue.

The room was noticeably warm from the heat of the fire. Mindlessly, Rhianna reached to open the window. It opened an inch or so, before a hook latch prevented further movement. She sighed, as all manner of scandalous thoughts were broken and she had no choice but to give the window more attention than she wished. Using her fingers as her eyes in the dark, she ran them along the edge of the sash in search of the bolt.

To her surprise, she heard murmuring below.

Rhianna held her breath and listened. Whether they were men, women, or both, she could not decipher from their muffled voices; and though the full moon gave off sufficient light to the ground below, her view was obstructed. Only two shadows along the portico were visible.

Clink.

The latch bounced against the sill before falling to the ground two floors below. Rhianna jumped, hardly aware she had found the latch when it broke at her fingertips. With her hand pressed tightly against her chest, she heard the second *clink* as it hit the stone ground.

The voices silenced and the shadows disappeared. An eerie sensation overcame Rhianna and she feared that those very shadows might be climbing the wall after her. Absurdity, of course. Still, nothing seemed to quell the impression that she was much too near something that she was not intended to be near.

Rhianna eased away from the lavender curtains and cringed as she crossed the creaky floor to her bed. Had it been creaky before? She couldn't remember. Pulling the covers up to her neck, she listened for voices that never resurfaced and hoped that morning wasn't far off.

*

At breakfast, Lord Kingsley expressed his hope that Rhianna had passed a comfortable night in the lavender room and seemed very pleased to find it was so. Rhianna sensed no change in his manner or hint in him regarding the events of the early morning. No, even as Lydia Kingsley and Desmond's eyes seemed glued upon her at his inquest, Guilford Kingsley was unaltered and she continued to find herself at ease, at least, in *his* presence.

The morning room of Kingsley Manor was everything it ought to have been, its atmosphere the superlative example of leisure, ideal in all ways for breakfasts, writing, and reading. Rhianna took her time, enjoying every moment, as well as the vast selection of dishes that lay before her. Some she was not familiar with and gratefully she accepted occasional, whispered hints from Audra, who watched her intently, apparently aware of her every puzzlement.

The day was to afford a tour of Kingsley Manor. Lord Kingsley was happy to conduct it and Audra was equally happy to join them, offering her own commentary along the way. Neither, however, was as delighted as Rhianna, who could think of no greater joy than getting to know the geography of the house and committing to memory each and every minute detail. It was also no great disappointment that Lydia and Desmond Kingsley were otherwise engaged and would not be joining their small party.

Kingsley Manor, a thirty-bedroom mansion, required they set out early to see as much of it as the day would allow. Rhianna's experience thus far consisted of the great front hall, the drawing and morning rooms, and the stairs and hallway leading to her lavender chamber. Lord Kingsley began his tour with the principal rooms on the ground floor, starting with the dining room—large, tastefully decorated, and not overly ornate, with finely carved, wainscoted, oak-paneled walls, which even with its crimson tones and masculine artwork could do no wrong. Then they walked through the gallery, a grand, well-lit room on the east side of the manor, with a high ceiling and equally high windows. Although no portraits were hung beyond immediate family, the gallery housed some magnificent pieces of art. Rhianna could have spent considerable time leisurely walking that long room, and was sorry to leave it, even after spending more than an hour there.

Over the course of the day, they continued to move throughout the house and immediate grounds, viewing the formal garden at the back of the house, library, and billiard room. It was clear that not just one tour, but several additional tours would be required. Visits to the kitchen, brew house, and wine cellar, as well as the schoolroom, theater, and ballroom on the upper levels would be conducted in the near future.

Rhianna, although having seen enough in one day to keep sleep away indefinitely, looked forward to touring the rest of what was within Kingsley Manor's walls. But she also longed to see what lay beyond them, not the least of which included the conservatory, stables, dairy, and apple orchard. Until then, she allowed, a little private exploration would most certainly hold her over.

*

With only a short time to dress, Rhianna hurriedly extracted her best mourning attire from the hanging rail of the mahogany corner cabinet. Various emotions swirled within her, but the foremost of all was excitement.

When the hour struck, she exited the lavender room and headed for the dining room. To her surprise, she found Desmond Kingsley waiting for her on the balcony. A tall man of twenty-eight, Desmond's features were distinctly his mother's, with an aquiline nose that fit his narrow face, and skin unusually rough for his age and station. Rhianna couldn't say she particularly disliked him, but something about him made her uncomfortable.

"I hope we did not wake you last night," he stated blandly.

There was no mistaking his meaning. With his words, Desmond Kingsley identified himself as one of last night's shadows and Rhianna felt her pulse quicken.

Before she could reply, he added, "My cousin, who has been staying with us as of late, is an early riser."

She made the connection to Pierson quickly. It seemed his departure from the manor had not happened as rapidly as it appeared the previous night, and no wonder. If he had been staying at the manor, and not merely visiting, he must have had bags to pack. Secretly, she wished she had caught a glimpse of the man who escaped in the early morning hours.

Smiling nervously, Rhianna said, "I am sorry I did not chance to meet him. Will he soon return?"

"It is difficult to say. His business was urgent, hence, the early departure. He can always be counted on to leave at a moment's notice."

"A lofty attribute, to be sure."

"To be sure," echoed Desmond, "so long as it does not interfere with the comfort and rest of others."

Anxious to end this conversation and be on her way, Rhianna authorized him not to worry. "I thank you for your concern, Lord Kingsley, but it is quite unnecessary, I assure you. My only, brief trouble last night was that of an overly warm fire—nothing an open window could not relieve. In all, my night was comfortably spent."

This seemed to satisfy him, but Rhianna could not help but feel his intention was to intimidate. Or was he simply concerned with the comfort of a guest? This question made her wonder if she could accuse him of the preceding motive. After all, Soleil had warned her many times of her overactive imagination.

"Are you on your way to dinner?" she asked.

"I will soon join you. Do you know the way?"

"I do."

"Very well, Miss Braden, I look forward to seeing you shortly."

Leaving this encounter perplexed, Rhianna chose to believe in Desmond's innocence and guided herself downstairs to the dining room. Her mind, however, filled with conjecture, was not ready to rest.

Guilford and Lydia Kingsley were already seated with Audra at the long, Chippendale table with its carved, cabriole legs. She was motioned to sit in a chair with a vase-shaped back splat and, though her tight corset made it difficult to sit and breathe at the same time, she took her place beside Audra. Her genuine compliments on the furniture unearthed the knowledge that it had belonged to Guilford's mother, and though Lydia seemed irritated at the mention of her, *he* was delighted at Rhianna's appreciation for the style. An inquiry into his mother's situation further revealed that she had passed, but Lydia's sour countenance deterred Rhianna from any additional pursuit of the subject.

Desmond soon after appeared and an elaborate dinner of several courses was served. The first consisted of two main dishes, venison and beef sirloin, accompanied by vegetable pudding, macaroni pie, preserve of olives and larded sweetbreads. It was a spread fit for royalty and appealing in both presentation and taste.

Still, Rhianna recoiled inwardly at dirtying so much of the Kingsley china as the entire company began the meal. This same dilemma tormented her a second time, as the next course of salmon and chicken fricassee, potatoes, almond pudding, and syllabub, bought a new set of china and crystal to sully.

With all the soups, side dishes, and pastries, Rhianna totaled twenty-five plates per course. All was perfection and, at the end of two hours, after consuming many delicacies, Rhianna was certain she could not look at another fruit tart for some time.

Conversation had been light and easy, led mostly by Guilford Kingsley, with occasional whispers from Audra, who apparently had been for some time deprived of a confidant and had many important things to communicate to Rhianna about her doll collection. Rhianna, a very willing listener, expressed her genuine interest and they quickly decided that a viewing of Audra's display was not only necessary, but should be expeditiously planned.

The rest of the evening passed uneventfully, as did the night. After dinner, Rhianna was invited to cards. She played for a time, though she looked very much forward to removing her corset, as well as escaping the company of Desmond, whose eyes seemed frequently upon her. Exhaustion was settling in from the full day and, as much as she wanted to savor every moment in Kingsley Manor, she took her exit at the earliest opportunity.

*

Early the following day, Rhianna expressed her wish to pay her respects to the departed. The *barouche* was immediately offered to her, though she politely declined. The day was turning out lovely and Rhianna preferred to walk, much to the alarm of Audra, who did not believe in taking any such physical pains to arrive anywhere. She urged Rhianna vehemently to take a horse, insisting that horseback riding could be equally good exercise as walking, as well as refreshing. But this was a solemn occasion that demanded reflection, and Rhianna considered nothing so given to meditation as walking. On such grounds, Audra allowed, albeit unwillingly, that walking might be permissible.

Rhianna also had veiled plans to make another visit—a visit to a place in which no *barouche* could accompany her. A certain friend had frequented her thoughts over the years. She could not help but wonder if that friend was still living and she was determined to find out as soon as possible.

After breakfast, Rhianna had a letter addressed to Soleil ready for the post. After handing it to Henry and informing a servant of the broken window lock in her room, she departed for the churchyard.

It had been ten years since she had stood before a grave. The last time, it was the grave of the previous owner of her beloved brooch. Now, Rhianna stood before the shared grave of her parents. The ground was still freshly shoveled over where the coffins had been laid and the inscription on their memorial stone was simple. Sheltered by sycamores and elms, the churchyard seemed a scene of peaceful dignity as Rhianna placed the flowers she had picked along the way.

When she cried, it was from the guilt of not crying over her parents' deaths. Looking to the heavens, she asked forgiveness for her dispassionate emotions. If only they could have but loved her, the way she wanted to love them. If only they had been but kind, she should have mourned them the way a daughter ought to mourn a father and a mother.

But they had not, and she could not. The black of her mourning clothes was all she could give them.

Soon, she found her mind dwelling on the Kingsleys, on the Vallières, on the smaller, unmarked grave beside her parents'—everything but what lay before her. And each time she caught her thoughts drifting, she chastised herself. Feelings of regret and blame quickly became overbearing. If their treatment toward her had been due, in some way, to an offense on her part, amends could never be made, nor could a new relationship ever be attained. These thoughts were enough to bring her already heavy spirits lower as she mourned what could never be.

*

Guided by the stream she followed as a child, Rhianna struggled to lift the heavy folds of her skirt above the wet ground. Even still, though she was cautious with her footing, there was no preventing the bottom of her dress from getting dirty. She hoped, when she returned later to Kingsley Manor, that she would be able to slip into her room to change before anyone noticed.

Traveling along the infrequently trodden, muddy path, Rhianna questioned the reliability of her memory of that dimly lit trail. Once the ivy-covered hunting lodge came into view, though, there was no mistaking it. With mixed feelings of relief and apprehension, Rhianna hastened to the lodge's door.

Looking around, she felt as though eyes were upon her. And though it was a sensation she had often felt here, Rhianna began to wonder why she had come. After all, even as a guest at Kingsley Manor, she had no permission to be *here*. As a child, perhaps she could have gotten away with such an intrusion but, as a young woman, was it not outright trespassing? She paused to listen, but heard no movement, aside that of a stiff breeze and an occasional birdsong.

She knocked.

There had been no communication between the two after Rhianna left for Madame Chandelle's School for Girls and, in those first moments after she'd rapped on the weather-worn, wooden door, Rhianna's mind raced with unanswered questions. Would anyone be able to answer them if her confidant no longer lived? And, who was this woman, who led so sheltered a life, hidden from the world? Would the mysteries that accompanied her, mysteries that Rhianna had so often dwelt upon, forever be concealed?

Perhaps she had no right to know, but that did not mean she did not wish to. It had become so very personal to Rhianna, almost as if their lives were fully connected with one another so that Rhianna *did* have a right, more so than anyone. This wonderful woman had especially provided a companionship to the young Rhianna, a maternal-like intimacy, at a time when she was in desperate need of it. Standing before the cherished lodge, Rhianna hoped that she had brought as much friendship to this woman in her lonely hours as Rhianna herself had enjoyed.

At last, all fears were dispelled. The door was opened and the long-lost confidant appeared. Rhianna expected a good deal of excitement, but no such reaction arose. Her appearance still very much resembled the woman Rhianna recalled. In her plain clothing, her braided hair wrapped into a large bun, she looked upon the younger woman instead with distinct bewilderment.

"Young woman, are you lost?" she asked with concern. "Do you need help?"

"You do not recognize me, Mauvreen?" Rhianna said with a smile, immediately recalling that although Mauvreen might appear the same, *she* certainly did not.

Whether it had been Rhianna's words, or her manner, it was all that need be said. The expected excitement then overcame Mauvreen. Rhianna could see it in her glassy eyes.

"Dear child!" she exclaimed, her hand pressed to her heart. "Ay, a child no more! Let me look at you—good heavens, I must look *up!*" After a moment of reflection, she implored, "Is it really you?" Rhianna could no sooner broaden her smile than Mauvreen embraced her. "Oh, but of course it is! I wonder that your red hair did not give it away instantly. Come in!"

A mysterious, middle-aged woman, Mauvreen seemed as much a figment of Rhianna's imagination as she always had. No one seemed to know she existed, and she had yet to give a clear explanation as to why she resided alone in the hunting lodge.

The lodge, too, seemed an invention of the mind, which had its own secrets, not the least of which was the tombstone for Haldana that sat just outside the kitchen window. And yet, this cabin, overgrown with ivy and situated in the most distant corner of the Kingsley property, was where she had first met Mauvreen, and it was here she had spent her happiest of days.

The natural inquiries immediately ensued of health and so on, and the two took their places by the fire as Mauvreen set a tray of tea on the table before them. Rhianna couldn't resist a glance toward Mauvreen's end table where a familiar drawing of a young woman sat encased in an elegant, silver frame. No matter how many times she had looked at it as a child, she never grew tired of it. The young woman, lovely in every respect, was holding a bouquet of roses. What stood out to Rhianna most was her gown—all that lace, all those ribbons! Rhianna wore that dress in her dreams on many a night.

"You always loved that drawing," Mauvreen said, casting a sideways glance as she poured the hot water.

Rhianna nodded. "I can't believe I'm here, Mauvreen. I thought I would never see you again."

"I must admit, I am more than surprised to see you so shortly after your return to England."

Taking the cup offered to her, Rhianna asked, "Did you already know of my return?" Mauvreen offered her a coy grin. "Your knowledge astounds me, Mauvreen! You must tell me how you hear such things."

As she spoke the words, Rhianna knew the ever-mysterious Mauvreen would offer her no such information.

"My child," she answered, "the trees whisper in these woods. One must learn to listen."

Aware, too, of her parents' deaths, Mauvreen did not hesitate to comment on the unfortunate events, and on this topic she was most comforting. Rhianna opened up to her even sooner than she expected regarding her own regrets, and Mauvreen was quick to soothe her. Rhianna was soon convinced that the distant relationship was what her parents had wished, and that a young girl in a foreign country could not be expected to maintain a one-sided connection.

A summary of the last ten years of Rhianna's life was requested and an abbreviated version of this happy tale she was glad to narrate. From the grandeur of her travels through London, to the steamship at the docks of Dover, to her first night at the gothic-styled Madame Chandelle's, to life with the Vallières, not a crucial detail was left omitted, no major experience wanting to be told. As should be expected, such a recount brought both amusement and seriousness. Humorous stories brought many laughs, whereas significant moments, such as Philippe's proposal, brought sobriety and thoughtfulness. Mauvreen was glad to know that the brooch she had given her had brought Rhianna happiness and comfort throughout.

"This young man named Philippe," Mauvreen said, musing, "have you given him an answer?"

"No," Rhianna said, growing solemn. "It was at that moment Lord Kingsley arrived with news of my parents' deaths. It would seem his relationship with my father was more than cordial."

There was no telling which subjects Mauvreen would open up to and there was a good deal Rhianna wanted to know about the Kingsley family. To her surprise, Mauvreen was not entirely silent on the subject.

"I am aware Mr. Braden was a comfort to him when Lord Kingsley was unwell." With a pause, she added, "I understand he has been more frequently ill."

This last was said almost as a question, but if such was the case, Rhianna had seen nothing to support her claim.

"If he has, I have not observed it," she told Mauvreen.

Mauvreen mumbled something about a fever running through Thornton and Rhianna knew better than to try further for particulars. She would sooner receive information from Mauvreen's whispering trees. Instead, she continued with another line of questioning, determined not to give in to Mauvreen's efforts at changing the subject altogether.

"What can you tell me of a Mr. Pierson? Is his a familiar name to you?" Rhianna asked.

"Mr. Pierson?" Mauvreen resounded. "In what way do you know of him?"

The whole of Rhianna's brief experience with him was relayed, from the initial upset his presence invoked in Lord Kingsley, to his mysterious departure early the next morning.

Mauvreen, for her part, listened attentively to these events—so attentively, in fact, that when the account was complete, Rhianna was not sure she could draw Mauvreen out of rumination. When at last she did, Mauvreen did not hesitate to share some passionate thoughts with her young friend.

"It has been some time since I have heard the name," said she. "Mr. Pierson is Lydia Kingsley's first cousin by relation. Lord Kingsley banned him from the manor some time ago, actually— not out of concern for his own good reputation only, but in fear of the poor influence Mr. Pierson might have on young Desmond. Of that, I hope I am mistaken when I say, it is likely too late." Mauvreen continued, "In addition to his gambling problems, Pierson was also heavily in debt and now owes Lord Kingsley a significant sum of money. I declare, if he returned to the manor, I am shocked."

This was more than Mauvreen had ever said together on such a scandalous topic and Rhianna was shocked nearly speechless by it, not to mention by the details themselves.

"Well, if such is the case," Rhianna told her, "I am glad he is gone."

"If he returns, Rhianna, I beg you will stay far away from him."

At the end of all this, Rhianna's visit had lasted some hours and she knew it was time to return to the Kingsleys. They parted with the promise to meet again, and often, for as long as Rhianna remained in England.

*

"Ah, our young guest, come! The men and Audra have gone out.

Let us take this opportunity to get to know one another."

Rhianna could not but reflect how strikingly Desmond took after his mother, not in manner only, but likewise in appearance. They shared the same sunken, piercing eyes, dark complexion, and domineering posture.

Lady Kingsley continued, "The weather is so fine today. I was just about to take a turn through the garden. Will you not join me?"

Despite the amount of walking Rhianna had done earlier, and her filthy skirt, she could hardly decline the opportunity to see more of the Kingsley grounds.

"Certainly," was Rhianna's reply, and the lady took her arm in hers.

Lydia Kingsley took pride in the formal gardens, which she proudly guided Rhianna along. "Our gardener, Stowe, is quite the artist. Some years back, the grounds were so overly ornate. I was quite anxious to move away from the formal, French style and what a work he has done! It is natural without being too natural. See how the trellis-covered walk offers the perfect transition to the garden . . ."

Rhianna was quick to compliment them, followed by the lady's wish that the visitors who "time and again" expressed their envy over "such beauty" were not so very dissatisfied with their own gardens. As she spoke, Rhianna found humor in such statements, recognizing that Lydia Kingsley was not the sort to regret any such envy her home may have evoked.

"My husband does not view his garden as seriously as he ought," she went on, "but that is where I take pride in our thirty-year union. I feel I quite complement him where he is lacking—and vice versa, naturally. Appearance is so very important when one is as visible in society as he is, you see. We could hardly go on with an unsuitable garden."

Rhianna listened courteously to her as she detailed her favorite features of the garden, the extent of the property and house, the size of the rooms compared to those in the surrounding manors, including a ballroom rivaled only by that at Ravensleigh, and the significant number of servants they kept. In the end, Lydia expressed her humble desire of only finding herself worthy of being called its mistress.

Thus seemingly absorbed with her own home and social rank, Lydia Kingsley made it clear almost immediately that she did not care very much about getting to know Rhianna—save for one subject.

"How long will you be staying with us?" Before Rhianna could respond, Lydia added, "Oh my, that sounds dreadful, does it not? I would never want to suggest you were *imposing* on us, Miss Braden. No, no, not at all. I am simply wondering how long we can expect to enjoy your company."

"Oh, I didn't . . . I'm not quite sure, exactly . . ."

"But of course you're not quite sure," she agreed. "You've only just arrived. How ridiculous of me! And do not feel you are at all in the way. The manor is quite large enough to accommodate a crowd without its members needing ever meet. And if my husband views you as his special guest, then I beg you to imagine I feel exactly the same."

Rhianna found herself nearly speechless by this, but managed a simple "thank you."

Upon nearing a grand, ivory-colored rotunda, its pillars draped in clematis and its dome reflected in a nearby, manmade lake, the two women paused for sanctuary from the sun. From a bench within, they had an excellent view of the back of Kingsley Manor and its courtyard. Having never seen the home from this angle, Rhianna was struck by its undeniable beauty.

"My husband, in his good intention of seeing you promptly settled," continued Lady Kingsley, "placed you in the lavender guest room. I have since told him that you would be much more at ease in the *rose* room. You can see its window from here. It has a positively enchanting view of this rotunda and is far superior to the room you are presently in. Besides, as my husband's distinguished visitor, you deserve the best."

"You are very thoughtful, Lady Kingsley," Rhianna expressed, speaking for what was almost the first time since they had left the house. "I am sure, however, that the present situation is most sufficient. I would never wish to be moved. It would be beyond unnecessary."

For a brief moment, Rhianna thought she sensed a feeling of disapproval from Lydia Kingsley. Indeed, the look that crossed her face proved she did not expect to find resistance. Rhianna hoped it was not ill-mannered of her to refuse such an action as the lady was suggesting. Never did she intend to insult her, nor did she wish to seem ungrateful. Rhianna's feelings were simple—they had already done quite enough for her and the idea of them doing more was a thing she could in no way accept.

Lady Kingsley seemed intent on persuading her. "Oh, but my dear, think of how you'll not have to deal with the stuffiness that comes with your current apartment. The heat from the fire is more in proportion to the measurements of the *rose* room."

"Thank you, and thank you again, but . . ."

"I cannot hear it," she interrupted. "I shall have you in comfort by the end of the afternoon. Besides, Katie is moving your articles as we speak."

With this last, her fate was sealed. To the rose room she must go.

Strange feelings accompanied this conversation. Something in the tone of it reminded Rhianna of her conversation with Desmond earlier. Perhaps it was merely speculation, but she was beginning to believe that there was a decided reason Lady Kingsley wanted her out of the lavender room.

Rhianna's things were moved upon their return to the house, and it was in the rose room she would prepare for dinner at Kingsley Manor. When the door was closed behind her, Rhianna conducted a brief inspection. The view of the rotunda, where only an hour before she had been a guest, she could not but fall in love with. But aside from being in the rear of the manor and a very little improvement in temperature, Rhianna was unable to distinguish any great differences between the rose and lavender rooms.

From this location, however, there were no carriages and no voices to awaken her. Rhianna would have slept peacefully through the succeeding nights, save for a few childhood memories come back to haunt her dreams . . .

*

Like the ivy that overtook the lodge, the roses overtook the garden and the white picket fence that enclosed the area. No post, no stone was free of them. To grow such flowers so deep in the woods undoubtedly took a great deal of energy and care, and these roses were as plump and brilliant as any Rhianna had seen in more favorable conditions. A break in the trees above allowed the necessary sunlight. Rhianna tilted her head back and felt its warm rays on her face. *Such a perfect, peaceful place,* she thought, while raising one particularly red flower to her tiny nose. The fragrance of them swirled in the air around her as she continued her exploration, tracing the short, stone walkway that led to the heart of the garden.

And there, at the end of the path, a gravestone emerged. A nine-year-old Rhianna caught her breath as she read the engraving: *My Beloved Haldana 1794–1813.*

The stone blended in so well she hadn't noticed it at first. It lay close to the lodge and was framed in roses and vines.

All at once, Rhianna felt as though the world fell silent. It was as if the woods around her were not only watching, but waiting—even anticipating—for something to happen. The roses, too, seemed to close in on her, to trap her. The world outside the garden seemed to grow farther and farther away. She began to feel lightheaded. Her pulse quickened. Her fingers tingled. Fearfully, she retreated to the outer edge of the garden.

Mauvreen appeared at the gate and the vision of her immediately eased Rhianna's disquieted emotions. Had she been in a dark room, Mauvreen would have been a glowing fire, her glorious light thwarting any encircling evils.

"What are you doing out here, child?" Mauvreen asked her.

Mauvreen's tone seemed different, uneasy, just like the forest. Rhianna felt she must have done something wrong.

"I wanted to see the roses," Rhianna explained, as the woman approached her. "Are you angry with me, Mauvreen?"

"Angry?" Mauvreen repeated in shock. "Rhianna . . ." She hesitated. "Don't be silly. I only wish you had waited for me."

She knelt down so that the two of them were of equal height and gave a passing glance toward the gravestone.

"I'm sorry, Mauvreen," Rhianna apologized. Then, following her friend's gaze, she faltered, "Who is this buried here? Who is Haldana?"

Mauvreen had a look of uneasiness on her face and she did not answer immediately. As she stalled, her weathered fingers combed a few unruly strands of her wiry hair into place.

"Someone who was very dear to me," she responded softly. Then, in a revealing statement, unlike Mauvreen to offer, she added, "She is the girl in your favorite drawing."

Rhianna's mouth fell. "I always thought that girl . . . was you."

"Oh! Goodness, child. I was never that pretty."

Rhianna suddenly saw the grave in an entirely different light. All fears associated with it were long gone. Curiosity began to take over. "Haldana . . ."

"We called her Hallie."

"She was young. What did she die from, Mauvreen?"

Shaking her head, as if trying to cast the sadness from her person, Mauvreen suddenly closed up. She would continue the conversation no further.

"Let us not discuss such things."

"But why is she not buried in the churchyard?"

"No, no. That is enough of that."

"But, Mauvreen!" Rhianna begged.

"Come."

Mauvreen rose to her feet and took her by the hand.

Rhianna had known Mauvreen long enough to know when the time for pressing her for secrets was up. With a reluctant nod, she obliged her, the image of a gravestone etched in her mind and the name *Hallie* echoing in her ears . . .

Even though she knew she was asleep, Rhianna could not wake herself. The memories would hold her captive until they had played out in full. Her body turned freely in her sheets, but her mind was imprisoned. Her fingers closed around the brooch she had placed under her pillow—Hallie's brooch—as she waited for the dream to release her.

*

As the weeks passed, not many hours were spent going through the items at the Bradens' cottage. Rhianna packed a few books, including a well-worn copy of *The History of Sir Charles Grandison*, but she had no interest in any articles belonging to either parent. Guilford Kingsley assisted her in selling a few items, but she decided to leave the majority there for the temporary minister found by Lord Kingsley, who was to hold the position until a more permanent resident could be installed. Overall, Rhianna preferred to spend her time becoming acquainted with Kingsley Manor's inhabitants.

Of the Kingsley family, Lydia and Desmond were the least to be seen, and Rhianna preferred it that way. When she did find herself in their company, usually in the evening, the former seemed always to look as though she was required to be elsewhere and the latter seemed never to take his eyes off Rhianna. On the opposite side of the spectrum, Guilford Kingsley proved consistent in personality and generosity. Rhianna also had opportunity to spend considerable time alone with Audra Kingsley, who, with the same large eyes, high cheekbones, and light hair and skin as her father, decidedly resembled the handsomer side of the family. Audra also seemed fortunate enough to have avoided inheriting her mother's snobbish personality or her brother's arrogance. She grew quickly attached to Rhianna, who found it quite natural to return the affection.

Of those in service, Katie, a housemaid, and Henry, the butler, were two with whom she made easy friends and whose company she enjoyed when she was not exploring the many ins and outs of the house.

In this area, she spent as much free time as she possibly could. One particular curiosity existed in the form of a door that lay down the northern corridor, on the first floor. Surrounded by many of the family chambers, it remained locked at all times and Rhianna could not, without seeming overly curious, find anyone who could tell her why or what lay beyond it.

When six weeks had passed, Rhianna received a letter from Soleil, with a few lines from Philippe enclosed. Because her first letter to them had offered little information beyond her safe arrival at the manor, Soleil's letter eagerly pressed for more details. Her writing seemed, from the very page, as an extension of herself. However, Soleil could not master the feeling that Philippe's words conveyed in only a few sentences. They reached a level of emotion that only he, in his adoration of her, could communicate. As her eyes scanned the words, Rhianna could almost feel his presence beside her.

It might have been an easy letter to respond to, with so much to communicate since her previous note, except for the last inquiry in Philippe's hand, namely, when she could be expected to return to them. For days, Rhianna was lost as to how to reply to this letter. As much as she missed France, she was in no hurry to return. Philippe's regard confused and unsettled her. Besides, there were still things she wanted to do in England. At the same time, she could not impose on the Kingsleys much longer. There seemed no choice but to leave—until an offer from Lord Kingsley opened the possibility of remaining.

It was a quiet morning at the Kingsley home. Lydia and

Desmond were out walking and Audra had just left to join up with them when Guilford Kingsley called Rhianna into his study. It was a dark, burgundy-themed room, with magnificent, fitted bookcases lining the walls containing a collection of books that far surpassed that found at Madame Chandelle's. Above a marble fireplace mantel hung a Greek sculpture of an Athenian couple, and antique pieces sat here and there. Marveling as she entered, Rhianna accepted the seat he offered before his writing desk.

"Miss Braden," he addressed, taking his own seat opposite her, "I hope you have enjoyed these last several weeks with us. That is, as much as possible, under the circumstances."

"I have, very much."

"I am glad of it. Be certain of our happiness in having you here. Additionally, be assured that you may stay as long as you wish."

Her conversation with Lydia Kingsley in the first days as a guest at Kingsley Manor was briefly called to mind. How different a feel such similar words had coming from Lord Kingsley!

"You are too kind, Lord Kingsley. Though, I expect to have other arrangements soon. As you know, my family in France is anxious to know my plans."

"Ah! This brings me to my purpose in calling you here. I promise to get right to the point. Hopefully, I have not pulled you from anything very pressing."

"No, indeed, my lord. Audra has just left me to find her mother and brother. I am fully unengaged."

He continued, "Well, then, let me not waste a moment, lest she should return for you. You realize, Miss Braden, that as the daughter of my departed friend, my help is infinitely extended toward you."

"Then I am infinitely grateful, sir."

"Something occurred to me recently," he told her, each word delivered with well-pondered thought, "and, as you have yet to respond to your letter, I think I shall suggest it to you, while the opportunity is still open."

There was a quality in Guilford Kingsley unique to himself. A characteristic that gave the impression a person could not only be oneself in his company, but that he truly enjoyed *having* one's company. He openly and willingly offered himself as a friend to any who welcomed the relationship.

"You have certainly captured my interest," Rhianna admitted.

"Audra," he began, "as I am sure you know, is so very fond of you. Now, I flatter myself as having an excellent grasp of the obvious and I have not *ever* seen her so fond of anyone."

Rhianna smiled. "The feeling is mutual, I assure you. She is a delightful young lady."

"I'm glad to hear you think so," he said gaily. "Audra's previous governess, Miss Barnesworth, married recently and is yet to be replaced. Miss Braden, there is no one I would rather have as Audra's guardian and teacher than yourself. In fact, it is my express desire. That is, of course, if you are interested in such a situation."

Governess to Lord Kingsley's daughter! The surprise of such an offer was more than she could have dreamed. Yet, he did not request from her a résumé, nor require references. He simply presented to her the position.

"Surely, you must first wish to find me qualified?" she managed.

He shook his head. "There is no doubt as to your abilities, Miss Braden. As a teacher at Madame Chandelle's for more than two years, I hardly think you *could* be unsuitable. No, I'm confident in your qualifications—both in intellect and character. I hope you don't mind my saying you would be a good exemplar to Audra. I believe she would also be more apt to learn from someone whom she regards and in whose company she finds enjoyment. Her interaction with you this last month or so has proven such is the case. My only wish is that you will inform me of your decision anon."

Rhianna was at once certain. "I can answer it for you now, Lord Kingsley, and the answer is yes! I would like it very much. Indeed, I hardly know what else to say! Thank you for your confidence in me. I will do my utmost not to disappoint you."

"I have no fear of it," he replied contentedly. "None, whatsoever."

And so it was settled. She replied to her letter with news of her new position, and instruction with Audra soon began. Classes included literature, history, geography, sciences, foreign languages, and religion, not to mention embroidery, painting, music, and art—essentially, all the workings of a proper education. Riding, too, was soon a daily custom, and the bond between student and teacher grew until Audra and Rhianna were, at last, inseparable.

Ere long, months passed of settling in, and somewhere between teaching, writing letters to the Vallières, and visiting Mauvreen whenever the opportunity admitted, Kingsley Manor became home.

*

"She is looking very well."

Mauvreen stated this matter-of-factly, as she took a seat before the cloaked man in the sitting room of the lodge.

"How would you know?" he returned. "Not that anything you know surprises me, Mauvreen."

Mauvreen offered a smile before answering. "She has been to see me. But you already knew that."

He shrugged his shoulders.

"What is there to be done?" Mauvreen continued. "You cannot place a barrier around Kingsley woods. Even if you could, I wouldn't let you."

"No," he returned. "I expect you wouldn't. Nor would I have any intention, if I could."

His eyes met hers with a knowing glance.

"I did not expect she would search for you after all these years, but perhaps some secrets are not meant to be kept."

Chapter Three

Lord Thayne Brighton was returning from London when he witnessed the accident from the window of his carriage. What had so frightened the horse he knew not—all he could see was *her*. Fear seized him while he helplessly watched the horse throw her from its saddle.

Thayne cried to his driver to halt, tossing his top hat and cloak aside. No sooner had the wheels slowed than he leapt to the road and ran into the field where the woman lay.

"Hello, there! Are you all right?"

There was no response, either audible or visible, as he neared. The horse moved some distance away as Thayne approached, agitatedly swinging **its** tail and huffing. Dropping to his knees beside the still body, he could not but despise the beast that had thrown her, an angelic beauty who seemed something out of Shakespeare's plays or Michelangelo's paintings. What relief he felt to see that she was alive!

Who was this striking creature, whose delicate self lay weak before him? Who was this young woman garbed in riding clothes, unaccompanied and unfamiliar, defenseless to whomever chanced to find her? He must know who she was. The steed she had been riding, Lord Brighton could discern, was a well-bred specimen from no ordinary stable. Perhaps, a new family had moved into Thornton since his departure?

Thayne lifted her motionless body from the ground and hastened to the coach. Her long, red locks, which had escaped their pins, lay strewn across his shoulder and arm.

"*To Ravensleigh at once!*" he ordered the driver, and the coach dashed onward.

Thayne rolled up his cloak and laid it beneath her as a pillow as they drove on. What was it in her face that kept him from looking away? He told himself he must learn the name of the family to whom she belonged and inform them of where she was, but he had other reasons for wishing to know her family. He wanted to know her name. He *needed* to know her name.

It seemed to take forever to reach Ravensleigh, the manor Thayne had inherited six years ago when his father, Reeves, Lord Brighton, Earl of Ravensleigh, passed away. His mother and younger brother, Crispin, resided there with him, along with more servants and attendants than he could count. He was glad to have many of them on hand when they pulled up to the house.

"Call my mother and her maidservant," Thayne directed to whoever was near enough to carry out the order.

There was a steady murmur amongst all, the excitement of Lord Brighton's return alone being more than Ravensleigh had seen in months. Now, as he lifted the girl from the coach, a girl unconscious and mysterious, her person in frightfully poor condition, such events were surely enough to keep the servants talking and speculating for many a dull afternoon.

Lady Brighton met him in the foyer, a look of alarm on her face. "Oh! Thayne, what happened to her?"

She hurried to his side to examine the girl, but Thayne did not pause.

"Let us take her to a bed. She was tossed from her horse." Turning to the butler, he ordered, "Remford, fetch Dr. Logan at once!"

Lady Brighton covered her open mouth with her hands and followed Thayne to the nearest guestroom. A servant turned down the sheets to lay the girl in.

"Who is she?"

"I was hoping you would know," was Thayne's preoccupied response, as he gently placed her down. "Her family will be worrying if we cannot reach them soon."

"They will be worrying anyway, dear, when they *do* know where she is." Lady Brighton placed her hand upon the girl's forehead. Turning to a servant girl, she said, "Susan, a rag and water, quickly!"

Susan at once left the room to fetch the requested items.

"Such a lovely girl. I've never seen her before. What of the horse?" Lady Brighton asked.

Thayne shook his head. "I was foremost concerned with her. The horse I left."

She requested a recount of the incident, which he relayed in detail. Visibly distressed, Thayne knew not what to do with himself once his tale was ended. He hardly noticed Susan as she returned and his mother took it upon herself to wipe the dirt from the girl's face and arms.

"Shall I send someone out for the horse? If we have the beast, perhaps we will be able to find her family."

"No," he said, rising from his seat, "*I* shall return for the horse."

Rising with him, his mother suggested, "Can we not send someone else? You've only just returned from a long trip. I hardly think it necessary for you to retrieve the creature personally."

"My apologies, Mother, but I feel it quite necessary," he told her, as she accompanied him to the door. "I am much too anxious to be unemployed. If I do not find occupation to keep me engaged, I will go mad."

"Ah!" cried she, relinquishing. "I wonder that I held any hope of keeping you here. Your brother is of the very same disposition, you know."

Thayne reached for the door. "Where is Crispin, incidentally?"

"Out with his governess. They went to town. He'll be so delighted you're home."

"I'll be glad to see him, myself," Thayne said. "I won't be long."

Lord Brighton kissed his mother goodbye and departed to carry out his purpose. That blasted horse was to unravel a secret that he could scarcely stand a moment longer to be kept.

*

After a week away on business, Guilford Kingsley was looking forward to arriving home a few days early. As usual, Audra was there to greet him the moment the coach was observed from the manor's windows. Unlike usual, Audra did not seem her characteristically jubilant self. Rather, there was an urgency in her manner as she descended the portico.

Something was wrong.

"Papa!" she cried.

Audra hardly waited for the carriage door to open and her father to step down before taking his hand.

"Make haste!" she exclaimed, urging him forward. "You must come and talk to Mama *at once!*"

His relaxed state of mind long gone, he asked, "Pray, what is the hurry?"

"It is Miss Braden!"

Her words were panicked. Guilford shook his head, trying to understand her meaning.

"What is the matter with Miss Braden?"

"She is gone! *Missing.*"

"Since when?" he cried.

"Today," she hurried. "She did not return from her horse ride this morning." Tears filled her eyes, and Audra confessed, "I did not go with her, Papa—if only I had gone with her! Then, I would know where she was . . ."

"Come," he told her. "Do not fret. All will be well. Where is your mother?"

She wasted no time in leading him inside the entrance hall.

"Lydia!" he called. Removing his top hat and tucking his walking stick under his arm, he called again, "Lydia!"

"My love!" she answered, appearing at the top of the winding stairs. "You're home."

"Yes, yes," he declared, as she approached him. "What has happened while I was away?"

"Oh, Guilford! Audra is so very distraught. I see she has told you about her Miss Braden. What should we do?"

"We must search. Where is Desmond?"

"He left the house early with a friend and is yet returned."

"Then I shall go alone. There is no reason to delay."

Guilford Kingsley put his top hat back on, and his walking stick hit the marble floor with a driving thud.

"I want to come! *Please*, Papa!"

"No, Audra," replied her mother. "Can we not send a servant?" she asked her husband.

But Guilford paid no mind to her. "I shall return," he said, and hurried out.

"Where will you go at this late hour?" cried Lydia.

He offered no reply. The door closed behind him.

*

For hours, Thayne searched for the stallion, but to no avail. Whether it had found its way home or run away, he knew not. But it was neither in the field that was the scene of the accident, nor in the surrounding area. Disappointed and empty-handed, he at last headed home.

Ravensleigh, a long house overlooking a curve of the River Thornton, its battlements high against the English skies, was one of the most admired of all the Thornton country homes. Its Jacobean style was updated in the early 1700s, adding two additional wings to its current appearance. Also, its gardens, not unlike Kingsley Manor, had undergone significant changes, with Roman-themed statuary and pillars, where during the day one could enjoy meandering walks through groves, paths, and woods.

Now, though, Ravensleigh's front, sloping lawns were dark as Thayne neared home. As he prepared to dismount, Lord Kingsley's carriage turned swiftly down the drive. Not the speed only, but the hour as well, caught Thayne's attention, and he rode up to greet him.

Dusk was upon them, and through thick clouds, a thin moon and pale stars began to make their first appearance of the night. The driver brought the coach to a halt and Guilford leaned out the window.

"Good evening, Lord Kingsley," Thayne greeted. "You are no doubt testing the soundness of your carriage. Under such speeds, I daresay it holds up quite well."

"A comfort, Lord Brighton, but not enough to ease my distress," he said, his manner noticeably affected.

"Distress?" Thayne repeated with alarm. "I trust all is well with your family?"

"I am searching for a missing girl who stays with us. Her name is Rhianna Braden."

A missing girl!

"Was she alone?" he asked him hurriedly. "And on horseback?"

"She was."

"And has she red hair?"

"She does!"

Thayne's heart stopped in his chest as the mystery that had tormented him these last several hours came to an end. Rhianna Braden—a guest of the Kingsleys!

"Well, Lord Kingsley, for now, rest at ease. She is here, at Ravensleigh."

He breathed a sigh of relief. "Is she all right?"

"Miss Braden was thrown from her saddle earlier today. Doctor Logan was called to examine her before I left. You've only just caught me returning from a search for the horse, but success did not accompany my quest."

"I thank you, at any rate," replied Guilford. "Likely he'll find his way home."

Thayne nodded. "Please come in. The doctor may admit us to see Miss Braden."

*

Halfway home from Mauvreen's, Rhianna heard the sound of rustling branches. Slowing her pace, she listened cautiously to her surroundings. Her heart began to race in her chest as the rustling drew closer. Suddenly, it sounded as if something was running toward her, indeed, *bounding* toward her.

Knowing the distance she was from her cottage, Rhianna ran. Dashing forward, crunching branches and leaves beneath the weight of her small, nine-year-old body, she disregarded the noise she was making, her only goal to travel farther and faster.

"Stop!" a voice called.

Startled, Rhianna felt the sound pierce her body and glanced over her shoulder, more frightened than before. With Mauvreen's strict emphasis on the secrecy of their visits, Rhianna did not know the worse evil: to happen upon a wild, hungry beast or a human who would reveal her clandestine friendship.

Rhianna had never run so fast in her life, nor been so terribly worried. She looked back once more, but saw no one, even as the voice called again.

"Stop!"

Just then, Rhianna came to the horrid realization that the voice was not calling to her at all, but worse still, to the overly excited hunting dog that chased her. With a scream, she fled down an incline and dropped to her knees in the muddy stream that guided her.

"Stop!" the person again cried.

A drenched Rhianna glanced, terrified, at the bank where the dog barked at her happily, his tail wagging so violently his entire body wiggled. Soon after, the figure of a boy emerged from behind the trees, laughing at the scene before him.

"You found him!" he quipped childishly to Rhianna.

She recognized the boy's face instantly. Certainly, there was no mistaking it.

"Have you drowned?" he asked.

Still kneeling in the stream, Rhianna's fingers curled into the mud at the sight of him.

"Yours was the carriage that spoiled my blue dress!" she burst out.

A rain-filled ditch in the soggy road outside Rhianna's cottage ought to have been enough to warn her and Brenna away as the Brighton carriage came along that morning. Alas, as if the event in and of itself were not humiliating enough, it was eclipsed by the face of a prepubescent boy as he leaned out the window and laughed at them.

"Well you certainly are ungrateful," he retorted playfully. "Here I am, checking to see that you have not perished, and here you are, yelling at me."

"You should apologize!"

His smile curled to the side as he placed his hands on his dog and petted him rewardingly for his catch. The dog, in turn, looked admiringly at his owner.

"You don't mean to blame that on *me*," he replied.

"You *laughed* at us," she reminded him, considering how the hound would respond if she advanced to the embankment and pushed the boy into the water.

The black-haired, blue-eyed child shrugged. "Well, what was I supposed to do? I found it amusing."

Rhianna could hardly believe what she was hearing. He was either completely wicked or had a very poor sense of humor.

"Look!" she cried, clambering to her feet and pointing to the bottom of the green dress she was wearing. The plain dress without a pearl button or piece of lace found on it was, in fact, her best frock. "Now this one also is spoiled, no thanks to *you*."

"Well, maybe *you* shouldn't walk so close to the stream. That goes for muddy roads, as well."

"Indeed!" she shouted angrily. "Well if *your dog* had not come bounding toward me, I would never have fallen. I would have been home by now."

Enraged, Rhianna turned and began walking toward town on the opposite side of the stream.

"Who are you?" he called out to her, jumping across the stream with his dog barreling through it behind him. "And what are you doing out here, anyway? This is the Kingsleys' property."

"I'd ask the same of you, if I cared a fig," she responded, her back to him.

Chasing after her, his hound faithfully at his side, he called, "I have more right to be here than you, peasant!"

His words brought her to a halt. She about-faced, and cried, "How dare you? I am the curate's daughter!"

"And I," he said, sauntering toward her, "am Thayne Brighton, heir to Ravensleigh, the House of Brighton, not to mention the title of Lord."

With revulsion, Rhianna shoved him using all her force. Master Brighton fell, landing rearward into the stream with a hearty splash.

"May you never live to see the day!" she cried.

With tears in her eyes, Rhianna stormed off toward home, without looking back behind her.

*

By the time she opened her eyes, Rhianna was conscious of very little around her. The one thing she did know was that she felt safe and the lady beside her was caring and concerned. An attempt to sit up in bed ended with a moan as Rhianna felt the full effects of a headache and she surrendered to her pillow.

Taking Rhianna's hand in her own and speaking in a soft voice, the lady said, "You're all right, my dear. Do not fret yourself with struggling to get up. Rest. You took quite a fall."

Rhianna could do little beyond examine the intricate strapwork of the ceiling from the comforts between four wood bedposts . . .

Fall?

"I beg your pardon?"

"What is your name?"

The question throbbed in her head. "My name is Rhianna Braden."

"Well, Miss Braden, you were thrown from your horse this morning, but the doctor says you're going to be just fine."

She focused her eyes on the lady's face. It had a soft, kind appearance, and her smile was sweet. Only a very few lines gave any hint to her age, and her manners revealed motherly instincts.

"Can you have any idea of what happened?" the lady continued.

"No, indeed, I do not remember it," Rhianna told her. Then, trailing off in thought, she recollected, "There was a man."

After some moments without a further description, the woman beside her questioned, "Who was this man?"

She struggled to recall details. "I remember a man with dark features. He was also on horseback, though behind me some ways. I am sure I have never seen him before and he seemed to be there for some time. That's the last thing I recall." Rhianna asked, "I rather had the feeling he was following me but, perhaps—did he bring me here?"

The lady's eyes widened at this account, but she did not press her further.

"No, Miss Braden. My son brought you here. He was passing in his carriage as it happened."

"I am very grateful," she struggled. Then, something occurred to Rhianna as the lady reached for a pitcher of water on the end table and began to pour her a drink.

"Forgive me, my lady, but where am I?"

"My name is Lady Moira Brighton, and this is my home, Ravensleigh."

*

The night sky blanketed Ravensleigh when Lords Brighton and Kingsley entered the drawing room to inquire of the patient. It was explained to them by Lady Brighton that the doctor had left only half an hour prior.

"She is resting now," she said. "He found it quite astonishing that she escaped such an incident with no more than a concussion and general soreness. He expects her to be up and about in a day or so."

"What a relief!" cried Thayne. "I ought to censure you, Lord Kingsley, for allowing young ladies out to ride unaccompanied, but under the circumstances I trust you've learned your lesson."

"Has she spoken?" asked Lord Kingsley. "Has there been an account of what happened?"

"She remembers nothing of the accident itself or what may have frightened the horse," the lady continued. She paused as the men accepted their drinks from the servants. "There is one thing that disturbs me, though, Guilford. Miss Braden claims that before the accident she thought she saw someone, a man, following her."

"Following her? A man, you say?"

"Yes."

"What sort of man?"

"She gave no clear description. He was at a distance, she claims, but of dark complexion." Turning to her son, she declared, "I thought perhaps you might have seen something, Thayne. After all, you witnessed the accident yourself."

"I did," he told her, "but I recall no man in the vicinity—no one at all but my driver and myself. You must allow, however, that in my fright for *her*, I was conscious only of Miss Braden and, even less so, the horse."

"All suspicions aside, a man in such vicinity must have also seen the accident. That he did not also hurry to assist is disquieting to me," Lady Brighton returned.

A pause of silence ensued, but nothing could be concluded in the matter.

"I am curious," said Lady Brighton to Guilford, "as it is the nature of all women, to know who this lovely young lady is. Is she new to the area?"

"Yes, Lord Kingsley," Thayne encouraged. "I should also like to know something about your guest."

"Miss Braden has been in the area for almost a year now," he told them. "She was my guest for part of that time."

"I cannot recall seeing her at any of the social gatherings," Lady Brighton continued. "She is quite stunning."

Guilford gave a brief account of her history as daughter of the curate, to her schooling in France, to her recently ended period of mourning.

"As of these nine months past," he concluded, "she is Audra's governess."

"Of course," mumbled Thayne, who in his disappointment slumped deep into his chair.

This disclosure made it impossible for him to appear cheerful. The most heavenly creature he had ever had the pleasure to look upon, whose presence he had thought unworthy to stand within, and through the unfairness of society the angel was damned to the working class. *Quelle horreur!* A rising condemnation for social attitudes and structure rose in his breast.

Curate . . .

Braden . . .

All at once, Thayne was transported to a moment he had not thought of in some time. A day in his childhood when his dog had led him deep into the Kingsley woods. A day he ran into a fellow trespasser: the curate's daughter. The very same red curls fell upon her neck then as they now lay upon the pillow in his guestroom. *Yours was the carriage that spoiled my blue dress.* The sentences that had passed between them came flooding back to him all at once and rendered him speechless. All that surrounded him now at Ravensleigh disappeared and he fell into a trance-like state. Thayne had always remembered their brief encounter, and the shock of this revelation was more than he could believe. *I have more right to be here than you, peasant.* Thayne's stomach turned at his words to her and his pompous attitude. *You should apologize,* he heard her young voice say, repeatedly.

Thayne must have appeared quite pained, and it is no wonder, considering the thoughts that inwardly tortured him, that Lady Brighton said suddenly, "You look very ill, Thayne. Perhaps you ought to retire for the evening."

For him, the return from these reflections was difficult. "Yes, Mother. I think I should," he struggled to say. Turning to his guest, he offered, "The hour grows late, Lord Kingsley. Permit me to have a room prepared for you."

"I thank you, Brighton," he declared, "but my family will be wanting news. May I continue to leave Miss Braden in your kind care, Moira?"

"It needn't be asked," she avowed, as all in company arose.

"Your goodness exceeds that in all of Thornton, my dear lady. I'll inquire of her progress in the morning."

"We look forward to your call," she declared.

"Goodnight to you both."

"Goodnight."

Thayne nodded as the butler saw Lord Kingsley out. When the door had closed, Lady Brighton gave her son an attentive look.

"You are out of spirits, Thayne. What is the matter?"

Thayne cared not that his countenance was now more clearly troubled.

"I am sure you will think me irrational, indeed, foolish," he began, contemplatively. "I'll have you know, Mother, that I am well aware of who I am. An Earl, Lord of Ravensleigh, owner of over fifteen hundred acres of country land, besides a house in town, with a family name that dates back generations, a seat in Parliament, and a fortune second only to Lord Kingsley's throughout the country. All this, and yet, I have no one to share it with. I have been introduced to many women, in England and France, Greece and Italy, those women considered the loveliest, from the wealthiest families, educated, refined, distinguished, daughters of peers, renowned for their talents, with the sort of well-respected reputations that would befit someone of my station . . ."

Lady Brighton gave him a moment's silence, before pressing him. "And so?" she encouraged.

He sighed. "So why is it," he said, turning his glance to the door, "that out of all of them, the only one—and, I declare, she is the *only* one—ever to catch my attention, to intrigue me and bewitch me, all without a word, not a single one, is *Miss Kingsley's governess?*"

*

Desmond paced the floor of the study, as he had for the last several hours, pausing only occasionally to look out the windows. The west faced a distant Ravensleigh and the south, the approach to Kingsley Manor. Earlier, the south had offered the most activity as Stowe, the gardener, tended to the grounds. He had seemed to enjoy his labor, but Desmond imagined it only a resignation, for who would prefer working in the garden to sitting comfortably in a study with a glass of port?

That was some time ago. At the moment, the west provided his only distraction, as a young manservant and a young maidservant met near a tree for a stolen kiss. *Such a dull, inferior existence,* thought Desmond. He felt relief he was not of their situation, born into poor families, damned to a life of drudgery. This thread of thought summoned Pierson to mind, a man born of a family whose connections were good, but whose habits brought him down in society. In Desmond's mind, Pierson's actions, though hardly honorable, ought not to sever him from the family. Lord Kingsley's reasons for banishing him aside, family was all that he had for support, and Desmond did not disagree with his mother for allowing Pierson still into their lives, though against her husband's wishes.

Suddenly, Desmond laughed to himself. *So many secrets,* he thought. *So, so many.*

Miss Braden was soon present in his thoughts. A beautiful

girl—among the handsomest he had come across in all his travels. Had her standing in society been different, he could easily see himself taking her for a bride and even, perhaps, being mildly contented with her for a short while. As it was, that could never be. Never could he publicly connect himself with such an unequal alliance. Privately was entirely different, of course. If she returned to the manor, she would make a very convenient mistress. He did not share his mother's view that his father had already taken her thus and he could not help wondering if she would be easily persuaded . . .

It did not matter, Desmond decided. He was not expecting her to return.

A knock at the door halted his musings and Lydia Kingsley entered.

"Here you are. I have searched the whole house over looking for you," she said, catching her breath. "The servants are already saying **Guilford** has found Rhianna Braden."

Desmond turned to her coolly. "Dead?"

"No."

Astonished, he ventured, "Well, go on."

Lady Kingsley paced through the room. "The servants only know so much. It would seem she was thrown from her horse, but not very harmed."

"I shall have to see for myself," he said.

"Soon you shall. Very soon, I hear. As early as tomorrow or the day after, they are saying. I expect Guilford home shortly with more reliable information."

"How interesting," he thought aloud. "How *very* interesting."

*

At once Rhianna recognized the name of Brighton. It was a name nostalgic of her childhood, but without the sweet indulgence such memories are oft to produce. The most arrogant, contemptuous, and insolent boy one could imagine—let alone confront in an actual existent representation (as such had been her misfortune)—was associated with it, and now he had come into her acquaintance once again. Yes, Thayne Brighton had grown to take his father's title, as he once boasted, and was possessor of the very house whose roof covered her.

Surely, thought she, *had he any notion of what position I held he would not have helped me.*

Only, he *had* helped her. Indeed, while she spent the entire next day in his guestroom, surrounded by a sea of blankets and pillows, he concerned himself with her hourly, inquiring of her at every opportunity. How often she heard his voice on the opposite side of the door and with what earnestness he expressed in his tone! Rhianna knew that when the hour approached to speak with Lord Brighton she must be cordial to him. Even if his character was one she could not excuse, he had done her a great service. For this, she did wish to thank him, for she truly was appreciative.

Dr. Logan had instructed Rhianna to remain in bed for two full days. During that time, Lady Brighton was frequently with her and Rhianna could not but take pleasure in the lady's company. She was certain that Thayne Brighton must have taken after his father's disposition, as his mother displayed everything that was good and generous.

As the pain subsided and her power to hold conversation returned to her, Rhianna, for the first time since her departure from France, enjoyed with Lady Brighton something akin to the family atmosphere she knew with the Vallières. Surprised by what seemed an immediate friendship, Rhianna was even more surprised—after it was decided that she should return the following day to Kingsley Manor—to hear Lady Brighton acknowledge, as a woman frequently surrounded by her sons, she would miss Rhianna's company.

On the morning of her departure from Ravensleigh, she saw him. Lady Brighton brought her to the drawing room where he and Lord Kingsley sat; both rose at her entrance. The walls were delicately adorned with Chinese wallpaper and the ceiling molding was finely executed in ivory-colored relief against a backdrop of pastel green. Rosewood tables and armchairs were strategically placed. As Rhianna was led near the fireplace where the men had been seated, she could not help but admire the lavish carving in the overmantel, an elaborate, marble chimneypiece. Opposite, a draped window curtain revealed a picturesque view of the drive she could not remember passing along three days previous.

An official introduction followed. Thayne, now a man of two and twenty, proved to have striking, even features, with dark, straight hair and sapphire eyes, outlined by thick, black lashes. She was surprised to see his face unveil a manly outline and square jaw that replaced the rounder, prepubescent face of the young boy she'd met years ago. Had Rhianna not disliked him so much, she might have even thought him handsome.

Lady Brighton offered an official introduction. Rhianna searched, but could find no hint of recognition in his gaze; neither could she find in his tall, strong frame any indication of dislike. On a further study of his demeanor, she found he presented himself most civilly. It was an unforeseen interview. Under no circumstances had she expected to find him at all mannerly.

Thayne bowed to her. "I took it upon myself to inquire of your health earlier, Miss Braden. May I again inquire to see if the report is as well now as it was earlier?"

"You may, and it is," she told him, while examining his careless black coiffure and straight nose. "I cannot begin to express the extent of my gratitude—"

"And you need not," he interrupted, all thoughts connected with the unpleasant event seeming to him very disagreeable. "Please, it is most unnecessary. We are only glad to have you as our guest. Let us not make mention of it."

She nodded assent. "Very well, Lord Brighton."

Thayne motioned her to a Grecian chaise-lounge beside a

mighty hearth where a great fire flamed and flared, and the four were soon seated.

"I neglected to mention last night," said Lady Brighton to Guilford, "how very glad I am to see you so well. You seem quite a different person than you were a twelvemonth ago."

"Quite so," he returned, cheerfully. "No doubt my returned health was, in part, due to the good counsel of Doctor Logan and spending more time outdoors. It was very bad times then, however, and Miss Braden's father was a source of great comfort to me."

Rhianna glanced toward Thayne, but found no reaction in him of what she expected. There was no start, nor wonder in his looks. Either he was an excellent actor or Lord Brighton was already well aware of her background. He might not perhaps remember their past confrontation, but he was sensible of her position in society, her station in life. And still, he treated her respectfully and courteously.

She sat amazed.

"You will be glad to know, Brighton," continued Lord Kingsley, with a change of topic, "that my steed found its way home last night. Desmond discovered him near the stables before I returned."

"Did he, indeed? This is good news," he affirmed. "Was there nothing indicating the cause of his fit?"

"Nothing, whatsoever. I honestly cannot imagine what caused him to go into such a frenzy."

The door opened and a servant entered with tea. Rhianna, growing anxious to be home, looked forward to their finishing it so that she might take leave of Ravensleigh. If she could not be alone with Lady Brighton, she preferred not to be there at all.

"I have an idea," cried Lady Brighton suddenly. "It has been too long since we have had a ball at the manor, Guilford, and I say that we have some things that call for a celebration! What with Miss Braden's recovery . . ."

"Yes, and your good health, Lord Kingsley," added Lord Brighton. "It has been far too long."

"It is a splendid idea!" Guilford agreed, the pitch of his voice lifting enthusiastically. "Lydia cannot object. The festivities shall be the greatest that Thornton has seen in some time. I shall plan for six weeks from today."

Lady Brighton clasped her hands together. "How wonderful it will be to again have a party at the manor!"

Rhianna, for her part, nearly fainted with the concept. To view a ball at Kingsley Manor would have caused her former nine-year-old heart to swell to twice its size, but now to be a part of it, as well! *Surely,* she thought, *I have not heard correctly. He could not mean for me to attend.*

Lord Kingsley planned onward. "Everyone shall be invited. I will call friends as far as London. Miss Braden, you have not said a word. Your opinion, please?"

The sudden attention directed toward her gave Rhianna a shock, and she could not form a word in response.

Seeming to sense her distress, Lady Brighton spoke for her, saying, "Oh, you must not put her on the spot, Lord Kingsley. Such a scheme is so remarkable you must allow that we are all lost in thought with the design of it. As I am contemplating," she turned to address Rhianna, "and if you would like, Miss Braden, we can perhaps get together to discuss costumes."

"Thank you, but I do not think Lord Kingsley means for me to participate," Rhianna whispered to her.

"Oh, but of course he does!" she confirmed. "My dear Miss Braden, if I understand correctly, he means very much for you to go."

"Without question," Guilford affirmed, overhearing this last, "your presence is essential."

An overwhelmed Rhianna could hardly hold herself up. She placed her hand on Lady Brighton's, unmasking her feeble condition.

"Oh, my dear, Miss Braden! You look so pale," the lady immediately perceived. "Guilford, that is enough planning for now. You must take her home this instant. I am sure the comfort of her own home is what she most needs."

"It must be all the excitement of these last days still lingering with me," Rhianna told her.

Lords Kingsley and Brighton were already at her service and the carriage was ordered at once.

*

My Dear Soleil, You cannot imagine what events I have to relay to you. I hardly know where to begin . . .

Thus Rhianna set out at writing her letter. Two days since her stay at Ravensleigh had passed, she sat at the window seat of her rose room. Folds of mauve curtain framed her as she held quill and paper in hand. Through the clear windowpane she could view the rotunda, the whitewashed frame bright as it reflected the sun's unclouded rays. It was here she rested her eyes while she dwelt on her next lines.

The day passed quickly as she wrote, and when Rhianna reached the end of her letter the morning was well along. Placing her papers aside, she rose to leave her room. She was in no hurry to go anywhere, as Lord Kingsley had suspended Audra's lessons for the week at least. She walked along the front balcony, whose tall windows shared the same view of the front approach—as did the lavender room where she had spent her first nights at the manor house.

A visitor caught her attention, a man on horseback who made his way through the gate. The Kingsleys often had visitors, and over the past several months she had begun to recognize many of them from a distance. But this visitor was new—or at least he had not been to Kingsley Manor since she arrived.

Suddenly, she guessed she knew *who.*

It was not long after she heard him enter downstairs that her suspicions were confirmed. As Alfred led him into the drawing room, she caught herself pacing. Wondering at her excitability, Rhianna forced herself back to the window to enjoy the scene she originally sought, only to find she could not remove her eyes from his horse, a muscular, brown-and-white stallion with a long, flowing mane.

A servant approached her from behind, breaking her spell. "You have a visitor, Miss Braden."

She turned to him with a start. "*I* have a visitor?"

"Yes. Lord Brighton of Ravensleigh is requesting you."

"Requesting *me*?"

"Yes, miss."

Thayne Brighton was requesting *her*? Rhianna struggled ineffectually to collect herself as the servant led her downstairs. When at last they reached the drawing room, Rhianna had resigned herself that there could be no preparation for this unexpected meeting.

Guilford and Thayne seemed delighted as she entered. Desmond was not in company, but then, Desmond was rarely home. It was a discomfort lifted from her not to have him there. Lydia Kingsley, looking characteristically irritable, summoned Rhianna to take a seat next to her, which Rhianna accepted.

Once the initial greetings had taken place, Lord Brighton wasted no time in inquiring after Rhianna. "How are you feeling today, Miss Braden? All of Ravensleigh has been wondering about you. I was instructed to speak with you directly, and told, additionally, not to return to the house until I had an answer, and a positive one, at that."

This notion could not but force a smile from her, awkward though she felt, being so addressed. "You may tell them to let you pass the gates, for I am well."

He appeared very sincere when he smiled, revealing a perfect line of white, straight teeth. She caught herself looking at them longer than she ought to have.

"Thank you. My mother will be especially glad of it. Where you are concerned, her worry has not rested," he expressed to her. "It is our joint wish to see you again at Ravensleigh when you are up to it."

Could she be dreaming? An invitation back to Ravensleigh?

"I would be glad to again visit Ravensleigh," she declared, astonished.

All of a sudden, Lord Kingsley rose from his seat.

"My dear Lady Kingsley, would you be so good as to join me in the study? There is something I must communicate to you and it cannot wait."

With what appeared to Rhianna shock and annoyance in Lydia's manner, the lady rose and followed him out of the room so suddenly that Rhianna found herself quite alone with Thayne Brighton.

What could Lord Kingsley mean by this? Rhianna thought in the moments of silence immediately following his exit from the room.

Thayne soon started conversation again, however, saying, "I imagine you must have many frightening recollections of the accident, Miss Braden. How are you coping with them?"

With her thoughts scattered, Rhianna had no choice but to allow herself a moment to consider the question at hand.

Finally, she said, "I have not been able to recall the accident, so, thankfully, I have been spared any such disturbing thoughts."

"You may, indeed, be grateful for that," he replied. "In this instance, you are doing better than I."

Rhianna looked at him in wonder, but overwhelmed by the return of his gaze, quickly lowered her eyes to the floor.

"I'm . . . sorry."

"No, no," he hurried. "You must understand it was just very . . . it was a fearsome moment. I did not foresee, from the appearance of it, that only days later we would be sitting here. You cannot imagine, after beholding you lifeless in the field, how seeing you here, alert, well, it is . . . it is greatly consoling."

This brief recount of what was undoubtedly only a glimpse into his side of the experience brought a flush to Rhianna's cheeks. The thought of her unconscious person in his care was one she had not dwelt upon; though suddenly she wished desperately that she could remember.

"I will never forget what you have done for me," she expressed, expecting him to cut off her thanks at any moment, "and I am well aware that the only reason I am sitting here speaking to you is because you were there to help me. I know not how to thank you."

He shook his head. "Seeing you here in good health is enough."

Silence followed until, at last, Thayne ventured to address her again. "Miss Braden," he began, with some eagerness, "this talk has turned far too serious. Besides, I have a confession to make. While your condition was, certainly, of utmost importance to my visit, it was not my only purpose in coming. I have come to request, that is, I am hoping at the upcoming ball I might trouble you for two dances."

Thayne Brighton dance with a governess? Rhianna imagined he must still be delirious with fear for her life.

"I would have applied at the ball," he concluded, "but I imagine your dance card has already long since been reserved?"

There is no figuring him out! thought Rhianna. *Is he sincere or in jest?* She did not know whether she ought to be flattered or insulted.

"Actually, they have not *all* been spoken for, Lord Brighton."

"Indeed!" he cried, with a very proper amount of surprise. "Then the other gentlemen have shown you far more courtesy than have I by troubling you so promptly after your accident. You must forgive me. Still, I will, however rude, demand those two dances, if you will allow me."

Rhianna consented, as Guilford and Lydia reentered the drawing room. The very idea of what had just passed was ridiculous to her on every level. Her only certainty in the matter was that he would certainly spill something on her dress.

Thayne shortly took leave of Lady Kingsley and Rhianna. He remained only to discuss some business with Lord Kingsley in his study before returning to Ravensleigh. The impression his visit left, however, was a powerful one.

"Well, that was a very odd sort of call," said Lady Kingsley. "Lord Brighton rather gives one the impression he did not come at all for his usual sort of visit. In fact, the gentleman seems quite to dote on you."

Rhianna had come to expect snide comments from Lydia in her year at Kingsley Manor, but this was more direct than anything she had previously experienced from the lady.

"Lady Kingsley, forgive me, but I am sure you are utterly mistaken. Lord Brighton may be the gentleman enough, indeed, to offer the most basic of kind expressions, but I am quite certain his main purpose in visiting Kingsley Manor is the same as ever— his business with Lord Kingsley."

"Your argument is not nearly convincing enough to sway my opinion, Miss Braden. I have never seen him behave thus. It seems to me you have become quite a favorite of his."

"Not at all, my lady! Had I not fallen from my horse, Lord Brighton would never have entertained an audience with me."

Lydia gave an indifferent shrug. "Well, I suppose there is no way to test that theory, is there?"

"I see no need if there were," Rhianna told her. "I am happy to accept kindness from wherever it comes."

"Yes, a good rule of thumb," she agreed. "My husband, Guilford, is very kind, would you not agree?"

Rhianna wished not to speculate on her possible meaning. Her next words intended to not only end this peculiar conversation, but end it on a lighter note.

"I have found everyone here at the manor to be very kind. Now, if you will excuse me, Lady Kingsley, I have much to prepare for Audra's next lessons."

Lydia inclined her head, and Rhianna quickly escaped her company for the quiet of the schoolroom.

*

Soleil wasted no time in responding to Rhianna's letter. Great relief was expressed in response to the horse accident, though they were sure it would produce nothing but nightmares for them all for weeks to come. With regard to the ball, knowing it to be another childhood wish come true for Rhianna, Soleil was delighted for her; Philippe, on the other hand, was not quite as thrilled. She had no doubt that his eyes would behold her note, which is why Rhianna had chosen her words carefully. Even still, what she did say of the upcoming ball was enough to put him in doleful spirits.

"Poor Philippe is rather heartbroken that you should be at a ball without him. He begs you to think of him once before the night is through."

Soleil also intimated that they would be soon traveling to see her. Precisely when she could not yet say, but they were looking to visit her in England within the next couple months.

On the morning that Soleil's letter arrived, it had been arranged for Rhianna to go with Lady Brighton to her dressmaker and cobbler. Guilford, unreservedly forgoing all convention, continued to insist Rhianna attend the ball. He also expressed his wish that Lydia see to Rhianna's costume, but Lady Brighton was quite determined to take over, and Lydia was quite willing to allow it. Rhianna, beside herself that she should be doing any such thing, would have been happy to go with either lady, but was *very* happy to go with Lady Brighton.

Never, thought Rhianna, *was a girl to be more elegantly attired for a dance in all of England.* A white-on-white pattern in French silk had been chosen, with Lady Brighton's guidance, designed with a fashionably wide neckline, small waist, bell-shaped skirt, and beret sleeves. The corsage was to be trimmed in horizontal folds, while knots of ribbon ornamented the shoulders and back of the gown. With Lord Kingsley's insistence that price be no object, Lady Brighton overlooked no detail in all complimentary accessories.

If Rhianna's mind had been torn between Soleil and Philippe's visit and the ball, the latter overpowered the former. She could only think to herself that all the things she had dared to dream of, but never attempted to wish for, were happening.

*

One week before the ball, Desmond was determined to request Rhianna's hand for the first two dances of the evening. It would be well before the majority knew she was a governess; therefore, with nothing known of her other than her beauty, which would paralyze even the most aloof of spectators, she was certain to be in the foreground. Not one to shy away from attention, he looked forward to claiming the source of many eager glances and whispers for at least the first hour of the ball. More importantly, however, it would be well before any other gentlemen had an opportunity to recommend themselves to *his* future paramour, placing Desmond at advantage to lay his groundwork.

On the week of the ball he approached her. Just as he had hoped, he found her alone in the schoolroom, collecting a French exercise book from Audra's desk.

"My dear Miss Braden," he called her as he entered. "How very glad I am to find you here."

*

Rarely did anyone enter the schoolroom besides Audra. A servant occasionally, to be sure, but otherwise it was something of a retreat for Rhianna, particularly when Lord Kingsley was out. In the months since her arrival at Kingsley Manor, she had yet to establish a comfortable rapport with Lydia or her son, the former being frequently ill-humored and the latter arrogant. Desmond's sudden entrance at once enshrouded the room with a disagreeable air.

"Lord Kingsley," she responded, with a start, "what a surprise."

She watched the young heir as he stepped animatedly passed Audra's desk and approached her. If his sudden appearance had not startled her enough, his insistence on standing so very close when speaking to her did little to put her at ease. She did what she could to keep at a distance of an arm's length, but found it was not in her power to do half as much.

"Now, really, when it is just us, must we continue to address one another so formally? It would be perfectly proper for you to call me Desmond."

To this awkward statement, he left her no time to respond. Likely, she could not have formed a composed reply give a considerable amount of time, so she was not sorry that he continued along. Privately, she resolved to do all in her power never to be alone with him on any future occasion.

He told her, "I have searched the entire house over and was beginning to wonder that you might be hiding from me. Certainly, you must know why I have come."

Rhianna declared she did not and, in a second effort to create some distance between them, moved to her desk by the window and placed down the book she had been carrying.

He followed her.

"How very modest you are," he said, with a twisted grin. "Very well, I shall not make you wait, though you cannot make me believe you are without your suspicions."

She had difficulty in meeting his gaze, which, as usual, was fixed intently on her. Frequently, she got the sense he was making advances at her with his eyes and today was no exception. His cocky manner and over confidence were more exaggerated than usual, and she found herself leaning very nearly backwards to gain precious inches worth of space between them.

"I really can have no idea," she admitted, hoping he would hurry with saying whatever it was he intended to say and leave.

And then he said the words that made Rhianna's heart sink. "I have come to reserve the first two dances from you at the ball Saturday."

She really was surprised that she should receive any request from him at all. And that he was given to the delusion she had been waiting for him to ask was unsettling, to say the least. Little did he know that the truth was quite the opposite—his request, although not unpleasant enough to ruin the experience altogether, was quite enough for her to hope the first two dances passed as quickly as possible.

"You mustn't be so astonished." He grinned, her speechlessness seeming to amuse him. "Did you really think I would *not* seek to secure you for as many dances as society would allow? If only I could request your hand for the whole of the evening!"

Thankfully, at this moment, Audra entered the schoolroom and Rhianna had never been so happy to see her.

"I know that you will not disappoint me," he stated under his breath, knowing his time was up.

Aware that there could be no declining it, she accepted with what graciousness she could summon.

"I look forward to it with pleasure," he concluded, and with his back to Audra he lifted her hand to his lips.

With this last, Desmond Kingsley left her, smiling as he had since the moment he entered the schoolroom. As the relief of his departure sunk in, Rhianna reflected that her impression of him had not changed; indeed, it was built upon. She already found Desmond Kingsley unpleasant, conceited, and vulgar; now it was very clear that he thought her attracted to him. What presumption! Probably, he thought *every* woman attracted to him.

While she pondered these things, Audra approached her with a question about her history lesson. With difficulty, Rhianna attempted to extinguish Desmond from her mind as she opened her copy of the book.

"Part three," Audra specified, as Rhianna turned there.

Fingering through the pages, she noticed some of her own notes were missing.

"I don't understand, it's all so very odd," she mumbled to herself.

Checking to see that she did, in fact, have the correct publication, she then resorted to checking the name in the edition, at which point she solved the mystery—or discovered one. A flush came over her as she feverishly examined the inside cover of the book. In that instant, all thoughts of Desmond were erased as she ran her fingers under the faint black ink of the name *Hallie*.

"Audra, have you any idea where this book came from?" Her voice was breathless, her composure lost.

Audra looked at her with a curious gaze. "Is it not yours?"

"No . . ." Rhianna could not hide the frenzy of emotions. "Audra, can you tell me who Hallie is?"

"Hallie?"

"Yes. Her name is etched in this book. Do you know anything about her?"

Audra leaned over and looked for herself. It was some time before she finally answered; Rhianna thought that perhaps she never would.

"I believe that was the name of Desmond's last governess."

Rhianna's breath froze in her chest. *Hallie, a governess at Kingsley Manor?*

"Is there anything else you can tell me about her? Anything at all?" she asked Audra desperately.

Little Audra shook her head. "I never knew her. Miss Barnesworth was my governess from the beginning."

"Do you know why she left?" Rhianna continued, anxious to know anything and everything that Audra could tell.

"No." She added, "I do hope *you* will be here a long time."

Realizing that Audra knew nothing else regarding Hallie, Rhianna let the subject drop, but it was quite enough to keep her busily in thought, with Desmond a distant memory. After Audra left, she took care to keep the book with her, resolved to mention it to Mauvreen in hopes her friend would now be willing to provide further detail.

However, the following week was all bustle and excitement around Kingsley Manor and she could not get away. Fascinated by the preparations that went into a Kingsley ball, Rhianna watched on. Within the month, a guest list was written and invitations sent out, decorations were prepared, professional musicians engaged, and the dance floor was polished. An elaborate supper would soon be prepared by not one, but three chefs. Servants hastened from one room to another, checking to see that no detail was overlooked, so that when the final days before the ball arrived, everything was taken care of and all that was left was anticipation.

Chapter Four

A fire blazed in the hearth that evening, its flickering light enveloping Rhianna in a blanket of warmth as she stood before it. The rose room was cozy and brightly lit, assisted by a handful of candles whose glow in the mirror on the opposite wall was reflected to the far corners of the apartment. Arrayed in her white gown and satin slippers, the twenty-year-old Rhianna lingered momentarily before proceeding upstairs to the ballroom.

It was expected to be an exceedingly good ball. Not a single invitation had been declined, and more than thirty couples from the most respected families would be in attendance. Twenty-five dances would play in the Kingsley ballroom, entertaining some of the most desirable young men and women in England. With difficulty Rhianna mustered her courage to face such society, and she was torn between feelings of fear and absolute, perfect happiness.

Eight o'clock was the set hour. Some concern was made over the condition of the weather, for an early snow had begun to christen the roadways. Fortunately, it was thinly spread and would not prevent the greatly anticipated occasion from proceeding.

In hopes of getting a view of the approaching coaches, Rhianna decided to leave her chamber in favor of the window at the first floor balcony. On her way out, she stopped briefly to take a final glance at her curls to ensure they were properly in place. She stood in wonder at the bandeaus of pearls carefully woven through her red ringlets and the matching choker necklace with its pear-shaped rhinestone drop that complimented the low neckline of her white, silky gown. She smoothed the skirt of her floor-length dress and marveled at her gloved hands. Hallie's brooch provided the finishing touch. Smiling to herself, Rhianna knew the girl who left the rose room that night would not be the same girl who returned.

Through the tall, frost-clouded Venetian window that overlooked Kingsley Manor's front entrance, she could observe in the moonlight the white-sprinkled trees that guarded the glistening, snow-dusted ground. In the north winds, snowflakes danced through the air blissfully, as if having their own celebration outside. Rhianna stood and watched, a grandfather clock chiming behind her eight times, as a carriage pulled up to the house. Soon after, several more carriages followed, the tread marks left by their wheels quickly hidden in a blanket of yet more snow. The guests were arriving.

"Miss Braden?"

She turned with a start to the servant that stood behind her. "Oh! Katie, I didn't hear you coming."

"Forgive me, I didn't mean to frighten. Lord Kingsley's good friend, Mr. Weathersby, has arrived from London and he wishes to introduce you."

Rhianna drew a deep breath. The time had come.

"Thank you. I'll be there directly," she said. "Will you be spending time with George tonight?"

Katie blushed. "The servants are having their own ball, of sorts. From the attic rooms, you can hear the music clearly. If you sneak away at all, come find us."

"I shall," Rhianna smiled.

With that, Katie disappeared as silently as she had come. Not wishing to keep Lord Kingsley waiting, Rhianna allowed only a parting glance out the window before leaving hastily for the ballroom.

*

The ballroom was all splendor and elegance. The chandeliers were lit, the decorations were opulent, paintings and priceless art were uncovered, and the orchestra was in position. Everything seemed full of liveliness and joy. In a short period of time, the room was a sea of ribbons and gloves, bonnets and feathers. Girls arrived whom Rhianna thought herself privileged to look upon. How lovely they were, in their satin, gauze, and crepe dresses! Broad lace outlined many of their small figures, and voluminous petticoats were not wanting. Many wore gold combs or coronets of silver filigree in their hair, and tiaras and wreaths of flowers were in abundance.

Rhianna observed one girl in particular, Miss Austine Leighart, daughter of Lord Leighart of Norwich, whom with both fairness and fortune on her side had the power to capture everyone's attention. With soft features, blond hair, and wearing a string of expensive Italian pearls, Miss Leighart complimented her physical appearance with social accomplishment and grace. Rhianna imagined she made women envious and men wild, but that all in the assembly could not but admire her above the other girls.

Rhianna made her way through the room to Guilford Kingsley, who upon seeing the gown Lady Brighton had chosen, appeared very much pleased with its effect. She admitted to herself she was flattered to hear him describe her as "highly becoming," though Rhianna noticed his eyes frequently and unsettlingly seemed to be cast upon her brooch. Lady Brighton was quick to find them both and voice her own satisfaction in the most indulging expressions, contributing to the warm flush in Rhianna's cheeks long after leaving to make her rounds of the room.

Black jackets and white cravats were plentiful among the gentlemen. Yet, though all wore their best formalwear and top hats, there was no man present who could match Thayne Brighton in his vest and dress coat. Rhianna first caught sight of him speaking with Miss Leighart and even she could not but admit he was looking his best. His sartorial splendor was second only to his statuesque frame and symmetrical features. His expression seemed inviting as he conversed with Miss Leighart, and Rhianna wondered what his opinion was of her.

Although vaguely aware her glance was lingering, she was

not caught out of it until Lydia Kingsley took notice. "They are intended for each other, you know," Lydia told her.

Swiftly did Rhianna lower her eyes, the words themselves hitting her with surprising unpleasantness, but eclipsed by her being found thus absorbed.

"They would make an excellent couple," she returned, mildly humiliated, before finding Lydia already conversing with a nearby acquaintance, her back turned.

Resultantly, Rhianna was unable to allow herself another look in Thayne's direction for some time. Meanwhile, Guilford Kingsley, oblivious to this exchange, provided her with a program and dance card, while busily introducing her to various arrivals. Several gentlemen wrote their names on her card at once. As they did so, Rhianna was shocked to overhear a few gossipy, older women considering her own best potential matches and forming wild speculations regarding her upbringing and education. It seemed because of her they would have plenty to entertain themselves for the whole of the evening.

Regardless of this last, Rhianna was so enraptured at the affair overall that she presently recovered from her awkward moment with Lydia. Until this point, she had had not a moment to concern herself even with her upcoming dances with Desmond Kingsley, but she soon recalled her misfortune after spotting him conversing with an older gentleman near the card room. Lord Whitehall of London was a large man, with a suspended middle and a thick, fleshy neck that nearly concealed his entire cravat. He held a very high seat in Parliament and his family had known the Kingsleys for generations. His wife was also in attendance, as well as his mother, a gravely frail, old woman who took considerable risk venturing into the cold to attend, but she claimed she "would not miss Claude's cooking for all the world."

Soon, Guilford Kingsley made his wish of commencing the ball known. Turning to Rhianna, he asked, "Are you engaged for the first dance?"

"I believe I am, sir, to Lord Kingsley."

This seemed to please him and he took a moment to catch his son's eye. Desmond soon realized the dancing was to begin and he hastened to his father's call and Rhianna's side. Taking her hand, he mentioned something about forgiving him for the delay and "how very charming" she looked. The next moment, he was escorting her, to her mortification, to the front of the set.

"Without a doubt," Desmond gloated, looking her over, "you are the most handsome girl of the night."

"Your compliments are more than a stretch, Lord Kingsley," she replied, hoping to discourage any such statements from him.

"Are they? I have observed guests stopping mid-sentence at the sight of you."

"I doubt that very much."

"You are a humble creature, aren't you? It escapes you, does it, that your natural beauty, enhanced by this costume and a pinch of mystery, attracts the notice of everyone present?" Rhianna met his gaze, as she often did, with speechless amazement, as he added, "You put Miss Leighart to shame."

These last words were whispered just as Miss Leighart herself, coupled with Lord Thayne Brighton, joined the set. Horrified that she should be placed before them both, Rhianna prayed Austine Leighart would not discover her situation until they no longer stood side by side.

"Lord Kingsley has an intriguing partner, indeed," said a less-than-enthusiastic Austine, in an undertone to Thayne. "Pray, who is she?"

Rhianna happened to overhear and distress nearly overtook her. How would Thayne Brighton explain her? Mortification was averted as, incredibly, he made no effort to promote her position as governess in the Kingsley home, as she expected of him. Instead, his answer was simple, even evasive, and his tone neither mocked nor judged.

"You must mean Miss Braden," he returned. "I understand she is come from France."

This seemed to be the end of the investigation. Austine did not seem to wish to know more, at least from Thayne, and the conversation moved on as the other couples also assembled in line. Desmond, for his part, grumbled about most of them, and mocked the rest, much to Rhianna's abhorrence.

"I cannot believe that Miss Leeds has the audacity to come and dance! She is very nearly *thirty*. I shall certainly never stand up with her."

"Lord Kingsley! How can you be so cruel?"

"Cruel? No, indeed," Desmond laughed. "At least, no more than every other male in this room. You may not hear their thoughts, but I daresay, in this matter, I have declared the sentiments of them all."

The music began. Guilford Kingsley opened his ball with a quadrille and at once the room was in motion. Rhianna tried desperately to immerse herself in the harmony of the piano, violin, and cello, ignoring Desmond as much as possible. Her heart beat severely as the moment neared for the surrounding couples to focus on her and Desmond's performance—but when the time came, Desmond led her masterfully and she could not but be comfortable with his style and grace. How confident he was, how easeful! He told her continuously how well she danced and how everyone must be in awe. Though his comments did little to calm her, she found that with his *skill* she was able to survive it.

*

Half an hour or more passed when, at last, the first dance was completed. It was now Desmond's turn to choose a dance and none would be chosen until he had the undivided attention of everyone in the room.

"I propose," said he, speaking to the crowd and pausing for effect, "a waltz."

Shouts of approval issued forth from the masses and the musicians did not hesitate. Music erupted forth as Desmond took Rhianna's hand and led her once again to the floor.

Rhianna could not look forward to dancing it. In only a few instances had she ever waltzed, and it had been uncomfortable enough even with Philippe. Now to be forced into it with Desmond Kingsley! It called for more courage than she believed she could muster. Her sole comfort was that it was the last she would have to dance with him for the rest of the evening.

Most dancers remained with their original partners. Miss Leighart appeared somewhat flushed and Rhianna observed Thayne gesture toward the refreshment room. She was astonished to discover that she was so absorbed with Austine Leighart's declination, and Lord Brighton subsequently placing his hand upon her waist, that she was fully unaware of Desmond Kingsley performing the same action with her until they began to dance.

Frequently, she caught herself watching Lord Brighton and Miss Leighart as they floated along the floor, their movements elegant, polished. Thayne returned Rhianna's glance on more than one occasion, and smiled each time. She wondered if he was truly smiling at her, or had been smiling from some witty remark of Miss Leighart's when their eyes happened to meet. Regardless, Rhianna smiled in return.

But what began as a curiosity started to happen so often that Rhianna fought herself *not* to look at Thayne Brighton, and in consistently failing to stop herself, found his eyes were *always* upon her. At length, their smiles faded, their eyes locked, and a connection of unknown meaning was bridged between them.

"Oh!" Austine Leighart suddenly stopped dancing. "My dress!"

Thayne looked down with alarm and noted, with one false step, he had torn the hem of her gown. With a profusion of apologies, he led her off the dance floor to Lady Kingsley, who undoubtedly assisted her to the cloakroom for mending.

This was enough to break Rhianna's spell. The event did not escape Desmond's notice and Rhianna discerned he gave Thayne an unfriendly glance.

"I do believe *everyone* is desperate to dance with you," he said to her, irritably. Then, in a softer tone, Desmond added, "Oh, come now, you cannot blame him. And you mustn't blame yourself. You can hardly help it. In fact, if I were you, I would expect to be the cause of at least a few more ripped hems before the evening is out."

Even if, for a moment, it had crossed her mind, Rhianna was in no way going to adulate herself by accepting she held responsibility for Miss Leighart's torn gown. Besides this, she *certainly* did not want to hold a conversation with Desmond Kingsley over it.

With a quizzical brow, she replied, "I cannot imagine what you must be thinking."

"Thinking? Not at all. Thinking is the very thing we men are unable to do in your presence. We are quite handicapped tonight. Surely, you must know this."

"You flatter me excessively, Lord Kingsley."

"Do I, indeed? Or have you so thoroughly deceived yourself as to the power of your allure?"

This statement perturbed her, but she was too terrified to know his meaning to allow herself to reflect on it, at least, while they continued to waltz.

"Oh, certainly, the allure of my connections and inheritance is very great," she laughed, hoping with all her heart that this reminder would deter him from any unwanted advances.

"I doubt you shall want a partner all night," Desmond predicted.

Whether he knew it or not, his statement would indeed prove true. Rhianna did not *want* for a partner the whole of the evening, even if she did not *choose* to dance all twenty-five dances.

In response, Rhianna politely shook her head. "No, sir, there can be no convincing me of anything you are saying. No one in this room is more aware of how undeserving I am of being here than myself."

"Undeserving? My lady, let me not hear such words spoken from you again. How very peculiar you are. Have you no idea of your worth? Have you no idea what an honor and privilege it is to be of your acquaintance? No, I see you do not."

"How you exaggerate!" she cried. "Such nonsense I have never heard. I can barely listen to you."

"I do not exaggerate, nor have I ever. I only beg you let me show you . . ."

A pause was necessary at this point, for the dance was over. The music concluded and applause issued forth from the crowd.

When it died down, and as new partners were chosen, Desmond leaned toward her ear, and said, "I could give you so much, if only you would allow me."

"What do you mean, Lord Kingsley?" she asked pointedly.

He kissed her hand and smiled. "Desmond," he replied, with a wink.

With this last, he disappeared into the assemblage, leaving her with no more than her own thoughts. How any one person could be so plain in meaning, yet, at the same time, so very vague, she hardly knew. One thing she quickly settled upon was that, for a man of his situation, it was unthinkable that he should reduce himself, nay, be so *imprudent*, as to sincerely address himself to his sister's governess. Of this fact, she could be certain. She also trusted she had given no encouragement for such intimacy as he was now taking the liberty of engaging in with her. This may not have been of any consequence, as Desmond Kingsley did not seem the type to wait for encouragement. Still, there was the question of his intent, and Rhianna examined with a degree of distress the one possible arrangement he might have in mind.

Before she was able to worry herself beyond her ability to conceal it, Mr. Weathersby approached her for a dance. A tall, thin man who had known Lord Guilford Kingsley since youth, Mr. Weathersby was a likeable gentleman. Grateful not to be left alone, she accepted readily, and thus continued the ball. Fourteen dances were played, and Rhianna neither saw nor spoke to

Desmond again until supper, where some few times she noticed him intent on making eye contact with her. She felt sure that given the opportunity to speak to her in private, he would undoubtedly revive the most unwelcome conversation.

Several dinner courses were served: endless quantities of soup, cheese, and oysters were provided, and Claude's veal was much talked about. Many of the guests were unable to decipher whether the food really was excellent and not just because their wine informed them so. Nevertheless, all were enjoying themselves immensely, and the old women and the young looked forward with eagerness to the time when the dancing would resume.

Despite Desmond's remarks of earlier, Rhianna allowed the melodic harmony of Vivaldi and Bach to penetrate her spirit. The masterpieces played that night could not but calm her soul. This second part of the evening ball found her more at ease with her surroundings, as well, because Lord Kingsley had introduced her to many more guests, and there were thus fewer strangers.

It was not until late in the evening that, drained from the activities, she escaped to a quiet seat. Her last partner, a young baron from the neighboring town of Bromley, brought her some refreshments before fulfilling his obligation to dance with another young lady. His wishes to remain seated with Rhianna were discernible through his effusive apologies for being otherwise committed. Despondently did he depart from her and lead his new partner to the floor.

Rhianna was not sorry to see him go. There was something magical in observing a Kingsley ball as a spectator and she enjoyed having the moment to herself.

Never, she thought, *I shall never forget this night.*

She enjoyed watching the happy couples as they skipped and twirled, the pastel gowns of the ladies offering just a faint splash of color against the gentlemen's black wardrobe. It was the perfect evening. Her seat, too, was perfectly situated far from Desmond Kingsley, who danced with a Miss DeWitt, rumored to be the lady that Lord and Lady Kingsley wished to secure for their son. Rhianna thought that was an excellent idea and hoped it would happen for them sooner than later.

Many of the older guests had long since scurried to the card tables, including long-time friends of Guilford Kingsley, Lord Whitehall and his mother, Dowager Lady Whitehall. Lady Whitehall, an eccentric, talkative woman, equal to her mate in measurements and overall embarrassing to those associated with her, was vocal that she would not miss a moment of the ballroom's liveliness for the world. She was, at this time, commanding a conversation among her contemporaries on the evening's entertainment, at a table not far from Rhianna. Rhianna decided to amuse herself by listening in on their conversation.

"Never have I seen such a skilled group of young dancers as are gathered at this ball! My word, the Kingsleys have done such a lovely job of collecting them together! See how gracefully they proceed—separate when required, together when required. Whatever the dance demands, no movement eludes them."

In her ramblings, she went on to comment specifically on Miss Leighart and another well-bred lady, Miss Mina Selwyn.

"Excellent examples of English nobility! Sheer excellence! Also, that young lady who began the ball with Desmond Kingsley—she is unfamiliar to me—how very flawless!"

"Oh, yes," cried another woman. "She gives Miss Leighart quite the run for her money. Who can tell me about her? I have not been able to get a word of information."

Rhianna instinctively covered her mouth with her hand and laughed at their ridiculousness. She wondered what they would say if they knew the details of her identity.

For a short while, her musings were uninterrupted. Time enough passed for her to become fairly absorbed in them so that when someone did approach to speak to her, she was taken by surprise.

"How is it that you are not dancing, Miss Braden? Your

countless partners have fatigued you, I daresay."

Roused from distraction, she turned to find Lord Thayne Brighton standing beside her. As he addressed her, she could not tell if she now felt awkward or completely at ease. She had seen him only occasionally since the incident with Miss Leighart, who often flirted with him between dances.

"You are very observant," she replied. "And what of yourself? Are you not dancing?"

"Dancing," he then answered, "is all well and good. Interesting conversation, however, is what I am now seeking." He gestured to sit with her. "May I?"

She nodded consent. "If it is conversation that you desire, Lord Brighton, how is it that you should need to leave the floor? Do you not speak to your partners?"

"Oh, yes, certainly," he acknowledged. "But you forget I specified *interesting* conversation—something lacking in my partners as of yet. I was left with no choice but to go in search of it elsewhere."

A blow to Miss Leighart, indeed!

"Well," said Rhianna, astonished by his frankness, "I cannot bear to keep you in deception. If you have not found what you are looking for in so many refined and distinguished ladies, you are certain to be disappointed at this very table."

"No, Miss Braden, indeed, you are mistaken. While *they* have had nothing to remark on beyond the ball itself, there is a particular matter you and I desperately need to discuss that is of the utmost importance. That is, if you are disengaged."

There was something in the way he looked at her and in the turn of his smile that made it impossible for her to know if he was sincere or jesting. Nothing of such a nature came to her mind that required immediate and private communication, as he suggested. Regardless, he had fully captured her attention and she could hardly refuse such a consultation.

"Of the utmost importance, you say?"

"The very paramount."

"Well, Lord Brighton," she professed, unable to prevent the corners of her mouth from widening, "I am all attention."

"You may not remember . . ." he began. "No, I know you must not. It was some time ago . . ."

Thayne searched for words and Rhianna knew he did not speak in jest.

"What I wish to say is," he continued, "I have come asking your forgiveness."

She looked at him wide-eyed. "I beg your pardon?"

"Miss Braden, I am aware you must now think me very odd." Thayne implored, "Allow me to explain myself."

He stopped and searched her expression for what seemed to Rhianna a long moment.

"Lord Brighton," she interrupted, with a coy smile, "I understand you perfectly."

"No," Thayne said at last, appearing broken from a spell, "You cannot in the least comprehend me. I speak of an incident—nay, two incidents—from ten years ago, and had they not tormented me so greatly these past weeks and had I not made mention of them, they were sure never to be resurrected. As it is, I must receive your forgiveness for the error of an undeveloped mind, the disposition of a foolish, imperfect youth, and gain closure, or I am doomed to live in constant regret."

Allowing no interruption from her, he continued, "You are no doubt under the impression that this is the beginning of our acquaintance when it is, in fact, a renewal. It must have been very shortly before you left for France that you met with a very stupid and insensible eleven-year-old boy. I imagine it means nothing to you today, but I must apologize for my appalling conduct then. To have thought that my upbringing was any sort of excuse for my ill treatment of you was ignorance at its very core. I see now that both then and today, I was utterly in the wrong, and your conduct at all times has proven you infinitely my superior."

All the while, Rhianna gazed at him in wonder and disbelief. To imagine she would receive an apology from that contemptible boy, that mean, heartless child who could not see beyond his own family crest! Was he sincerely confessing to her the wrongs of his behavior and asking forgiveness? It could not be, she thought, and yet, how earnestly he spoke, and what angst he tried vainly to suppress.

Lord Guilford Kingsley arrived, suspending their conversation.

"Dear friends!" he called to both Rhianna and Thayne. He was in excellent spirits. "Shall I flatter myself? I think the evening quite capital! Pray, set me right—are you having an abominable time?"

Rising to greet him, Thayne Brighton shook Lord Kingsley's hand. Beside him, Rhianna ascended from her seat.

"It is always a pleasure to be with such fine company, sir. I own it is a splendid ball."

"Good, good!" he cried, happily. "And what of Miss Braden? I trust you are enjoying yourself?"

"I am exceedingly happy, Lord Kingsley. I cannot form words expressive enough to thank you for such a night," she assured him.

A new song was about to begin and before Guilford could respond, Thayne declared, "If you will excuse us, Lord Kingsley, I was only just about to request Miss Braden's company on the floor." Turning to Rhianna, he said, "I would like to claim my promised dances. Will you do me the honor?"

Thayne offered his hand to Rhianna, and she accepted.

"Enjoy yourselves, by all means," Lord Kingsley insisted. "I am off to attend to my other guests."

Thanks were again offered to him and he left them presently. A country dance was chosen, and Rhianna was conscious of many eyes riveted on them as she and Thayne made their way through the assemblage.

"I do not ask that you pardon what you cannot," he concluded pleadingly, as they took their positions, "only what your feelings will allow. You must know, however, that to find pity on myself, remorseful and afflicted as I am, will free me from a suffering which you cannot imagine."

Thayne Brighton had, in those few sentences, recommended himself most highly to Rhianna. The music began, and the dance brought them apart momentarily, but Rhianna did not need a moment to form her answer.

When they were brought together again, she took his hands, and declared, "You shock me exceedingly. Very well, let us forget the past. Let us be friends."

"So you *do* remember?"

She merely smiled, and said, "I suppose such an apology, not to mention the kindness you showed after my accident, must make you pardonable."

With an air of genuine relief, Thayne declared, "Fate has looked upon me favorably today. Let us be friends, indeed."

She could not despise him after this tête-à-tête. In fact, with her opinion of him entirely altered, feeling that he was now both handsome *and* amiable, Rhianna was quite willing to, and already did, like him.

After this, there was nothing but to enjoy her time with Thayne Brighton. They danced, they laughed, and the leering eyes of Austine Leighart and Desmond Kingsley went almost wholly unnoticed.

At the end of their second dance, Thayne declared, "No man was ever happier to find that reconciliation was not too much a thing to be hoped for. Will you be very uncomfortable if I boast of having danced with the most charming lady in the entire house?"

A scream issued forth from amongst them, silencing the music and the crowd. The cry was close to Rhianna and Thayne; she instinctively tightened her hold on him as they looked around. Guests moved round about, separating, allowing space to the person from whom it had come.

Dowager Lady Whitehall was very pale. The object of her glassy gaze was indubitable. The longer she looked at Rhianna, the more frightened she became, sinking into the arms of Lady Whitehall who held her afoot.

"Catherine!" cried she, wide-eyed and shivering.

Rhianna felt her heart stop as Lord Whitehall and Lord Kingsley rushed to the dowager's side and tried futilely to calm her.

"Guilford! Guilford, do you not see her?" she cried continuously.

"Mother, you are hallucinating," declared her son. "What can you mean?"

She ignored him and spoke only to Lord Kingsley. "Can you not answer me, Guilford? Surely, *you must see her*!"

In a very low, calm tone, he spoke to her, saying, "My dear madam, you are mistaken. What you are seeing is only a guest of ours."

"It is an *apparition*!"

He assured her, "There is no such thing before you. You must believe me. Catherine is not here."

At this moment, and at this moment only, did Dowager Lady Whitehall remove her eyes from Rhianna and lock them upon Lord Kingsley.

"You will never convince me of it," she swore.

Taking another look in the direction of the young couple, the old woman fell unconscious.

Rhianna gasped and commotion filled the ballroom. Mr. Weathersby and another, younger man lifted the dowager and carried her off as Lady Kingsley guided them and the Whitehalls out of the dance hall for quiet recovery.

Feeling that every eye must rest upon her, Rhianna kept her head and eyes down, inwardly traumatized. Hardly was she aware that Thayne still held her hands in his and even less was she aware of the concern in his eyes. Only when Lord Kingsley approached could she unflinchingly look up.

"Miss Braden," said he, in a private tone, "are you well?"

"I am sure I do not know," she returned, her voice shaky.

He placed a caring hand upon her arm. "She is a confused, old woman. There is no meaning in her words. Pray, do not let it alarm you."

While he spoke, she gained enough courage to ask the only question that seemed to matter. "Who is Catherine?"

Lord Kingsley answered, "Obviously, she is not in her right mind." With a glance at Thayne, he added, "Seeing as you are in good hands, I must withdraw to see about the dowager. Excuse me."

Guilford Kingsley thus left them, raising an arm to the orchestra, signaling them to play. Music resumed, and those who did not care enough about Dowager Lady Whitehall's scene to allow it to ruin their fun chose new partners. A few stood to the side and further observed Rhianna.

"Come," said Thayne, guiding her to a seat, "you must sit. You are grown almost as pale as the dowager."

She only had time to thank him before an impertinent Desmond approached.

"Ah, Brighton, my good man! I appreciate your assistance in helping Miss Braden. Now that I am here, however, I am glad to relieve you of your duty so you may continue to enjoy the ball."

Rhianna knew not what subtle reaction she must have given in response, but Thayne was directly mindful of her desire not to have Desmond around.

He rose to meet him, saying, "You may call it a duty, if you are so inclined, but even if it were such, I should have no wish to be relieved of it."

"I do not want to cause trouble to anyone," Rhianna injected, with little energy.

"You are no trouble. Let the concern not enter your mind." Turning once more to Desmond, Thayne said, "You may safely continue to enjoy the ball that is in your father's honor. Your services are not needed here."

Desmond's displeasure was surprisingly ill concealed. Coldly, he excused himself and walked out of the ballroom altogether. Fortunately, the tension his presence created quickly dissipated with his exit.

Lady Brighton soon joined Rhianna and Thayne. Rhianna last had the opportunity of speaking with her only briefly at supper, but now she was glad to have her companionship again. Such a good-natured woman, and so unaffected by anything dramatic, Lady Brighton was precisely the sort of company Rhianna welcomed after the troubling event.

"Curious what she said," whispered Lady Brighton to Thayne and Rhianna. "I can think of no one by the name of Catherine."

Thayne sat leaning toward Rhianna protectively. "I think that you make too much of it, Mother. I believe Dowager Lady Whitehall was, as Lord Kingsley said, not in her right mind. The woman is ancient—her son ought not to keep her up such late hours."

All expressed a hope that the dowager would quickly recover. Soon, Lady Brighton made a comment on the dancing and the general elegance of everyone in attendance, which further progressed into small talk about supper and the weather. Both her and her son's attempts to take Rhianna's mind off the troubling event did not go unnoticed by her, and though it did not produce the desired effect, she was appreciative and thought they gave it a wonderful effort.

"I admit, I am very interested to know how the snow is getting along," said Thayne. "I propose we take a look outside."

"Oh, no, no," said Lady Brighton, "not me, indeed. I have no energy to leave the comfort of this seat, but do not let me stop you."

"Miss Braden, will you join me?"

She hesitated, and he pleaded further for her company.

"Well, perhaps a walk will do me good," she at last conceded, taking his hand.

They bid *adieu* to Lady Brighton and the two set forth toward a far corner of the ballroom, where crowding was minimal and the windows easily accessible.

"How were the balls in France, Miss Braden? Does excitement follow you?" he asked along the way.

"By excitement, do you mean old women screaming at me?" she asked, with a smile.

"Or having cross gentlemen vying for your attention," he smirked.

She chuckled under her breath and momentarily recalled her coming out ball in France. Rhianna was sixteen years of age when Marquis Vallière hosted the ball in her honor. She and Philippe opened with a minuet. It was a sacred and cherished occasion.

This quickly triggered the memory, not only of that night gone by, but of Philippe himself and Rhianna caught herself in a comparison of her feelings for him and Thayne Brighton. The very presence of the latter had a tremendous effect on her. Never had she discerned such a perfect mix of emotions. His kindness, his words, his company brought her pleasure, yet his person—a turning of his head, the movement of an arm, the prospect of being with him alone—forced her to acknowledge that within only an hour's time, Lord Thayne Brighton procured the power to make Rhianna's heart flutter.

"No, I would venture to say this has been quite the evening. Not to mention," she added, "the addition of new and unlikely friends."

They stood beside the window as she spoke and he watched her with—was it admiration? He seemed to halt his glance suddenly, and had there not been the barrier of situation and position in society, Rhianna might not have attempted to check her feelings.

"Quite the evening," he returned.

Thayne distractedly drew back the drapery. She could not help but watch him closely, in part out of curiosity, in part because he was mesmerizing.

"Perhaps all of us will have to rely on the Kingsleys' good hospitality and remain at the manor this night," he said to her, before looking out.

"Let us hope it is not the case, or you may be sleeping where you now stand," she jested.

"After such a night, even the best of circumstances would not place me in a mind for sleep."

What this suggested, she hardly knew, but she afterward turned her attention to the window with little interest as to what lay beyond it. Rhianna barely perceived the ground of the courtyard was dry and the few flurries that swirled above were dispersing.

"I see Lydia Kingsley is up to her old tricks," Thayne remarked, awakening Rhianna at once. "Lord Kingsley will not be happy about this."

She squinted through the glass at the two shadowy figures that had eluded her previously. Despite the darkness, there was no mistaking the persons who now united covertly below. It was a brief meeting, something passed between them, and they separated.

"That is the man I saw before my accident!" declared Rhianna.

Thayne looked at her sharply. "Pierson? Are you sure?"

Rhianna's mouth fell open at the name. "*That* is Mr. Pierson?"

He nodded confirmation. "How do you know of him?"

Rhianna relayed, "The night I arrived from France, Lord Kingsley seemed very much upset to hear Mr. Pierson was at the manor while he was away."

"I suppose it explains why," Thayne said, "if he did see you fall from your horse, he did not come to assist. He would not want Lord Kingsley to know he was in the area. But why would he follow you . . . ?"

He trailed off in thought as Rhianna's mind followed a different path.

"So it is as I thought," she said to him. "Lady Kingsley will not banish him, despite Lord Kingsley's wishes."

"So you have never met him?"

"I never met him, no. That same night we came to the manor, he was nowhere to be seen."

"As can only be expected . . ."

Her interest was piqued at the prospect that Thayne knew something more than Mauvreen had told her. Rhianna looked eagerly upon him. Skillfully, she asked no question, but allowed him to read it in her expression.

He hesitated, before proceeding cautiously, "I would not wish to speak inappropriately with you, Miss Braden. Perhaps I have said too much."

For Rhianna, he certainly had said too much to stop at this point.

"Is what you refer to of general knowledge?" she asked, not knowing her own desperation.

Choosing his words carefully, he said, "I would find it surprising if you have lived in Kingsley Manor these months and not known the nature of Lydia and Pierson's relationship."

Rhianna gave pause. "Are they not cousins?"

"Yes," he laughed. "That they are."

Despite her general naïvety, Rhianna began to follow his train of thought. "You don't mean to say . . ."

Once again her look said the rest, and Thayne nodded apologetically.

"They are lovers," he confirmed. "But, Miss Braden, I fear I have offended you."

"Not you, indeed!" she cried. "But poor Lord Kingsley!"

"Pierson only affects Lord Kingsley's wallet. He does not affect his heart," he replied. "If you feel for Lord Kingsley, you must feel more that his own lover is long gone."

"Lord Kingsley, as well?" she despaired. "No, I cannot believe it of him. He is . . . a good man."

Thayne retreated immediately. "He is, indeed."

Rhianna, despite such a shock, could see that no joy or even contentment seemed possible with Lydia. After a short time, she processed this information and still wished to know more.

"Lord Brighton," she begged, "I do so wish Lord Kingsley to be happy. Do you suggest he found a measure of happiness with . . . his mistress?"

Thayne had a pained expression on his face. "They were known to have been very much in love," he told her. "So much so, in fact, their devotion became somewhat legendary. Lord Kingsley has never recovered from the loss of her."

Rhianna suspected he could have said much more on the subject, but he quickly fell silent. He almost seemed as if he had something else on his mind entirely.

"Goodness . . . who was this woman?" she asked.

"Desmond's last governess."

"*Hallie* . . .?"

Her sudden passion in saying this one word seemed to surprise him. "So you have heard of her?"

With determination she released herself from speechlessness. Hallie—*My Beloved Haldana*—Lord Guilford Kingsley's mistress! Rhianna drew a quick breath as she recalled him gazing at her brooch.

"I know very little. Does anyone know what happened to her?"

He shook his head. "She disappeared suddenly. To this day it remains a mystery."

At that moment, Austine Leighart approached them, coming from a table where sat six or so young men and women who had all appeared to be of a close-knit clique the whole of the evening.

After examining Rhianna insolently, she ignored her, saying, "Lord Brighton, I think you have been gone for hours! Will you not come and visit your friends before we are departed for the evening?"

Her posture, the look in her eyes, all screamed of jealousy. Rhianna understood her and felt she had the right. If she and Thayne Brighton were intended for each other, as Lydia Kingsley suggested, and had Rhianna been in Miss Leighart's shoes, she should have felt the same way.

"Yes, of course. I will meet you there in but a moment."

Triumphantly, Austine dismissed herself to where she had come, leaving no opportunity for an introduction.

Thayne sighed, more visibly than Rhianna thought he intended.

"Miss Braden, you will have to excuse me. I wonder to where Desmond Kingsley has now gone? He would see firsthand the definition of *duty*."

"Of course, you must go. I shan't attempt to keep you."

He hesitated.

"We will have to continue this conversation at another time." Rhianna nodded, with the belief he would never remember their conversation, when he asked, "Perhaps tomorrow? Lord Kingsley no doubt allows you time to yourself?"

She could not hide her surprise. How torn she felt! Already, she had predetermined that her free time would be spent with Mauvreen.

"I . . ."

"You have plans," he determined. Before she felt forced to hasten an answer, Thayne hurried, "I mustn't ask you to alter your plans for me. I dare not be so selfish. However, I—I would like very much to see you again. That is, at a time convenient to you and . . . if you so desire."

This last caught her breath. She could hardly think.

"I take Audra for riding lessons Monday . . ."

"Allow me to invite you both to Ravensleigh's stables," he returned. "Audra is very fond of my brother, Crispin. Perhaps we all can go. They are of similar age and he would be very happy to see her, as well."

"I'm sure we would be delighted."

Thayne seemed very happy. "I shall have a carriage sent for you both that morning."

So it was settled. He bowed, she curtseyed, and Thayne Brighton left to appease Austine.

Such incredible plans, all decided so suddenly! Rhianna was in high spirits and, as she accepted a dance with a young man whom she barely recalled meeting, her mind was already far into Monday. Any and all unpleasantness from the evening was a distant memory. How he had done it, she could not figure out, but Thayne had changed her feelings toward him entirely.

*

Following an elaborate fireworks display, the night was nearing three o'clock when the first family called their carriage. As the last few dances went underway, the dance floor thinned and the crowds lessened, with the exception of a few couples who remained determined to see it out to the last. The evening was coming to an end, as was Rhianna's energy. At Lord Kingsley's suggestion, (he himself would not quit his last guests until after daybreak), she retired without ceremony to the rose room, with his word that it would not be the last ball she would attend at Kingsley Manor. It was the perfect conclusion to a perfect night.

Chapter Five

"It's been some time since you've come to see me." Mauvreen pressed her fingers to her mouth, her eyes searching through him. "You are not looking well, again."

"Overtired, perhaps," the cloaked man replied. "I have had a long night."

"And . . . ?"

She stopped here and leaned back in her seat, as though she said enough for him to respond. Perhaps she did, but his mood called for specific questions. He begged her to elaborate.

"I only wish to know if she danced," Mauvreen pressed him. "Will you deny an old woman?"

He coughed. Whether it was real or feigned to buy him time she hardly knew. The cloaked man leaned forward, running his hand through his silver hair.

"You make this so difficult for me—yes, she danced. From the moment she entered the room, there was not a fellow who had not fallen at her feet."

Mauvreen smiled brightly and nodded her contentment. "I expected as much. She must have looked—"

"Like an angel," he finished. "Or, a ghost, if you ask Dowager Lady Whitehall."

Mauvreen raised a quizzical brow. "Oh, dear . . ."

"It is the least of my concerns. I have more oppressive matters to handle."

"Lydia," she stated, blankly. "How is she behaving?"

His countenance suffered at this. "Poorly, I'm afraid. There is no controlling that woman," he opened up. "How she can be so openly defiant baffles me exhaustively."

"Have you spoken with her? What does she say to it?"

There was a knock at the door, and a voice calling Mauvreen's name. "Hello!" it cried, and it was no mystery as to whom the voice belonged.

"I will leave through the back," said the cloaked man.

But the opportunity was gone. The handle turned, the door opened, and Rhianna entered the lodge.

"The door was unlocked, Mauvreen, I hope you don't mind . . ." Her words froze, as did her body and her gaze. "Lord Kingsley."

*

He rose with his companion, mumbled an indistinct "Miss Braden," and stood awkwardly beside Mauvreen. The latter said nothing, and Rhianna, too, could think of nothing to say. A moment or two of the silence that followed did little to allay the uneasiness. Something must be said and Rhianna at last felt it her responsibility to explain herself.

"Lord Kingsley," she began again, "I'm so sorry, I . . ."

Embarrassment set in and she could not immediately continue. Lord Kingsley remained silent and turned to Mauvreen. The old woman caught his glance, but did not hold it.

"I did not expect to find anyone else here," Rhianna finished, feeling the necessity of departure.

"Not at all," Guilford told her, snatching up his walking stick and putting on his hat. "I was just on my way out."

His voice was calm, comforting. He tipped his hat to them both and flashed Mauvreen a glance, which seemed to convey his permission to proceed with the visit. The old woman's face lit up and she smiled at Rhianna with open arms, calling her to her side. Taking her up on the invitation, Rhianna made her way to her friend, trading places with Lord Kingsley who moved toward the door.

"Good day to you," said Lord Kingsley as he left the lodge, closing the door behind him.

Rhianna turned to Mauvreen and the two took each other's hands.

"How very strange, after all the times I have come, to finally cross paths with another visitor!" cried Rhianna. "Mauvreen, does he come to see you often?"

She shrugged and looked out the window at him as he made his way through the woods toward Kingsley Manor. "There was a time I would see him every day."

"Does he mind that I am here?" she asked anxiously. "I shall never forget what a secret you stressed our visits must be."

"Yes, well," she said, as the two assumed their usual positions in the lodge sitting room, "let us keep it between us three." Once sitting comfortably on the sofa, Mauvreen continued, "How was the ball? I have heard hardly a thing about it."

Rhianna smiled to herself at the recollection, a hint of warmth rising in her cheeks. "Lord Kingsley has not, I hope, left you without at least some details?"

"I have heard the gentlemen were in quite a frenzy to claim their dances with you."

"Oh, Lord Kingsley has cheated you terribly! The number of my partners is nothing to the music, the decorations, the gowns! Has he given you nothing further?"

"No," her friend told her, "but besides, through your eyes, I shall have an entirely different description of it than he could give. It requires a woman to properly describe the charm of such an evening."

With this, all the loveliness of the ball was detailed with a passion only Rhianna could have communicated. Not a fabric or tiara went undescribed, even musical notes were given their moment. But a narration of the ball would not have been complete without relating Dowager Lady Whitehall's accusation, which she recounted in full.

"My heavens," Mauvreen exclaimed, in response to her account, "how very frightening for you. It would seem she suffers from dementia."

"Indeed!" she laughed. "Or else, I am a ghost, but I tend to think I am not."

Rhianna now came to the point she had wanted all along to discuss. "Mauvreen, is it true," she began, delicately, "that Lord Kingsley and Hallie were . . ."

She paused. Mauvreen appeared intrigued and leaned forward in her seat. No doubt their names together in the same sentence caught her attention. As usual, there was a look in her eyes that gave one the impression she already guessed what Rhianna was going to say.

". . . in love?"

Mauvreen smiled at her delicacy. "Yes, it is true."

It was only the second time she had ever given more than a vague and uninformative response. Rhianna sat astonished. She believed Lord Brighton, but hearing it confirmed from Mauvreen was more shocking than the intelligence itself.

"What makes you ask?" Mauvreen questioned.

Rhianna told her everything from discovering Hallie's name in the schoolbook to learning she was Desmond's governess to Lord Brighton alluding to the affair and everything in between.

"This Lord Brighton fellow—I like the sound of him. He seems quite all right."

"Yes, he . . ." Rhianna blushed. ". . . does seem quite all right."

Mostly concerned with the account of Lydia and Pierson, Mauvreen asked, "And you believe Lord Brighton has spoken to Lord Kingsley about what you saw?"

"I do, but I leave it to your discretion as to whether you ought to speak with him, as well." Mauvreen continued to absorb it all as Rhianna continued, "Mauvreen, is that why Lord Kingsley comes to the lodge? To visit Hallie's grave?"

Her friend sighed as though she ought to have anticipated a return to the subject.

"I'd like to think my company is part of the appeal," she

jested, "but mostly, yes." Knowing where her young friend was heading, she added, "There are many things I would like to tell you, Rhianna, but they are not my stories to tell."

Rhianna recognized Mauvreen's skillful conclusion of the subject. She knew this was all the information she would gather from her, but she was not entirely disappointed.

She soon returned to Kingsley Manor with all the exhilaration of her visit to the lodge, as well as the morrow's plans. But there was one essential thing left to be done.

Lord Kingsley was easily found in the foyer when Rhianna entered the manor. She greeted him, and he turned to her with a smile.

"Lord Kingsley, Audra and I have been invited to Ravensleigh for her riding lessons tomorrow. On behalf of both of us, I would like to ask your permission to go."

He nodded, knowingly. "Lord Brighton informed me of the invitation at the ball. I think it is a marvelous plan and have no objection."

"Thank you, sir. He offered to send a carriage for us in the morning, then."

"Very good," he agreed.

She curtseyed and headed for her room to prepare for supper.

"Oh, Miss Braden?" he called.

"Yes?" she turned.

"The next time you visit . . . *your friend* . . . please, always feel free to take one of the horses. It is a long walk."

*

Audra cupped her palms over her ears. Her eyes, too, were shut tightly as if it would help keep the sounds out. There were few things she could bear less than the sound of her parents arguing, an experience that was becoming all to frequent. Even the happiness that accompanied the addition of Miss Braden as her governess, previously enough to carry her though such similar nights, could not lift her above it. She attempted not to listen, but in the stillness of her own, dark bedroom there was little she could do to avoid it. Their voices carried through the walls and along the wood floors of the manor. She at last resorted to muffing the words with her hands.

"I will not be humiliated under my own roof, Lydia!"

"Oh, is that so? Hypocrite! You and your governesses!"

"Do not test my patience. After thirty years of marriage to you, I deserve your respect."

"Thirty years of marriage, Guilford? That you even bother to count is a shock to me. Ours is no marriage, nor has it been from the start."

"That was your decision, Lydia. Now, certainly, we are what we are, but I'll be damned if you'll continue to bring him into this house!"

"By all means, pretend it matters one iota to you with whom I spend my time. I laugh at the notion."

"There was a time that I cared very much, Lydia. Fortunately, those painful emotions have long since passed. Only Kingsley Manor is dear to me now, and you'll not defile it if I have anything to say about it. This is my home, and you are nothing but a guest to me."

Audra pulled the covers over her head. The full meaning of their words eluded her, but the emotions behind them were clear. In her twelve years, she could not recall a time she witnessed them happy in one another's presence. She doubted there ever was such a time.

For a moment, all was quiet. She lowered the sheets to her chin, her eyes searching the still air. Her father's words must have struck a chord.

"But, that it were different," her mother at last regretted. "I imagine we are thirty years too late for that."

"Indeed, madam, we are," Guilford returned coldly. Then, he added, "Lydia, I will not ask you again. Respect my house."

Audra turned onto her stomach and twisted her pillow over her head. At last finding peace beneath its feathers, she repeated her prayers and went to sleep.

*

The Brighton carriage arrived bright and early. Audra was as outwardly thrilled as Rhianna was inwardly, and the latter was amused to listen as Audra chatted on excitedly about Crispin. Not to mention, it did much to calm her own anxieties and distract her from the fact they were going horseback riding with Crispin's elder brother.

Ravensleigh seemed a house straight out of a fairy tale, its grounds something from a painting. Her first visit had not provided the best opportunity for viewing the estate, though she knew it was something exceptionally lovely. Now, coming up the open country separating the two properties, Rhianna saw from her seat in the coach that, excepting only Kingsley Manor, Ravensleigh was unequaled by any other home in Thornton. Even during the early winter season, the grounds entirely without color, there was no denying its beauty. A rectangular-shaped, grey brick manor, with innumerable, tall windows, and four round columns at the entrance gate, Ravensleigh gave the appearance of a miniature castle and its grounds were the very definition of picturesque.

As they traveled the tree-lined drive and pulled up to the front, a footman was seen standing at the door. An older man with a gentle manner, he appeared welcoming as they came to a stop.

"Good day," said he, with a nod. "Miss Kingsley and Miss Braden, I presume?"

"Good day," both replied, as they were assisted down.

As each smoothed her woolen riding habit, Rhianna somehow managed appreciation for the frilled collar of her shirt and the jacket bodice that had been netted for her by Soleil. She recalled Lady Brighton washing them both for her after the accident, lending Rhianna some of her own bedclothes while she recovered.

"Please follow me," he said.

He led them to the green drawing room, the room most familiar to her, other than the guest bedroom where she spent her recovery from the horse accident. As she and Audra sat on the rosewood-framed furniture, she recalled the Chinese wallpaper and the marble chimneypiece. More than this, Rhianna recalled seeing *him* for the first time standing beside it, and his concern and anxious inquiries into her health. She smiled to herself as she recalled how she disliked him, and how little reason she had to do so.

"I will let the family know you are here," the servant told them, disappearing into the house.

Rhianna could not deceive herself into believing she was not nervous. It had been two days since the ball, two days since she had seen him last. What if by now his opinion of her had changed? Suppose he woke up the following morning and realized he had made a dreadful mistake? Undoubtedly, he did not wish to waste his time riding with a governess and her pupil, but he would be too much the gentleman to rescind the invitation. Rhianna envisioned him awaking in horror at the recollection of his behavior at the ball, and in front of Miss Leighart! The impression that he must certainly have left with other guests, acquaintances of his, would be a shocking reality. The shame, the gossip that he would now endure! How he must have been dreading this morning!

We ought not to be here, she thought to herself, as the doorman returned to them. *He does not want us here. We do not belong.*

"Lady Brighton," he introduced, as she came smiling into the room. Both girls rose to greet her and she received them warmly.

The servant continued, "Lord Brighton and Master Brighton send word . . ."

No, he would not come to greet them. Rhianna was sure that the doorman was returned with Lord Brighton's regrets that he could not join them. Tea with Lady Brighton would most certainly be offered as a substitute and she wondered how quickly she could get Audra away from Ravensleigh. How she wished to leave and never return!

". . . that they will be here in a moment," he concluded.

In a moment.

Her heart fluttered.

"I am so glad you have come," Lady Brighton declared. "Miss Kingsley, it has been such a long time since I have seen you. Pray, how old are you now?"

Audra turned to her at once, and said, "I am twelve now. However, Crispin is still four years older. He is in such a race."

Lady Brighton's grin widened. "Yes, I imagine he is."

"Will you be coming with us?" she asked.

"No, not I, but I do hope you will take tea with me after you return," she invited, with a glance at Rhianna.

"Certainly, we should love to," Rhianna accepted, automatically and much too quickly.

"Has Miss Braden told you how lovely the ball was the other evening?"

Audra lit up at the thought of it. "She has. I was with her when she dressed for it. You have such taste in gowns, Lady Brighton! I hope when I am old enough to go to a ball that you will help me choose one, as well?"

"I should like nothing better," she returned, genuinely.

Suddenly, the door burst open and a young man entered excitedly. His hair was lighter than Thayne's, but his face reminded Rhianna of the boy she once met in the Kingsley woods. From this, she was certain he must be Crispin, but before any of the ladies could rise, before an introduction could be made, he was standing before Audra.

"I have something to say to you, Audra," he declared seriously. "I am too old. From this moment forward, you must be known to me as Miss Kingsley."

His posture was very erect and showed his anxiety over this

matter. Thayne entered behind him, grinning. He nodded to the ladies, signaled them to remain seated, and remained otherwise silent so his brother could conclude his declaration.

Audra began to giggle at him. "You are the silliest boy I have ever known! Very well, what shall I call you?"

He thought for a moment. "Lord Crispin," he told her, awkwardly.

"Lord Crispin, if you insist on being so proper, will you not allow me a place to stand so I can greet you formally?"

Crispin smiled widely. "You're not mad, Audra?"

"Of course not. It only means we're getting older. That's not so bad."

Perfectly happy with this, Crispin took one, giant step back and the ladies rose from their seats.

"Crispin," said Thayne, "allow me to introduce you to Miss Rhianna Braden. Miss Braden, my brother Lord Crispin Brighton."

"A pleasure," she told him.

Crispin, having suddenly seen for the first time someone other than Audra in the room, turned to Thayne at once.

"She is very pretty, brother." Before anyone could respond beyond looks of surprise, Crispin continued to Rhianna, "Thank you for bringing *Miss Kingsley* here today. She is my greatest friend and I have not seen her in less than a twelvemonth."

"You can thank your brother for the invitation," she replied, embarrassed.

"Go on along," Lady Brighton encouraged. "Enjoy yourselves. The weather is very fine today. I shall see you all when you come back."

Audra and Crispin were first to the door, he having opened it for her before a servant could blink. Moments later, the four of them were on their way to the stables and it was very obvious to Rhianna that neither Audra nor she would be focusing on riding lessons.

*

Her fingers twisted the reins of her bridle, her black coat seeming to her a stark contrast to the magnificent, white horse she was seated upon. Of course, her eyes did not remain upon these items long, as Thayne appeared from the stables, seated upon his tall, chocolate-brown-and-white-spotted stallion, d'Artagnan. How gracefully he handled the creature—too frisky for most riders—and how excellent he himself looked as he advanced closer, his long riding coat exhibiting him handsomely and fitting well his powerful frame.

"I am glad to see you back on a horse, Miss Braden," he said, as he approached the trio. "Although, I must confess it does come with a measure of anxiety for me."

It was the first time she had been riding since the accident, but Rhianna had not until this moment given it any thought at all. Thayne Brighton was more distracting than she wanted to allow.

"At least, if any accident were to occur, I know I am in good company," she teased.

"May you not even jest."

Audra and Crispin, riding equally elegant creatures from Ravensleigh's stables, quickly galloped ahead. Thayne and Rhianna found themselves exchanging amused glances before catching up to them.

"Miss Braden," cried Audra, "would you please tell *Lord* Crispin that he is always to let the lady win a race?"

"Miss Braden," cried Crispin, in return, "what Miss Kingsley fails to understand is that she would *know* that I allowed her the win. Would it not be much better for her to see me win and, therefore, have confidence in me as a man?"

"Well, let's see," Rhianna returned, struggling to hide her amusement. "Lord Brighton, what have you to say on the matter?"

"Crispin, my dear brother, I am not entirely sure you had the win—Miss Kingsley is among the swiftest ladies I have seen in a sidesaddle."

"Aha!"

Audra was triumphant. She raised a shoulder to Crispin, the corners of her mouth stretched from ear to ear.

"Either way," Thayne continued, "I would suggest putting the lady's wishes ahead of the race."

"Is that so?" Crispin returned, riding his horse up to Audra's and pausing closely beside her. "Well, brother, I think you are not the only one who can give advice on how a man ought to treat a lady."

With that, he leaned over and gave Audra a kiss on the cheek before his horse broke into a full gallop. Audra chased after him.

"My brother is shameless," Thayne commented to Rhianna.

Feeling surprisingly more relaxed, Rhianna was glad to have this moment alone, though to what point and purpose she could hardly say. Even still, as Audra and Crispin continued happily in the far lead, neither Desmond Kingsley nor Austine Leighart could interrupt them here.

"Before this morning, I had never seen Audra in such anticipation," she admitted. "Twelve months seems a long time not to see one's neighbors."

"Yes," Thayne admitted. "Well, Lydia Kingsley is not particularly fond of my mother—or anyone, I believe." He smiled. "And, of course, Crispin and Miss Kingsley could use a few more years apart."

"I had no idea they were so fond of each other."

"Yes, they are." He paused suddenly, before quickly blurting, "May I . . . be so bold as to ask who *you* are fond of, Miss Braden?"

Rhianna could hardly believe the words that had escaped his lips and she suspected he was feeling the same, though she could not look at him after this.

"Forgive me," he hurried. "That was entirely inappropriate."

With his sudden apology, she smiled, and stole a quick glance at him. He looked disconcerted and she decided to engage him with witticism.

"If I were to say to you Desmond Kingsley, would you believe me?"

"No," he admitted with a chuckle. Seeming to find further courage, he added, "But surely, there must be someone? If not here, then in France?"

The thought of Philippe erased her smile and Thayne was

quick to notice.

"So, it is France, then?"

Rhianna let out a quick sigh and wondered at the odd turn their conversation had taken. "No, not, exactly."

He watched her closely, and she felt him trying to read her expressions.

"Philippe and I," she told him, surrendering, "practically grew up together. The only son of the family I lived with these last years, he proposed before I left France."

Why she was sharing this with him, she hardly knew.

"Proposed?" he repeated, nauseously. "Are you engaged?"

She shook her head. "I am not."

Thayne allowed her a moment to elaborate, but she did not.

"So you have refused him?" he asked.

Rhianna hesitated. "I . . . have not. Though, he and his sister are to visit me shortly and I suspect the matter will be settled at that time."

Rhianna felt a tinge ill. In over a year's time, she had not convinced herself of the appropriate response to Philippe. The one thing she knew for certain was that she could not always be guaranteed employment at Kingsley Manor. It was a subject she wished very much to avoid thinking about.

"Well, it ought to be a simple matter, ought it not? Are you in love with this Philippe? Because if you are at all uncertain of it, you ought not to accept."

"And what of you, Lord Brighton?" she asked, turning the subject on him. "Who are you fond of?"

She dared to steal another glance at him, but panicked as his eyes alone seemed to betray him—or were her own eyes deceiving her? Of course, Thayne Brighton could have no feelings for her, as much as she was beginning to wish it.

"Austine Leighart, no doubt," she declared, before he could answer.

Thayne laughed. "Ah, Miss Leighart. Miss Leighart is not happy unless she is the loveliest, most accomplished, most admired girl in a room. She rather dislikes you, I imagine."

"She can have no reason," Rhianna declared vehemently. "First of all, we weren't even introduced. And I daresay, from what I could tell that night at the ball, she was everything you just described."

"That can only be your feeling because you were not at an advantage to see yourself. If you ask me, Miss Leighart had every possible reason in the world to have a miserable evening." Rhianna could hardly breathe, as he concluded, "Miss Braden, do you believe in love at first sight?"

She was surprised to find that with such a question, her first thoughts turned, not to Philippe, but to Thayne Brighton. She thought of the first time she saw him in the Kingsley woods, and how she despised him.

"No," she declared.

In his face, she saw the man she *was* falling in love with, the love she knew to be the only kind one should marry for, if one's circumstances would only allow. Suddenly wrestling against the ache in her heart, she fought such hopeless emotions fruitlessly.

"Perhaps," she added, boldly, "at second sight."

With this, she rode on ahead of him toward the children. He followed shortly after, his last words lingering in the air for some minutes until their small party was reunited.

"The two of you seem to have gotten on well without us," announced Thayne to Audra and Crispin.

"Without you?" replied Crispin. "Were you not right behind all along?"

With a raised eyebrow, Thayne said, "Had you not noticed? Miss Braden and I have only just caught up."

"A fine joke, Lord Brighton," injected Audra. "We heard you the whole time."

"Heard us?" Rhianna asked her young pupil. "Whatever do you mean?"

"Your horses," she responded.

Instinctively, both Thayne and Rhianna looked about them and her heartbeat began to pick up. Obviously, Audra and Crispin had not heard *them*, so whom had they heard?

"Both horses, or only one?" asked Thayne, glancing suspiciously toward the woods on their left.

"Both," they replied together.

"You're certain? You heard more than one horse?"

Both girl and boy turned white as they realized he was not in jest and remained silent to stand by their claim. Each giving a glance to the south woods, only the nods of their heads followed this last query.

"You really weren't right behind us, were you?" Crispin affirmed.

"No," answered Thayne. "We had best return to Ravensleigh."

No argument succeeded this. The four riders about-faced and headed toward the house with no amount of sluggishness.

*

Crispin and Audra darted into the drawing room to meet with Lady Brighton. Meanwhile, Thayne requested a moment to speak with Rhianna outside.

With a concerned gaze, he took her hands and addressed her, saying, "Miss Braden, have you any reason to believe or, rather, to suspect you are being watched?"

He stood very close to her and she could not but admire from her advantageous line of view both his height and the square shape of his jaw. It was becoming more and more difficult not to catch her breath each and every time she met his gaze—and had he shown a thinly veiled attraction to her? Or was her heart misleading her yet again? Her eyes fell to the hands that enveloped hers and she could not deny that such a liberty as he had taken there was odd, indeed. Yet, she felt no inclination to widen the space between them.

Suddenly, she realized what he had asked her.

"Watched?" she repeated.

"My intent, Miss Braden, as your friend, is not to frighten you, of course. It is only—the fact that Pierson was at the scene of your accident . . ."

"That is quite a theory, Lord Brighton," she returned, not at all convinced. "Mr. Pierson may have been in the area, but there is nothing he could possibly want with me."

Thayne examined her for a moment.

"Lord Brighton, I have no doubt that there were, not one, but two persons in the woods back there, but it was smugglers more than likely. Men who no doubt want nothing to do with us so long as we want nothing to do with them."

Thayne shook his head. "I am going to make arrangements for you and Audra to return to Kingsley Manor shortly. In the interest of your safety, I will personally join you on the trip and speak to Lord Kingsley when we arrive."

"My goodness, I am sure we will arrive safely at Kingsley Manor without an escort."

"Miss Braden," he entreated, "do you think me able to allow such a thing? Do you imagine I could be at rest without any confirmation of your security?"

Before she could reply, Thayne pulled her gently forward and kissed her cheek, catching just the corner of her mouth. He lingered, and Rhianna was suddenly conscious of the scent of his skin and the feel of his breath upon her own.

"I beg you would think better of me," he said.

*

The following day, Austine Leighart and her mother came to pay a visit to Ravensleigh. The sight of the Leighart family carriage revealed their call to Thayne, who, unable to sleep the previous night, had gone out for an early ride. It was now a few days since the ball and he imagined they had come in search of a few, last compliments before returning to Norwich.

Thayne, far from pleased by the visit, wished they had come one day previous. He would have enjoyed seeing Austine's face at the sight of Rhianna. The thought of such an encounter was highly amusing and it helped put on a smile on his face as he entered his home.

Thayne entered his drawing room to find Austine alone. The unexpected situation left him, for a moment, confused. She noticed this at once and did not hesitate to explain.

"What an unexpected pleasure to see you, Lord Brighton!"

"Is it unexpected to find me in my own home?" he questioned dryly.

"Oh, you see, when your mother explained you had gone riding, we feared we would not cross paths. I say *we*, you must be wondering whom I mean."

"I am," he responded.

She was dressed to the nines, but Thayne was not impressed. Although she was stunning, her vanity was undeniable. Her very presence aggravated him and he wondered what excuse she contrived to create the situation he now found himself in.

"My mother has accompanied yours to the garden. I started with them, but as you can see, I've come back for my muff. The grounds are breathtaking in any season, but it is far too cold to be walking about without the proper attire."

"I find it incredulous that you forgot it to begin with."

Austine smiled. She had not forgotten the muff. He always saw right through her.

"You blame me for wanting to see you?" she asked, with an inflection of innocence. "I thought perhaps without company we could speak openly."

Thayne watched as she seated herself in a corner chair. She intended this meeting to last longer than he did.

"There is nothing I have to say to you that I cannot say in the company of others," he told her, bluntly.

"Are you quite sure?" she urged, playfully fingering the arm of her seat. "You are an amazing dancer, my lord. I had a mind to tell you how skillfully you handled the waltz."

"Did you?"

"Yes. I suppose you must have had a great deal of practice to make a woman feel as comfortable as I did. The dance floor can be such a daunting place, with great room for embarrassment. Almost as if one were standing before the crowd with no clothes on."

"It never crossed my mind."

Miss Leighart rose from the corner chair and approached him. Stroking the lapel of his coat, she continued, "No, I suppose it wouldn't have. But women are such timorous creatures. It's the very reason that a man like yourself, who has the skill to make his partner feel at ease, is so appreciated."

"Forgive me, I do not see the timidity in you, Miss Leighart."

Saying nothing in immediate reply, Austine held her eye contact. A moment passed before she responded to this last blow.

"What must I do, Lord Brighton?" she asked, flirtatiously. "Surely, I am attractive enough for you?"

Thayne removed her hand from his chest and stepped toward the door. Opening it for her, he said, "My heart is full of another. The best I can offer you is an escort to the garden."

A rage flushed over her with his words. "Full of another?" she cried, all efforts at cordiality gone. "I have to demand you tell me who this woman is!"

"On what basis?" he returned.

"Are we not intended for each other? Do we not have an excellent future together? Between my fortune and yours, how very influential we could be! Think of how everyone will look up to us. Surely, this is not something you intend to give up."

Thayne remained steadfast. "Our families might have encouraged the match, Miss Leighart, but I have certainly never hinted at its fruition. I intend to marry for love and no amount of money or prominence can change my position on the matter. The truth is, I do not love you, nor could I ever love you."

"You are cruel to me, Lord Brighton!"

"It would be cruel of me if you loved me. You, though, love only my position, my fortune, and my name. That is why I say these things to you without remorse. Were not you the one who suggested we speak openly? To lose me would mean disappointment for you on account of my wealth, not heartache on account of my person."

"No, my lord, you are entirely mistaken. What can have made you come to this unbelievable conclusion? Surely, these cannot be your true thoughts of me. I love you madly, as I could never love anyone."

Tears arose in Austine's eyes as she spoke, but Thayne was not deceived.

"I imagine you told Lord Cosworth the same, no doubt from the comfort of his bed, until he lost his riches."

In an instant, the vision of a victimized and desperate woman in love that stood before him transformed into the repugnant, gain-seeker that she was. Her open hand met his cheek with great energy.

"How dare you speak to a lady in this manner! Such ill-bred behavior I have never seen! You shame yourself and your family. What woman would ever find you a prize?"

Thayne extended his arm toward the door. "Good day, Miss Leighart."

A servant was sent for her mother at once. She met Austine in the carriage and they left Ravensleigh immediately.

*

Soleil's last letter was quickly followed by a second. It read, in part:

"*. . . we can no longer bear the separation. We must come and see you. Besides, I have been keeping a bit of good news with the hope of telling you in person. As you are reading this, we are already on our way . . .*"

Rhianna dropped Soleil's letter to her side and gazed listlessly out her chamber window overlooking the rotunda. She so wanted to be happy at the prospect of seeing them, but she knew what lay ahead. During the last year Rhianna had become rather deft at putting the matter out of her head. Presently, though, it weighed heavily upon her mind. Now that her mourning period was past, there was no escaping Philippe's request for an answer.

Of course, she began to reason, perhaps there was hope. After all, it had been more than a year. It was not altogether impossible that Philippe's feelings had changed. He had not seen her in some time. He'd had plenty of opportunity to reconsider his choice and her absence surely contributed to his being of a clear mind. She imagined him in social settings, introduced to various ladies, and finding one he admired and loved, and who admired and loved him in return.

The thought stopped her. Was that what she wanted? Philippe had loved her as well as any woman could ever hope to be loved. And though Rhianna knew she did not feel a passion for him as she imagined she would feel for the man she would marry, she did love him in return, as well as his family. How she would love to truly be a sister to Soleil! Not only that, but Philippe had the equivalent of five thousand pounds a year. She would never want for anything. France felt very much her home. Perhaps Mauvreen would even come with her.

Rhianna found herself battling the fear she had so desperately repressed. If Philippe no longer loved her, what did her future hold? Immediately, she had a place to live, a position she loved, a friend or two, but beyond that was uncertain. Suddenly, she felt guilty. When she hoped Philippe would still marry her, was it because she really, deeply wanted to be married to him? Or was it when she eliminated Philippe as a marriageable option, she simply eliminated her security? Above all, could one ever know the right reasons to marry?

Thayne Brighton inevitably penetrated her thoughts. He had been something of a fixture there since the ball, but even more consistently did she find herself drifting off because of him since their outing the previous day. It was not only his physical attractiveness, nor their unexpectedly intimate conversation, but hardly could she believe he had actually *kissed* her. How often she relived that moment! His lips, cold from the chilled air, warmed quickly against her cheek, the faintest hint of whiskers brushing against her smooth skin. She knew not what to make of it. Although she could not accuse him of the schemes she attributed to Desmond Kingsley, she also could not imagine him acting on any feelings he might have for her.

She heard a rap at the door.

"Yes, Katie?"

The servant curtseyed. "Lord Kingsley wishes to speak with you in his study, Miss Braden."

Grateful for any distraction from her thoughts, she responded to the summons without a moment's delay. Especially did she appreciate this particular interruption; Lord Kingsley had a calming manner that was contagious and Rhianna so wished to feel calm.

It was unnecessary for Katie to guide her. Rhianna knew her way around the manor well by now, even the upper floors seldom traveled by her, and had memorized every hallway, every door.

And one door in particular.

It was on the first floor, and she passed it whenever she could. The handle would never turn, for the room was always locked. She checked it as often as she had reason to pass it, or as often as she made up reason to do so, as she did on her way to Lord Kingsley that afternoon. As she expected, that day was as any other and she wondered what lay beyond the door. It was not infrequent for her to lie awake at night, pondering the potential contents of this room, situated just beyond the family chambers.

A servant announced her, as he led her into Lord Kingsley's study.

"Miss Braden, you come so quickly. I have only moments ago sent Katie for you."

He placed down the letter he was examining and removed his reading glasses.

"Yes, well," she replied, leaning onto the balls of her feet, "I was unemployed."

He gestured her to have a seat in the armchair before his desk. "I am glad to offer some mental stimulation."

Rhianna chuckled as she sat. "Mental stimulation I have in abundance, Lord Kingsley, however, a mental *diversion* would be most welcome." Realizing she did not want to address her concerns about Philippe, she hurried, "You've spoken with Lord Brighton, I understand?"

He nodded. "I have. He tells me that, aside from its abrupt ending, you all enjoyed a pleasant morning ride together yesterday."

"We did," she confirmed happily. "Audra and Crispin are very . . . fond . . . of each other."

Who are you fond of, Miss Braden? she heard Thayne's voice echo.

"Ah, yes," he chuckled, "I daresay, I ought not to allow her to come out any time before her sixteenth birthday." Lord Kingsley continued, "Miss Braden, I have a request to make of you. Will you humor me?"

This regained her focus. "Of course."

Guilford Kingsley inhaled deeply, his eyes, fixed on a distance object at the other end of the room, deep in mental vision.

"I share Lord Brighton's concerns to a degree," he began guardedly. "It is possible, what with yesterday's events and your previous accident . . ."

Here, he paused, but it was enough. Rhianna had not been much concerned with the idea of being followed, either during yesterday's outing or after her accident, until now. Something about Lord Kingsley expressing it made it more possible in her mind; something to be taken more seriously.

"It is my humble request," he added gently, "out of concern for your safety, that you not travel anywhere alone for the time being.

Also, I would like to extend the offer to escort you to Mauvreen's, if at any time you wish to see her."

Hardly could she speak. Had she been so consumed by her captivation of Thayne Brighton in both instances that she was blinded to a very real threat to her person? And for what reason could anyone have to single her out in such a manner?

"If you think it necessary . . ."

"Good," he said, in a way that seemed not only to finalize the matter, but to vaporize the gloomy air that had penetrated the room. "Besides, it ought not to be a difficult thing when your friends arrive."

Rhianna yet held her letter from Soleil in her hands. Suddenly conscious of it, she smiled weakly, her mind between topics.

"Yes, I have received news of Soleil and Philippe's visit only moments ago. How can you have heard?" She looked at him expectantly, her eyes full of amazement.

Lord Kingsley raised his own letter before her. "I have been in regular communication with Marquis Vallière since your arrival. From his letters, it seems they very much consider you as part of their family."

"As do I," she told him, astonished to learn of such correspondence. "Lord Kingsley, I would like to request some time to spend with them. I hope it is not asking too much. Audra can always accompany me, of course. It would be an excellent opportunity for her to practice her French and improve her accent."

He nodded agreeably, while clearing his throat. "Indeed, I insist on it. When I learned they had accepted my offer, I was very pleased to hear it."

She stared blankly at him. "Your offer, sir?"

"To stay at the manor, of course. Guests always give the servants a renewed vigor while cleaning."

"Lord Kingsley! Have you truly offered as much? To be sure, it is more than is necessary . . ."

"Not at all! They seem a very pleasant family with whom I

would welcome the opportunity to become more intimately acquainted. It is no inconvenience to anyone. We have more than enough rooms. There can be no objection on any side. I only regret that the Marquis and Marquise Vallière are unable to join their children for the trip."

Soleil and Philippe at the manor! For a brief moment, Rhianna's spirits were lifted. She anticipated nothing but joy and, for a time, felt no anxiety at all connected with the matter.

"Lord Kingsley," she began, "thanking you seems inadequate. You know not the happiness having them here will bring me."

Guilford coughed forcefully into his hand, before telling her, "I look forward to it, as well."

With concern, Rhianna asked, "Are you quite well, Lord Kingsley?"

"Yes, yes," he assured her, hoarsely. "Pray, inform Audra of the matter. Also, she will be delighted to know I have invited the Brightons to dinner tonight and, as it is a small group, I intend to include her."

Butterflies instantly danced in her stomach. She knew exactly how Audra would feel. The mention of the Brighton name was beginning to have its effect on Rhianna.

"You must also join us, Miss Braden," he said. She attempted to decline, but he would not have it. "It is not my wish only, but I will need you to keep an eye on Audra."

She could no longer refuse, but she could also not tell which part made her more anxious: being requested to dinner or deciding what to wear. Rhianna immediately had a mental vision of her closet and nothing seemed adequate. She compared the idea of herself in either her brown or cream dinner dresses to what Lady Brighton and Lydia Kingsley would undoubtedly be adorned in, and shuddered.

"Something troubles you?" he noticed.

"Oh, no, indeed," she declared, recovering.

Only she was not convincing and Lord Kingsley was not deceived. "Pray, tell me your concern. I want nothing but your comfort."

"There is no concern whatsoever. I shall certainly find something to put on," she insisted, revealing her disquiet unintentionally in her hurry to ease him.

At once, she regretted her words, recalling all he had done for her with her gown for the ball. Lord Kingsley, however, for his part, seemed glad for this comment and was quick to understand her.

"Rhi—" He stopped himself suddenly. "Miss Braden," he continued, "I have kept several gowns of my mother's. She was about your size and height, and they only want some minor adjustments to update them."

Even as he was speaking, Rhianna was shaking her head. "Lord Kingsley, I could *not* . . ."

"I can think of no better use for them, as they are quite lovely and it is a shame they are currently hidden away in an old closet."

"I really must protest—"

"I will have the seamstress gather them. You may expect her in your room within the hour."

The horrified look in her eyes brought a warm smile to his face and he chuckled, bringing on a fresh fit of coughing. No further objections would be entertained and Rhianna was soon dismissed from his study with the understanding that they would meet again at dinner.

Chapter Six

In a few hours time, with only a few stitches needed to tighten the bodice and a petticoat to add fullness to the skirt, Rhianna had a new, pale yellow dinner dress, trimmed with bands of satin, as well as a satin sash and buttons. She wore a necklace and earrings of turquoise that had been a gift from Marquise Vallière, as was the lace scarf she draped over her shoulders. As they waited to receive the Brightons, she sat uncomfortably in the drawing room, wondering what Lydia Kingsley would think at the sight of her in her mother-in-law's costume, but the lady did not seem to recognize it as such. Soon, with a smile of approval from Lord Kingsley, Rhianna relaxed and enjoyed its fabric of rich, fine silk, perfect in its condition, without any show of wear.

Barely were general pleasantries expressed when a servant announced that dinner was served. Lord and Lady Kingsley, followed by Thayne and Lady Brighton, started toward the dining room. Desmond took Rhianna's arm, as Crispin did Audra's, and the procession continued. Dinner—elaborate as ever, with numerous selections of meats, vegetables, fruits, and breads—sat displayed on the long table as if a work of art. Guilford sat at the head, merrily taking in the spread before him, with Lydia, followed by Desmond to his right, and Lady Brighton, Thayne, and Crispin to his left. Audra skipped happily to Crispin's side, instead of her intended place beside Desmond, but no one seemed to notice or mind. Rhianna regretted that she had no choice but to assume the unpleasant seat herself.

Guilford cleared his throat and thanked all for coming, followed by a short fit of coughing.

"Lord Kingsley," cried Lady Brighton, "we are all so glad your health has improved enough that we could be here tonight. But this cough of yours is worrisome."

"I, too, have noticed it," added Thayne. "You did not seem yourself, even at the ball."

"Oh, it's nothing at all, I assure you," he promised, encouraging all to proceed with the meal. "Now, no gloomy conversation allowed. I want nothing but to enjoy your company."

Thayne and Lady Brighton consented to his wish and joined in taking wine with the group.

*

"Miss Braden has had some very good news today," Guilford announced, wiping away the claret that escaped from his glass to his chin. "Good news, indeed, for all of us."

This intelligence did little to excite Lydia or Desmond, who clearly were already aware of the news to which he referred. Lady Brighton, however, was all smiles, looking very attentive; and Thayne, grateful for any opportunity to gaze at Rhianna, gave her his full attention as Lord Kingsley allowed her to declare the particulars.

Thayne gathered that the sudden focus on Rhianna was not what she would wish. Nonetheless, she handled herself beautifully as she addressed the group.

"I have just today received a letter from my friend, Soleil Vallière, whose family I lived with in France. She and her brother, Philippe Vallière, are coming to England to visit me."

"How wonderful!" Lady Brighton cried. "It must be some time since you have seen them."

"Over a year, Lady Brighton."

"They will be staying with us at the manor," Guilford added, jovially. "There is nothing like new friends, is there, Brighton?"

"I should like very much to meet them," Thayne managed, struggling against his character to lie convincingly.

A few further words were said on the subject, as Lady Brighton declared her wholehearted anticipation of the visit. Lydia Kingsley somehow achieved a comment, albeit an unbelievable one, of how "glad she should be" to have them as guests at the manor. The conversation of the table moved on, but the new topic could not hold Thayne's interest.

Rhianna smiled faintly and lowered her eyes to her meal, her slender fingers stirring the curve of her spoon disinterestedly around her soup bowl. Thayne was soon mimicking the action, as the idea of a smitten Frenchman coming to claim his long-lost love turned his stomach. The unpleasant thought only temporarily desisted as he dared raise his eyes and let them rest upon Rhianna—and was quickly mesmerized by the arch of her lashes as her eyes examined the steamy broth before her. He was soon lost in the creamy curve of her neck, only partially hidden by the red curls that danced along her collarbone. The occasional sparkle of an earring, as it caught a flicker of candlelight, would distract him momentarily, in between tracing the outline of her feminine shoulders and following the plunging neckline of her silk gown . . .

"What are your thoughts, Lord Brighton?"

His name rang in his ears as all the objects of the room—the table, the chairs, the ceiling, and the walls, which only a moment ago seemed so far removed—came rushing in at him. All at once, details emerged from obscurity, everything from the paintings to the curtains, the meal and the lighting, the eyes upon him, especially *hers*, and advanced to complete visual clarity in an instant. It was as if his eyes adjusted faster than his mind, and he consequently glanced toward Desmond Kingsley, the source of the voice, as he continued to awaken.

Lydia, for her part, looked at him sharply, with a quick turn toward Rhianna, and Desmond's glance was no less piercing.

Lord Kingsley was quick to come to his rescue. "Of course, Lord Brighton, you agree with me that there has been quite a bit of chaos in Bristol—a violent business, to be sure."

Fully alert now, he nodded his agreement. "Indeed, Lord Kingsley, I do agree with you there."

"Oh, Guilford," cried Lydia, "I beg you, parliamentary reform is a gentlemen's topic to be discussed over port and cigars. Pray, wait until the ladies have escaped to coffee and cards."

"Quite right," he agreed, taking a large bite of his lamb cutlet, "quite right. Brighton, would you pass the asparagus? Thank you."

*

"You're looking particularly handsome tonight, *Miss Braden*."

Rhianna shuddered at the emphasis on her name, recalling Desmond's wish that they address one another on a more informal level. His compliment, too, was unwelcome and she thanked him briefly with hopes of turning the subject.

"How do you enjoy your fish, Lord Kingsley?" she asked him, her voice a little louder, hoping to avoid engaging him in private conversation.

"Have I eaten fish? I hardly noticed." Smiling devilishly, he whispered, "What *have* you done to me?"

"You, sir, are a hopeless flirt," she discouraged, taking a sip of her wine and refusing to look him in the eyes.

"A flirt, indeed, but *hopeless* . . ." he stressed, ". . . I should hope not."

She turned to him, but as was usual when Desmond wished to emphasize his point, he turned away and joined the conversation of the table, allowing Rhianna no opportunity for rebuttal.

In this moment, she met Thayne's glance. As there seemed to be an understanding that he had observed and understood the type of unpleasant communication that had passed between her and Desmond, the unspoken exchange had an unexpectedly calming effect, and she smiled at him. From across the table, he returned the expression and stole a glance at the corner of her mouth that only the night before his own had touched. Her lips warmed at the recollection, as did her cheeks, and when he met her eyes again, her smile widened. His action revealed the thought that diverted his gaze, and to Rhianna his seat on the opposite side of the table no longer felt so very far away.

*

It was a familiar sensation to Lydia Kingsley, one she could not quite place her finger on, but unpleasant nonetheless. Of course, she had little time for such mild irritants. Indeed, Lydia had greater things to concern herself with than Rhianna Braden's presence in her dining room, even if she was all but certain the governess was her husband's mistress.

This, in itself, was no small matter. Lydia had held the same ideals on her wedding day as did most young brides—not that she intended to give up her Pierson, but she hoped to enjoy Guilford, as well. Not only that, but she'd always had a lingering sentimental attachment to the husband of her youth, so that even the most meaningless affair would give her a pinch.

But that alone would not have caused the uncomfortable sensation she now felt, and she felt it tonight more than any other with Rhianna. It was not altogether new to her, but something she had known some time ago, a feeling familiar, distasteful. Lydia could not put her finger on it, but it was almost as if the girl's presence was . . . watchful.

And she shuttered.

*

After dinner, the ladies endured a little awkward silence in the half-hour they spent alone in the drawing room. Crispin had been invited to stay with the men, which he did begrudgingly; therefore,

Audra sat by the fire, silently inconsolable. Lydia's presence alone was enough to put a pall on the mood, though, as hostess, she did make an effort to comment on the fruit tarts. Had she not been there, Lady Brighton and Rhianna might have enjoyed themselves quite thoroughly. As it was, each was left to raise a few humdrum, universal topics until they were exhausted, with little more than a few knowing glances exchanged here and there to relieve them.

Crispin was the first to bounce into the room. With only a quick greeting to the others, he went to Audra's side.

"You think I had fun without you?" he asked her, seeing her dejected position in the chair, her chin resting on her arm, her eyes gazing into the fire.

She refused to look at him. "Of course you did," she said, with what Rhianna recognized as pretend anger.

"They allowed me to try the port," he told her, mildly intoxicated.

"How was it?"

"It makes you look lovelier."

Only her eyes turned to him. "I'm not entirely sure that's a compliment."

Crispin's face contorted, giving one the impression he was rethinking it with some difficulty. "It was meant to be."

She grinned, her eyes returning to the flames.

"Audra, please look at me. I can't stand it."

"It's Miss Kingsley to you."

"That's what I said, isn't it?"

"No."

Audra sat upright in her chair and socked him in the arm, forgivingly.

Meanwhile, Guilford, Desmond, and Thayne entered the room and the overall spirit improved dramatically. The desserts already enjoyed by the ladies were now extended to the men, as Lord and Lady Kingsley, Desmond, and Thayne began a game of cards. Rhianna proposed to Audra she play a couple of songs on the piano for everyone's enjoyment, and with Crispin's added encouragement, she consented.

"She plays very well," Lady Brighton complimented to Rhianna, halfway through her first song.

Swelling with pride, Rhianna nodded. "She has a talent for it."

"Certainly, as well as a gifted instructor, I am sure."

Overhearing their conversation, Lydia gave a smug look from the card table. "Why don't you play for us, Miss Braden?"

Although convinced that Lydia's intention was nothing if not meant to either embarrass or overwhelm her, it had no such effect. Audra, Lydia's own daughter, had been thoroughly enjoying herself at the keys and Rhianna could think of nothing but her feelings.

"I, too, should like to hear you play," added Desmond.

"Lady Kingsley," Rhianna returned, respectfully, "Miss Kingsley has only just begun to play. Surely, I can play for you all some other time?"

"Oh, I'm sure Audra would not mind, would you, dear?"

Audra, who had already stopped playing, seemed more than aware that her mother was not really giving her a choice. She slid off the bench and walked over to Rhianna.

Lord Kingsley interposed. "Miss Braden, you do not have to perform for us tonight."

His words had a finality to them that Lydia did not presume to challenge.

Audra, taking Rhianna's hands, chimed in, "Actually, I think Miss Braden plays and sings very well. I would like to hear you," she added, standing before Rhianna.

"As would I," added Lady Brighton. "But only if Audra promises to resume her concert afterward."

"I agree," Thayne declared, placing down his hand of cards, "I cannot possibly listen to Miss Braden if Miss Kingsley will not continue immediately afterward."

Rhianna caught his eye as he said this last, and wondered at the curious grin that crossed his lips. Then, she turned to Audra, who tugged on her to encourage her to rise from her seat.

"One song," Rhianna told her, "if you promise as Lord and Lady Brighton have suggested."

Audra, not seeming at all bothered by the temporary dismissal, promised to resume her playing after Rhianna was done and plopped into a seat near Crispin.

"Do sing, as well, for us," Lydia interjected, as Rhianna took her seat at the piano.

Rhianna let her fingers rest upon the keys. She had always felt comfortable at the piano, but it had been some time since she had performed before company. Also, she fought desperately to block the thought that Thayne was in the audience, listening. She took a deep breath, chose to sing a French song that she learned from Soleil as a young girl, and allowed the first notes to play out.

The moment passed more quickly than she imagined it would. The tune itself transported her back to her younger years in France and she felt as though Soleil were beside her. She felt at home with the melody and her mind even ventured away from it as she considered how much she truly wished to see both Soleil and Philippe—just how much she missed and loved them. With these thoughts, she concluded her recital, unaware of the effect she had on the group.

Her glance first met Lord Kingsley's. He sat overcome, his eyes appearing glassy, and she turned away awkwardly. Lydia said nothing; Crispin suddenly stood and erupted with applause.

"You see, I *told* you she sang very well," cried Audra, to the speechless crowd.

Lady Brighton was the next to comment, her hand pressed to her chest. "Breathtaking, Miss Braden. I have never heard the like."

"It reminds me of someone," declared Desmond, "but I cannot recall whom. In any case, *bravo!*"

"To whom do you credit your gift?" asked Thayne, who had joined Crispin with his applause. "Undoubtedly, your mother or your father was very talented."

Rhianna shook her head. "Actually, neither was very musical."

"Well," Lady Brighton concluded, "God has given you quite an ability, I declare! I hope you will do us the honor of singing for us again soon."

Rhianna humbly thanked them, as Lord Kingsley quietly excused himself from the room. Her eyes followed him anxiously, but Audra soon distracted her by hopping onto the piano bench beside her.

"I'm going to play my song now, but afterwards, Crispin and I would like to go to the library to play backgammon. Will you take us?"

Lydia had no objections; looking frequently aggravated by the both of them, she gave permission in Lord Kingsley's absence. Thus, Rhianna conceded, though her disappointment at leaving the drawing room—and Thayne—was more than a little heavy.

Audra concluded her song. Rhianna was glad to see that at some time during it, Lord Kingsley returned looking his usual self. Crispin gave a second standing ovation and they prepared to leave for the library.

"Miss Braden," called Thayne, hurriedly, "do you play chess?"

Rhianna turned to him, as he sat with a handful of cards with the group. Quickly making the connection that the chessboard was also in the library, Rhianna wondered if it was too much to hope this was where his thoughts were leading.

"No, I . . . I should like very much to understand it, however, I have never had the opportunity to learn," she ventured.

Thayne nodded definitively. "You ought not to waste another moment. Mother," he turned, "would you do me the favor of taking over my hand? I think I'll be joining the group to the library."

"Of course," Lady Brighton agreed, smiling and rising at once.

Thayne seemed unashamed that he deliberately chose to leave the drawing room to remain with the children and their governess. Lord Kingsley seemed to have no position on the matter and Lady Brighton seemed to highly support it by taking over his hand, while

Desmond looked highly irritated, and Lydia appeared stunned.

*

Audra and Crispin had been talkative with Rhianna and Thayne during the majority of the trek from the drawing room to the library, but as they ascended the stairs to the top floor they began to skip ahead and chat animatedly between themselves.

"I hope it was not intrusive of me to accompany you," Thayne remarked to Rhianna, seizing his opportunity at private conversation.

"No, of course you are welcome to join us," she promised him. "I am glad of your company."

"And I of yours," he told her.

He stunned her momentarily, before she continued, "I only regret that you are missing out on socializing with the rest of the group."

"And pray, what is there to miss? I think it comes as no surprise that Lydia and Desmond Kingsley are not high on my list of persons with whom I wish to associate for an entire evening, or even, for any part of an evening." Rhianna held back a smile, and he went on, "Lord Kingsley and my mother I may see as frequently as I wish. But," he emphasized, "when is it that I get to see *you*, Miss Braden?"

Curiously, she glanced at him. "Did you not see me yesterday at Ravensleigh?"

"Was that only yesterday?" he returned facetiously. "Humph, it seems much longer."

"Yes," she told him directly. "And two days before that, at the ball, did we not dance together?"

Thayne gave a thoughtful look. "An eternity ago, to be sure."

His playful banter gave Rhianna pause as they reached the uppermost floor of Kingsley Manor and turned down the hall toward the library. She found it inconceivable that Thayne would be so unrefined as to knowingly tease her into false hopes of any romantic intensions. Surely, she thought, even *if* his heart were at all inclined toward her, he was too well-bred and gentlemanly for that. She felt it necessary to remind him of exactly the sort of decision he had made in leaving the drawing room.

"So, am I to take it that you would rather spend the rest of your evening with the Kingsleys' governess than with the Kingsleys themselves?"

"That is not how I see it," he told her. "Are we not friends, Miss Braden?"

She wrung her fingers together as she walked, unsure of her response. "Certainly," she managed, with an unconvincing inflection.

Thayne's tone was pained, as he declared, "It is not as impossible as you believe."

He caught Rhianna's eyes with a pleading expression, and she sighed. With every word, Thayne Brighton made it increasingly difficult for her to keep detached from her emotions.

"Well," she acquiesced, "I suppose it is forgivable to want to spend time with a friend."

This last seemed to lighten the mood. "And Miss Kingsley, of course."

"Of course." Suddenly, looking about her, Rhianna questioned, "Where *is* Audra?"

They heard a distant giggling, as well as footsteps.

"Crispin!" called Thayne, authoritatively.

Quickening their pace, Rhianna and Thayne entered the library, but found no sign of them there. Again, distant laughter led them directly next door to the empty, echoing ballroom. They entered hopeful, but to no avail.

"They're . . . *hiding on us?*" Rhianna wondered aloud.

"We probably should have seen this coming."

"Audra!" called Rhianna anxiously. "How could they have run off without us noticing?" she asked Thayne.

"Crispin!"

They found themselves in the middle of the long dance floor, the room itself appearing vastly larger without the throngs of people that had occupied it only days before. Around them there was only silence, until Thayne chuckled and the sound reverberated through the room.

Rhianna turned to him disbelievingly. "How can you laugh? They are so openly affectionate together. They ought not to be alone."

"They ought not," he agreed, smiling. "For that matter, neither should we."

Her concern for the children had eclipsed the realization that she was, indeed, alone with Thayne Brighton.

"Miss Braden," he said, consolingly, "try not to over concern yourself. They are undoubtedly watching us from some dark corner, laughing at our powerlessness over them. When they have lived out their moment, they will reappear." She considered giving in to his more optimistic outlook, as he added, "Besides, this could be far worse."

She was not blind to his feeble attempt to ease her worry, but she did not resist either.

"Do tell," she encouraged.

"Well, for instance, you could be alone with Desmond Kingsley, rather than myself."

Rhianna shuddered at the thought, recalling the last time she was alone with Desmond. She thought of him entering the schoolroom giddily and requesting the first two dances of the ball.

"Yes, I imagine that would be a *trifle* worse than the present circumstance."

That this last was uttered strictly tongue-in-cheek there could be no doubt. Finally, she laughed at the stark contrast and Thayne seemed pleased.

"The room feels so different from the other night," she recalled, after banishing those first two dances from her thoughts. "With its grandeur and liveliness gone, it is so very . . . unlike a ball."

Thayne looked about the vacant room and then back to her. "I like it better," he confessed, cheerfully. "Actually, the orchestra sounds especially captivating tonight, does it not?"

She looked wonderingly at him. Thayne bowed to her, grinning. Then, he held out his hand.

Rhianna, making the connection, submitted to his mock ball with a curtsey and took his hand for a pretend waltz. Thayne willingly slipped his hand around her waist and drew her close to him as they began to circle the room.

"I'm not entirely sure you were on my dance card, Lord Brighton," Rhianna teased.

"I beg your pardon. Was there another gentleman promised to this dance?"

"Not that I would have such pleasure to dance with."

Her words flowed quickly and without thought. Rhianna reconsidered them after they were pronounced, but it was too late.

He smiled wryly, and said, "I think Desmond Kingsley is looking very ill. I daresay he is rather jealous of me at this moment."

At once, Rhianna looked around them, but saw no one. Recognizing his comment again as farce, she happily played along.

"Does he look ill, indeed?" she returned. "Perhaps I should dance with him, considering that Miss Leighart is anxious to partner with you."

"Is she?" he asked, disinterestedly. "Well, she has used up her two dances already. Besides," he paused, holding her gaze, "I would cut our dance short for no one."

Her instinct was to look away, but his blue eyes held hers prisoner. Her feet would not obey her; her dancing slowed and her smile faded. What could the Lord of Ravensleigh want with a governess? Her expression begged him not to play with her heart.

With a seriousness that startled her, he mimicked her words, saying, "There is not any other that I would have such pleasure to dance with."

They stopped. Rhianna's heart raced as Thayne raised one hand to her face and gently ran the backs of his fingers along her skin.

"I made a terrible mistake last night," he said suddenly.

Rhianna looked at him blankly. Hardly could she think. She recalled only his lips against her cheek outside Ravensleigh.

"What mistake was that?" she managed breathlessly, as he took her face in his hands.

"I missed."

With that, he pressed his open mouth to hers, engulfing her lips completely in his kiss. Urgently, his full lips moved against hers, deeply and eagerly, and she reached for his wrists to steady herself. Seeming to sense her unbalance, Thayne took her hands and eased her arms smoothly over his shoulders and around his neck. As she interlocked her fingers there, he allowed her arms to lead his hands back to her body. Without breaking the kiss, Thayne pulled her into him, crushing her small frame into his embrace, yet even as her racing heart beat wildly against his breast it seemed she was not close enough. He clutched her tighter.

Thayne tapered his fervency only when she responded with a kiss of her own—only not a frenzied, desperate kiss, as he had displayed. Rhianna molded her lips to his mouth tenderly, searchingly, but desirous in their own way.

Rhianna's lips peeled slowly from his when she noticed his sudden stillness. His breath, sweet and intoxicating, flirted with her senses and his eyes even more so. When they met, they drew her deeper into his spell. Captivated by him at every angle, Rhianna observed all the smallest details that she could view only from this close distance—a small, flesh-colored mole directly before his left earlobe, the thickness of his upper lashes, and a brownish hue in his blue eyes. Just as those same eyes fell upon her lips a second time, he drew her in again and kissed her feverishly.

With a sudden gasp did she pull back, her breathing heavy and her parted lips pulsing. She turned to the children with a flush of embarrassment sweeping over her.

Crispin raised one eyebrow. Audra stood beside him, suppressing a giggle.

"Well done, brother," declared Crispin proudly, and the two walked passed them for the stairs. "Incidentally, we're not at all interested in backgammon anymore. Miss Kingsley and I will wait for you in the hall."

While her eyes followed them, she sensed Thayne's eyes—and hands—remained upon her. When she turned back to him, the tips of her fingers covering her mouth, he smiled widely.

"I am jealous of these fingers," he said, taking them in his own hand and raising them tenderly to his lips.

She opened her mouth, as if to speak, but there were no words at the ready.

Finally, he suggested, "Perhaps we ought not to lose the children again."

At last, Thayne released her and took a step back. He bowed, as though finishing their dance. Rhianna smiled nervously, just as he took her by the hand and together they hurried after Crispin and Audra.

*

As the families gathered in the Great Hall, Thayne hurried through the sea of goodbyes to Rhianna's side.

"I have to go to London for a week or two," Thayne whispered, looking as if he were struggling not to kiss her again. "I shall think of you every moment."

This confession, however private Thayne imagined it, did not go unnoticed. There was one person who noticed this brief interchange and Thayne was not long out the Kingsleys' door when halted by the sound of his name.

"A word, Brighton?"

As his mother and brother entered their coach, Thayne turned to find Desmond sauntering toward him.

"Certainly," he allowed, cautiously.

"I'm just curious," Desmond began, stalling until all ears were out of range, "wouldn't it be easier to keep a mistress who lives under your own roof? In my experience, I have found that anything else is, well, hardly convenient."

"I am not sure I understand you," said Thayne. Though instantly understanding him and instantly incensed, he hoped to force something more from Desmond that would excuse his fist against the man's jaw.

"I think you do," Desmond returned obnoxiously.

"Well, then, you mistake me grievously, for I have no intentions of pursuing anyone as a mistress under my roof or any other."

"Pardon my error," Desmond smiled.

"I am inclined to offer much more than occasional, clandestine lovemaking."

Desmond's smile melted into a scowl. "You can't be serious."

Thayne warned, "I would advise you to be wary of whom *you* pursue as a mistress."

"Would you, indeed? You know," he taunted, "she's no better than that."

Hardly had Thayne's clenched fist had time to turn white around the knuckles than it unleashed a punishing right hook to Desmond's face. Thayne's body thrust into action, following the lead of his shoulder; the blow was hard, and a loud snap was heard upon impact. Desmond fell sideways, but caught himself halfway down.

Meanwhile, the servants had seen enough to summon Lord Kingsley, with Lydia on his heels. Lady Brighton and Crispin had been close enough to hear the scuffle and they disembarked the carriage.

Desmond turned his head to both sides, the vertebrae in his neck cracking each time. After a time, he rose and stood face-to-face with Thayne. A trickle of blood ran down from the corner of his mouth.

"What is the meaning of this?" cried Lord Kingsley. When neither gentleman answered, he approached them. "Lord Brighton? Desmond?"

"Desmond!" cried Lydia, who at the sight of the injury rushed to his side.

The men's eyes locked, each ready for the next move. Desmond's nostrils flared. All looked on anxiously until, at last, Thayne took a step back, easing the tension.

"A misunderstanding, Lord Kingsley," he managed.

"I should say so. Desmond, what have you to say?"

He wiped the blood from his chin with the back of his hand and, upon reviewing it, stormed into the house. Lydia followed him immediately without a word.

Crispin stood, his mouth open, at the side of the carriage. Lady Brighton quickly instructed him to get back in. He obeyed her, and she approached Thayne and Lord Kingsley. Neither she nor the latter said anything; their looks urged their questions.

Thayne took a deep breath. "I cannot apologize for my actions, Lord Kingsley, only to you, if I have offended you by them."

"Ought I not to be offended?" he asked. His tone reflected a willingness to hear an explanation from his longtime friend.

"No," he said, confidently. "You ought not. Lord Kingsley, it is no secret to my mother the feelings I have developed for Miss Braden. I feel I reacted appropriately to the suggestions Desmond Kingsley has spoken of her."

"And what suggestions are those?"

"He has dishonorable intentions toward her. You cannot expect me to say more in the presence of my mother."

"Good heavens, Thayne. I'll be in the carriage." Lady Brighton offered her hand to Lord Kingsley. He accepted readily, as she said, "My apologies, Guilford. I hardly know what to say."

Guilford shook his head. "Go in peace, Moira, and good night."

She nodded and returned to the vehicle. Guilford raised his

hand to his forehead and sighed.

"Lord Kingsley, I know you cared for her father. And I know you care for her. Desmond says she is nothing better than a *whore,*" he stressed, visibly distraught.

Guilford, too, was visibly angered by this. The blood rushed through the veins of his forehead and the skin of his cheeks flushed red.

"I cannot make excuses for him there."

"I do not trust him, Lord Kingsley." Thayne pleaded, "Watch over her."

Lord Kingsley seemed to ponder this for a moment and he nodded. Then, his countenance softened and he placed a hand upon Thayne's shoulder.

"Is Miss Braden aware of your feelings for her?" he asked.

Thayne fought hard not to become lost in thoughts of earlier when, with a gentle passion, she conquered him entirely.

"I imagine she has an idea . . ."

"Do you intend to make them clearly known?" he pressed.

Thayne examined him. "You think me injudicious?"

"No," he told him, dropping his hand. "I know you better than to imagine you do not know exactly what you are doing."

With this, Thayne had little hesitation. "Then the answer to your question is yes."

Lord Kingsley paced to and fro. "Do you suppose she returns your affection?"

"I can only hope."

"Indeed," he mumbled distantly. "Brighton, if that truly is what you have decided, I would urge you to make your declarations sooner than later. Her visitors from France are arriving momentarily and one shares your hopes."

"Yes, Miss Braden has mentioned it."

"Has she?" he said, with surprise. He ceased pacing. "The Vallières seem to be a good family. I have been looking forward to their visit. But I have also been under the impression from Marquis Vallière's communication that Miss Braden would not stay long in England thereafter." He shrugged. "For Audra's sake, I think my daughter would like Miss Braden much better settled at Ravensleigh."

Thayne smiled. "I should like very much not to disappoint Miss Kingsley."

Guilford nodded, a pleased expression on his face. "Safe travels, my friend. In the future, do what you can to refrain from striking Desmond. I realize what I am asking will take considerable restraint."

*

News of the incident traveled quickly throughout the house and reached Rhianna just as she had changed into her bedclothes. A breathless Katie fell onto the edge of the bed to tell her of the account. Rhianna sat beside her, her eyes wide and her breath still.

"What can the fight have been about?" she asked, after Katie was finished.

"No one seems to have been close enough to hear," she told her. "Not even Henry."

Guilford and Lydia could be heard arguing on the lower floor, though their voices were indistinct. Soon, Rhianna heard a light knock at the door. Katie rushed to her feet to answer it, and found Audra standing teary-eyed at the threshold.

"Miss Braden?" the girl asked, a lump in her throat.

"Come in, come in," called Rhianna. "Whatever is the matter?"

Audra rushed into her arms. "May I sleep with you tonight?"

Katie silently excused herself as Rhianna stroked Audra's hair. "Of course, you may. But why do you not want to stay in your own lovely room?"

She sniffed and wiped her moist eyes with her fingers. "I can't hear them as well here. And we can talk of pleasant things."

"Oh, there," said Rhianna, resting her hand on the girl's damp cheek. "Pleasant things like Lord Crispin?"

She giggled through her tears. "Yes."

It was not the first time Lord and Lady Kingsley could be heard arguing within the manor, but it was the first time Audra Kingsley had come to her governess for comfort. Rhianna was touched and immensely happy that the girl thought to come to her.

"Well, hop in," she invited, pulling the bedcovers back. "Tell me everything he had to say tonight."

Instantly uplifted, Audra said much in a short span of time. It was not long before the comfort of the pillows, blankets, and Rhianna's company—as well as her exhaustion from a full night—overcame the girl. Audra fell asleep contentedly beside her governess.

Rhianna, her mind racing—not only with Katie's report, but the night as a whole—did not hope to have it so easy. Nor did she wish it. As Rhianna blew out her candle, she looked forward to hours of silent meditation, ready to fight sleep away if ever it came to claim her.

Chapter Seven

Guilford Kingsley sat as still as he possibly could while Audra put the finishing touches on his portrait.

"Is it very like me, Miss Braden?" he asked, fighting a grin.

"Oh, yes," she confirmed, standing behind the easel as Audra stroked her brush liberally on the canvas. "Very like, indeed."

There was a hint of humor in her tone, but Audra seemed oblivious. She squinted over the finer points, holding her breath as she made adjustments and smiling when satisfied.

"May I take a look?" Lord Kingsley requested, attempting to rise.

"Do not *move*, Papa!" cried Audra. "It is almost finished."

"You mustn't interfere with an inspired artist at work, Lord Kingsley," Rhianna reminded him, smiling.

"Certainly not," he agreed.

Moments later, a servant entered the schoolroom and announced an impending carriage.

"Oh!" cried Rhianna happily.

"Your friends must be here!" declared Audra.

Rhianna hurried to the south window and looked out over the approach.

"Why do you not go to them?" suggested Lord Kingsley. "Audra and I are almost done. We will follow shortly."

Rhianna spun around, biting back a wide grin. "Are you quite sure?"

"We insist, do we not, Audra?"

"Oh, yes! We will be there directly."

"Thank you both!"

Rhianna flew down the stairs, through the Great Hall, and out the front door to the gravel drive. In the open gig they had rented at the inn, both Soleil and Philippe nearly stood at the sight of her, despite two horses at full trot and several yards of travel yet to go.

"We nearly jumped from the carriage half a mile back, certain in our excitement to outrun the horses!" cried Soleil.

"And outrun them we would!" declared Philippe. "But we feared a broken leg or two might dampen our adventures."

"Good heavens, that you should conspire to do any such thing!" cried Rhianna, as the carriage slowed to a stop. "Never mind, now that you are here. Make haste!"

Both brother and sister leapt to the ground before any servant could assist them, and both took their turns embracing Rhianna. Rhianna's hand, when once intertwined with Soleil's, could not be pried away, and she was less than anxious for Philippe to remove his hand from the small of her back. For a moment, everything seemed right, with the best of both England and France joined in one location. Rhianna had never felt more at home than at that moment.

"Welcome!" called Lord Kingsley, approaching them from the manor house.

Audra raced ahead of him to greet them. "*Bonjour!*" she called, in an exaggerated French accent.

"*Bonjour!*" Soleil and Philippe echoed, amused.

Their bags were removed from the carriage by the time Lord Kingsley reached their small group. His movements were slow and he struggled to catch his breath. Since dinner with the Brightons two weeks past, his health seemed to be steadily declining, though he would not admit it.

Rhianna made the introductions, her heart swelling with unimaginable joy.

"Welcome," Lord Kingsley repeated, extending his arms warmly. "I know I speak for the rest of my family when I say how glad we are to have you stay with us. I hope you will make our home your home. Stay as long as you wish."

Effusions of thanks followed as the happy group made their

way inside. Once they were comfortably seated in the drawing room, conversation flowed effortlessly while all manner of refreshments and cakes were served and enjoyed. Even when Lydia and Desmond arrived to greet them, awkwardness could not exist amongst Soleil and Philippe's animated expressions and high spirits. Every compliment was paid to the Kingsleys themselves, their home, and their generous spirit. Lydia even seemed not to mind them, and Desmond, although Rhianna imagined he could do very well without Philippe, did not appear at all adverse to the presence of Soleil.

Rhianna could not have been more content. It was as if no break in their association had ever transpired and she felt none of the anxiousness she'd imagined she might with Philippe. Their company relieved her of all worry and, in ways she did not expect, renewed her feelings of familial attachment.

There was no want of dialogue. For some time, they could hardly keep up with the questions each had for the other. Much was covered, all promises of health for the Vallière family were ensured, and a general review of the previous year not already communicated by letter was fully established by all parties, albeit modified for a general audience.

The tears burst forth later, long after the afternoon and evening had passed. Rhianna hardly knew how the day had escaped, as she and Soleil languished blissfully on her bed in the rose room. Here, enjoying their first moments to themselves, all the emotions at last caught up with them. Soleil and Rhianna laughed at themselves as they sat with moist eyes, their handkerchiefs in hand.

At last, Rhianna felt at liberty to make a very important inquiry. "Now you *must* tell me. For weeks, I have waited and I cannot wait another second!" she declared, her hands clasped tightly around Soleil's. "What is it that you could not tell me except in person?"

Soleil glanced at her with the greatest of smiles before answering, "Armand has proposed! We are to be married in the spring!"

The explosion of delightful feelings this news released could only be fully expressed by an embrace.

"Oh, Soleil! This is the most wonderful of news!"

"I am so very, very happy."

"I can imagine! Certainly, I recall him being very agreeable the one evening we met," Rhianna recollected. "And Marquis and Marquise Vallière? What do they say to it?"

"They are very pleased," Soleil declared blithely. "And I shan't be very far from them, not more than fifty kilometers."

"And what does Philippe say to it?"

"He has told me that Count Deveraux is an excellent man, and I could not have done better had chosen the gentleman himself!"

"Well, that settles it, does it not? It is the most desirable of situations!" admitted Rhianna. "And, you really love him, Soleil, do you?"

"I do," she affirmed. "I love him, truly. I wish everyone could feel as I do."

"Well," Rhianna said, satisfied not with her friend's words only, but with the whole of her countenance, "I cannot begin to tell you how very delighted I am for you. He is a very fortunate fellow!"

"No, indeed, it is I who am the fortunate one."

A brief recount of the engagement itself was relayed, but for Rhianna it would hardly satisfy. "I want to know *all* the details," she declared at once. "I must know everything about him, and how you came to this point."

"Why do we not save that for tomorrow?" Soleil suggested. "The hour has grown late and I want us to get our rest so we can fully enjoy every moment of tomorrow. Lord Kingsley's suggestion of this Thornton Gardens seems just the place for such pleasant reminisces."

Rhianna agreed. She walked Soleil to the door and goodnights were exchanged. When the door was closed and Rhianna lay down in her bed, she fell soundly and peacefully asleep.

*

Philippe held the invisible reins of his imaginary horse, donning a large feather hat that he discovered in the theater costume closet. He gestured dramatically from the stage of the Kingsleys' theater, while Soleil, Rhianna, and Audra sat as spectators, giggling riotously.

Rain beat wildly against the windows, shattering all hopes of their going to Thornton Gardens for another consecutive day. Not one of them was sorry for it, however, as they easily entertained themselves simply by being together.

Philippe addressed them, saying, "This story is incomplete without a lady in distress."

His eyes turned toward Rhianna daringly, but she had no intention of volunteering. Audra, meanwhile, was quick to step forward, saving her governess from any further insistence from him.

"I shall be your lady!" she cried, hopping onto the stage. Dressed in an oversized cloak from the same wardrobe closet and tied at the waist with a golden rope belt, she cried, "Hark! The dragon!"

"*En guard!*" Philippe thrust a fictitious sword wildly into the air. "I believe we have frightened it away," he declared, catching his breath.

"No, indeed," answered Soleil, rising also to the stage, "for I have only ordered it away. I am queen of this land and the dragon answers to me. I warn you to leave and never return!"

Audra's eyes widened with the story and she tugged on Philippe's sleeve. "We must go at once, and save my older sister, as well!"

Philippe looked ready to stay and fight, but suddenly echoed, "Older sister, you say? Are not *you* my lady in distress?"

"Behold!" Audra pointed to Rhianna, holding her arm to her forehead theatrically. "You must save us both, or *neither of us!*"

"No, indeed," Rhianna laughed. "I am enjoying this far too much from my current point of view."

Philippe leapt to the floor before her with eagerness. With

straightened shoulders and an arched back, he held out his hand to her.

"Fair maiden," he implored, "I beg you to come with me. I promise you will find protection both from the wicked queen and her wretched dragon. Not only that, but your little sister has sworn to perish if you refuse."

Such a display could hardly go unrewarded. Rhianna took his hand and rose.

"To where shall we run?" she asked, the corners of her lips turned upward.

Philippe quickly pulled her near to him. "Running is out of the question," he said, in a tone more serious than the role required. "I am going to fight for you."

"Hurry!" called Audra. "The dragon has returned!"

Philippe hesitated, his gaze locked with Rhianna's and his acting skills failing him miserably. Finally, he gestured for her to take her place beside Audra. She did not waste a moment in joining the girl on stage, as Philippe's pretend arrow pierced Soleil's heart.

"Oh!" she groaned, reaching for a feigned wound.

As Soleil collapsed to the stage floor, Audra laughed heartily, her hands around her stomach. "This is fun, Miss Braden, do you not think?"

"It is very much fun," Rhianna returned.

Philippe approached them. "Just as when we were children," he reminisced.

Rhianna had many fond memories of performing with Philippe and Soleil in the privacy of the Vallière ballroom. Frequently, a temporary stage converted it into a theater when close friends were invited, either to observe or be included in the cast of their amateur theatricals.

Philippe's reference to these happy times was clearly intended to invoke sentimentality in her, and she did not wonder at his intentions. Several days had passed since their arrival and Philippe had not been secretive about his continued feelings for her. He left no doubt that those feelings had not only been renewed, but intensified, and he had all but spoken of the subject aloud. Rhianna anticipated it was only a matter of time before he did so.

In a quick instant, a different ballroom flashed through her thoughts. This one, conversely, was not filled with an audience, but rather only herself and a particular Englishman whom she had not seen in more than a fortnight. Her eyes rested on Philippe, but it was Thayne who looked back at her.

She had not heard any mention of him from the Kingsleys, and though she suspected that neither Lydia nor Desmond was anxious to receive the Brightons as guests in the near future, Rhianna expected Thayne's regular business visits with Lord Kingsley would continue upon his return to Thornton. Despite the inclement weather that continuously dampened her hopes of his coming, each day she allowed herself a little anticipation.

With difficulty, her mind returned to the moment at hand. After acknowledging the pleasant childhood memories to which Philippe had referred, Rhianna offered to continue their tour of Kingsley Manor, which at the discovery of the theater had been nearly irrevocably hindered.

The rest of the household was very little inconvenienced by their visit, and they spent the following rainy days confined to Kingsley Manor without any interruptions to their felicity.

*

Cold and bare as it was, Thornton Gardens never lost its beauty. Regardless of the time of year, one could not but enjoy a walk along its long, winding pathways, or admire its verandas and columns. An assortment of stone and wood bridges connected one corner of the garden to another and promised serenity with every stroll. In this very place, countless young ladies' hands were requested in marriage, not to mention the precious memories of many a stolen kiss.

It was the first day of pleasant weather since Soleil and Philippe's arrival. The rain had afforded them many hours to enjoy each other's company from the comfort of Kingsley Manor. But now, as the skies cleared and the roads dried, they prepared to set out for the gardens.

Audra was to join them, as her quick attachment to both Soleil and Philippe, combined with her inseparableness from Rhianna, left this singular option open to them. Barely did they avoid extending an invite to Desmond, who without actually asking was very blatant in expressing his desire to accompany them. In the end, their wish of being without him was greater than his wish of joining them, and when a carriage—provided at Guilford Kingsley's insistence—awaited them at the door, they were a final group of four.

As they prepared to leave, a visitor detained them. "Miss Braden!" he called from his saddle.

Urging d'Artagnan forward, Thayne halted his steed before her. With a quick glance at the Vallières, he removed his hat and bowed. His sudden appearance set Rhianna's heart aflutter.

Since the night of their kiss— so uncertain was she of his meaning by it—she had often imagined their next meeting and what his behavior would reveal to her. Each reverie left her guessing as to its significance, and she was anxious to see what impression he would leave her with. Surely, she anticipated, the next time they were brought together, she would see in his manner, in his speech, if he regretted it—and if such was the case, the sooner she knew, the better for her own heart's sake.

With the reality of this moment thrust upon her, she opted to curtsey, not rushing any sentence from her lips, as there was none fully developed.

"It is a pleasure to meet you this morning," he said, smiling.

"Of course, that goes without saying, as you are always a pleasure to meet."

His flattery was a welcome surprise, whereas his presence, his very *being*, was all consuming. Were Soleil, Philippe, and Audra still behind her? She knew not.

"You are too kind, Lord Brighton," she managed. "I am glad to see you have returned safely from London."

Thayne dismounted. As a servant led away his horse, he approached Rhianna. With each step, it was as if Cupid struck her with another arrow. Was she imagining it, or was Thayne Brighton suddenly standing a little closer to her than perhaps he ought?

"I returned to Thornton as soon as I was able," he confessed to her, in a tone that seemed only for her ears. "Had the weather been more cooperative, you would have seen me sooner."

She felt a warm flush of color rise in her cheeks as Thayne threw a glance at the rest of the group, which included a giggling Audra.

"I almost missed you," Thayne observed, raising his voice for the group. "Miss Kingsley, good day to you!"

In that moment, as introductions were made and civilities exchanged, Rhianna wished with all her heart they were not going to Thornton Gardens.

"How long will you be staying in England?" Thayne asked the Vallières. "If I know Miss Braden," he added, casting her a furtive glance, "I daresay she would have you stay infinitely."

"I would, indeed," Rhianna professed, smiling at his hint of intimacy.

"Our plans are uncertain," Philippe answered, "but as long as possible, of course. The company alone could certainly keep us here infinitely, but my sister has a wedding to plan."

Thayne congratulated her and Soleil thanked him, grinning with all the joys of prenuptial bliss.

"Well, I insist you all come to dine at Ravensleigh as soon as possible," invited Thayne.

"And me, as well?" cried Audra, excitedly.

"Of course," he confirmed. "Crispin would never forgive me otherwise."

"It would be an inestimable pleasure," declared Soleil, with a glance at her brother.

"Yes, we should like very much to come," echoed Philippe.

"Well, that settles it, then," Thayne smirked. "What say you all to tomorrow evening?"

"Rhianna," asked Philippe, "does that interfere with any other plans?"

The sound of her Christian name from Philippe's lips seemed to take Thayne by surprise. Rhianna, for her part, had long been accustomed to the sibling-like liberties they took with each other, but Thayne's ill-masked reaction did not leave her unaffected.

"Lord Brighton could never interfere with my plans," she daringly responded.

Her smile followed this, and Thayne seemed quickly recovered. The date was happily fixed upon and, as Thayne had business to discuss with Lord Kingsley, they prepared to part without further delay.

"Good day, Lord Brighton," said Rhianna regretfully, as Philippe assisted Soleil and Audra into the carriage.

Thayne bowed, and with that single act sealed Rhianna's fate. Her day would go on without him, and Thornton Gardens was drained of all its appeal.

*

This brief exchange rendered Rhianna conversationally useless. She found herself able only to respond to others' observations and, even then, it was perfunctory. At last, she steered the conversation toward a subject Soleil could command for some time—her engagement to Armand—while Rhianna battled her own inattentiveness.

It worked precisely as planned. Soleil was delighted to express every detail of the proposal, as well as events before and after, with all the original enthusiasm of her first communication of it, until the subject was exhausted. Having this to occupy them was of some relief to Rhianna, though it could not ease her completely. The closeness of the topic to one she wished to avoid with Philippe kept her stomach in constant knots, and she felt sure he must bring it up at any moment.

Philippe Vallière did not, however, raise any such disastrous matter to her. Romantic a setting as Thornton Gardens was, Philippe attempted not to engage her in talks of past declarations nor their significance one year hence. Rhianna even fleetingly imagined him disinterested in her as a wife, but such thoughts were entirely of her own invention. The way Philippe looked into her eyes, the way he held her arm in his, quickly dispelled any such idea from proceeding further. He was more devotedly attached than ever, proving once again, that absence unfailingly *does* make the heart grow fonder.

As they stopped while crossing over a bridge, admiring the view of a rocky stream, Soleil concluded her musings. "I must say, I find the country very much to my liking," she declared. "If only Armand was here, I might never leave."

Philippe agreed with her. "There is much to like," he confessed, looking affectionately at Rhianna. "I could see having a home in the English countryside to visit a few months out of the year. It would be the best of both worlds. What do you think, Rhianna?"

Briefly, Rhianna found herself considering his vision. She felt she owed him at least that, and Philippe's clear intention of inducing her to see the possibilities with him had its effect. A home in France and another in England was no small thing. Her heart lay in both places and it was no empty promise. Philippe was more than able to provide this, and more.

This last altered the path of her thoughts. That she should have someone in Philippe's position . . . a *count*, no less . . . offering her all the love and comfort of the world, should she really imagine that more than one such man would come along in her lifetime? More specifically, that the Lord of Ravensleigh should see her as a prospective mate, as Philippe did? Was it not more reasonable to believe that Thayne, unlike Philippe who had already proposed marriage, was interested in her in the way that Desmond Kingsley had implied?

Philippe Vallière was not the most handsome of all men, but he was not unattractive. He was kind, he was generous, he was well-bred, and his family had welcomed her as one of their own. Rhianna knew in her heart that though she would not be passionately in love, she would not be unhappy if married to him.

"I think it sounds lovely," she told him.

It was as much as Philippe seemed to expect in this public setting. Rhianna could see him mulling things over, and she made an attempt at nudging the conversation in a less serious direction. In the end, their day at Thornton Gardens proved just as pleasant as each day had been with them all along and any awkwardness Rhianna feared never made its appearance.

*

Soleil and Rhianna were anxious for a moment to speak privately. So the two young women arranged that when all had retired for the evening, Soleil would meet Rhianna in her room—a frequent pastime for the girls as of late. That night, as Kingsley Manor slept, she quietly tiptoed to Rhianna's bed, placed her candle on the nightstand, and crawled into the sheets beside her friend.

"I must know two things," she whispered to Rhianna. "First, *where* are you getting your gowns? I insist you take me to your dressmaker at once!"

Rhianna laughed under her breath. "You will never guess, but they are Lord Kingsley's mother's."

Soleil did not say a word in response, but simply stared with disbelief.

Rhianna continued, "The seamstress altered them for me at his request. It does sound rather odd when I say it aloud, but he insisted on it."

Soleil thought for a moment, before asking, "Can he have an ulterior motive? You must imagine why I would think it."

"No, none whatsoever," she assured her. "Lord Kingsley is an honorable man. He has never given me reason to feel uncomfortable. It is only his giving nature, I am sure of it."

"Lady Kingsley has not said anything of the matter?" Soleil questioned, with one chocolate eyebrow arched suspiciously.

Rhianna shook her head. "She does not seem to recognize them. Also, the mention of Lord Kingsley's mother only arose once with Lady Kingsley, and she did not seem to like her very much."

"I see," Soleil allowed. "Well, Lord Kingsley has been nothing but wonderful since we arrived here. He must truly be one of the most generous persons I have ever known."

Rhianna agreed, and Soleil did not press the matter any further. Instead, she addressed a different subject.

"As to the second thing I must know," Soleil said, "Lord Brighton is very handsome."

Rhianna's heart stopped at his name. With wide eyes she looked at Soleil, not at all having suspected Soleil would mention him.

"Rhianna, you know there is nothing that could part us. There is no choice in life you could make that would separate me from you, no matter what country you live in or whom you choose to marry."

"Soleil!" cried Rhianna, "I am not marrying Lord Brighton. We have no understanding at all. You know I would have told you as much."

"Yes, of course," she told her, "but I hope that, *if* any particular gentleman were to catch your eye, you would feel comfortable confiding in me." She paused, before adding, "I would not tell Philippe."

Rhianna's shoulders fell and she sighed—with relief. She could never hide her feelings from Soleil and she found comfort in having someone to whom she could unburden her heart.

With one, fair hand held against her cheek, she asked, "Am I blushing?"

Both girls laughed together and Soleil put her arms around Rhianna. Little could she know how invaluable was her support.

"Does he know how you feel?"

Rhianna shook her head. "We have discussed nothing."

Soleil waited for further details. Her eyes were wide with anticipation, her aura was all excitement.

"He can have no interest in me, Soleil," Rhianna hurried. "I am a curate's daughter, remember. A *governess*."

Soleil dispelled this thinking at once. "Gentlemen marry governesses all the time. And one as lovely as you, surely, he must know what a treasure you are. Has he given any signs? Any reason to believe he may share your sentiments?"

Rhianna smiled shyly. "We kissed."

Soleil's mouth fell and she reached excitedly for Rhianna's hands. But Rhianna was quick to calm her.

"It does not mean he wants to *marry me*, Soleil."

"What of his invitation to dinner?" she pointed out.

"He is friendly," Rhianna excused.

Soleil gave her a knowing glance that Rhianna tried to ignore. It was the same look she gave her anytime Rhianna was being completely and utterly ridiculous.

"Well," said Soleil, after a moment's thought, "tomorrow we dine at Ravensleigh and *I* shall be watching Lord Brighton very closely. We shall see what his intentions are."

Rhianna smiled, but could not but feel tranquil as she thought of Philippe. Soleil seemed to understand her immediately, but said nothing.

"I do love Philippe, Soleil," Rhianna expressed solemnly. "Has he said . . . ?"

Soleil hesitated. "Although I believe what you are looking for is seen plainly in his behavior, I'm afraid that is still a subject you will have to discuss with Philippe."

Rhianna nodded ascent. Soon, another thought came to her mind.

"Soleil," she began, curiously, "what does true love feel like?"

"Ah, love!" she mused, falling back onto the pillows. "Love is not one feeling or another. Love is a collection of many emotions. Love evolves. Young love is entirely different from mature love and one person's experience of love is not the same as someone else's. All in all, love is mysteriously indescribable."

"How did you know you were truly in love with Armand?"

"I just knew," she said, with a sly smile. "That is what makes love, *love*."

*

A hint of a French accent had returned to her voice and it tortured him. Rhianna must have lost the faint inflection when she returned to England, but in the company of the Vallières it was plainly distinctive. The painful effect of hearing it surprised Thayne, who thought every utterance from those lips a pleasant sweetness, for it was the product of time spent with *him*. It seemed, however, each time it nearly overwhelmed him with jealousy, *she* would relieve him of his sufferings by catching his glance and curling her lips at him. The weeks apart made it easy for him to become hopelessly lost in her smallest gesture, and he was sufficiently alleviated— that is, until Philippe leaned over and whispered something in her ear not meant for the rest of the dinner table.

"Do you hunt, Count Vallière?" Thayne asked him, on one such occasion.

Philippe turned to him, a comment from Rhianna no doubt still tickling his ears and a smile spread across his face.

"Indeed, no," he told him, with a friendly air. "Of course, I see the occasional necessity of it, and I hold no grudge against those who practice it, but I prefer shooting to hunting."

"A shame," returned Thayne. "I was hoping you might join me on a lawn meet at the Gatewood Estate, just west of here. They run regularly this time of year and have a very good pack of hounds."

"Yes, and my brother has a fine collection of pistols," announced Crispin.

Philippe thanked him and politely declined.

"Are you a very reckless hunter, Lord Brighton?" Soleil asked, teasingly.

"Only occasionally," he grinned, catching Rhianna's gaze.

"Thayne knows better than to discuss his high speed gallops and dangerous leaps before a worrisome mother," Lady Brighton remarked, smiling.

"I am sure," whispered Rhianna to her, loudly enough for all to hear, "Lord Crispin hopes someday to join him and Lord Brighton is eager not to ruin his chances."

"You know me too well, Miss Braden," Thayne bantered.

Overhearing his name across the table, Crispin concurred. "I very much look forward to my first hunt. Now that I am sixteen, I hope my brother will allow me to accompany him soon."

Audra crossed her arms at once and cried, angrily, "Well, if you harm one, single, helpless little fox, I shall certainly never speak to you again."

Crispin stared at her blankly, while her comment drew laughter from the rest of their small party. This particular evening, the Brightons enjoyed the company of only Rhianna, Audra, and the Vallières. Thayne's attempts at reconciliation with Desmond had not gone as hoped and both he and Lydia had refused to come to Ravensleigh. Guilford Kingsley, on the other hand, was not only willing to let go of the other week's altercation, but was more than wishing to join them for dinner, had his health not prevented it.

Thayne hoped, in having the Vallières at Ravensleigh, that his curiosity would be mollified. Instead, Philippe's close relationship and level of comfort with Rhianna raised only feelings of doubt as to her own emotions and, though she did not openly flirt with

Philippe as Philippe did with her, Thayne allowed himself to think the worst.

*

A conversation with Thayne had been Soleil's goal from the start of the evening and the opportunity presented itself in the drawing room after dinner. She found herself in a far corner near the piano when Thayne commented to her that he was glad the weather was fine enough for them to come, despite a sudden drop in temperature.

Soleil glanced upwards at him and agreed. "If it were the gloomiest day of the year, I could not be unhappy," she added. "I can hardly believe I haven't seen Rhianna for over a year."

"Such exceptional friends are few and far between," expressed Thayne. "With Miss Braden alone I considered myself indeed privileged; only now I have two more in addition. I wonder at how I came to be so fortunate."

"Well," responded Soleil, *sotto voce*, "between you and me, it is my hope that soon I shall have her as closer than a friend."

Soleil watched Thayne carefully after this, taking note of his every movement. There was one thing, and one thing alone, that could comfort Soleil if she could not have Rhianna as a sister. Indeed, she would rejoice if the man who kept Rhianna's heart from Philippe had himself given his own heart completely to Rhianna.

"How so?" was all he said.

His discomfort was obvious from the start, but Soleil would not be so easily satisfied.

"I have such delightful hopes," she added, happily. "But shall I tell you? How well do you keep a secret, Lord Brighton?"

Soleil played her part well, while Thayne grew visibly flustered. She could see the effect her insinuations were having on him, as his knee twitched anxiously and he sipped his brandy with intensity.

Not wishing to anguish him more than was needed, she found it unnecessary to force him to respond.

"I hope to call her sister," she finished.

Thayne did not know the curious eyes that examined him when he involuntarily glanced at Philippe. Soleil peered at him as his composure was lost and regained with a single word.

"Hope?" he repeated.

Thayne's face contorted in such a way as to attempt to appear interested, but he did an ill job of hiding his angst. In that moment, Soleil was certain of his affection for Rhianna and had no wish of his continued suffering.

"Oh, *hope*, yes," she affirmed, quickly. "They are not engaged. You have known Miss Braden for some months now—no doubt you can understand my reasons for wishing the connection."

Thayne seemed mildly relieved. "Certainly."

"Come along, *ma chère soeur*," called Philippe. "You must play something before we go. Our evening is passing along before us. Lord Brighton, surely you can spare her."

Thayne held out his arm and escorted Soleil to the pianoforte. Soleil seated herself on the bench and began playing from memory a soft, romantic number for her audience.

*

Lady Brighton seated herself beside Philippe for Soleil's performance, occasionally exclaiming how moved she was, while Audra and Crispin continued their game of jacks near the fire. All were employed, and Rhianna felt a tremble run through her as Thayne seated himself beside her.

The whole of the evening, they had had little interaction. A glance here and there and occasional quips directed toward each other among group conversation, yes. But an opportunity to speak privately had not yet presented itself. Rhianna hardly knew her hand had tightened nervously around the arm of the chair until she felt Thayne's fingers brush against hers.

She turned to him with surprise.

"I missed you," he quietly confessed to her.

Rhianna's heart nearly stopped and her breathing became erratic. Her gaze fell to their hands and then, after a moment, back to him. She loosened her grip on the chair and allowed his fingertips to meet hers. Soon, Thayne urged her arm to fall between the chairs and their fingers intertwined.

"I miss you still," he told her, glancing about them. "There is nothing like a room full of people to inspire a detachment almost as unbearable as literal separation."

Rhianna drew a short gasp of breath before venturing to speak to him.

"Can London have been so boring?" she returned. "Surely, there were distractions enough to keep your mind far from Thornton."

"Tell me you thought of me," Thayne entreated her, a hint of lovesick desperation in his voice. "If you thought of me but once I could recover from these last weeks, the effects of which I still feel."

"Lord Brighton . . ." she breathed, rendered further speechless by his admission.

He allowed her a moment, but she knew not how to proceed. His expression quickly fell and his delicate hold on her hand loosened.

"Perhaps the company in Thornton was sufficiently distracting," he said, with a glimpse in Philippe's direction.

"No," she hurried, dispelling this suggestion at once, but Thayne seemed barely to hear her. His pain penetrating her at the core, Rhianna mustered all the bravery she could, and told him, "I hoped every day to see you."

Thayne watched her mouth as she spoke and Rhianna wondered if it was the memory of a kiss that drew a faint smile to his lips.

"I thought of nothing but you," he professed, unabashedly, "every moment of every day."

He leaned toward her, his eyes examining the details of her face. It was the same look he gave her the night of their kiss—the last moment before he left Kingsley Manor, the night before he left for London.

"Please, do not look at me so," she begged. "I have seen that look before. It resulted in our not seeing each other for some weeks."

"Miss Braden," he said, with a spirit nothing short of urgent, "I must speak with you."

"*Snow!*" Audra pointed excitedly out the window. "Look! Is it not beautiful?"

Their hands separated as Soleil's song came to a sudden halt. Lady Brighton made her way to where Audra and Crispin were holding back the curtains and examined the conditions.

"It is a wonder the servants did not tell us sooner. They must not have seen, or surely they would have."

With concern, Rhianna asked, "How bad is it?"

Meanwhile, Soleil and Philippe made their way to the windows. As they rose from their seats, Rhianna anticipated the worst, namely, that she and Thayne would not be able to continue their conversation at present.

"It is very bad," Lady Brighton declared, worriedly. "You are, of course, all welcome to stay here, but by the looks of it, you may be here a few days."

"Lord Kingsley would be so worried," declared Soleil.

With one look at Audra, Rhianna agreed.

"You should go at once, then," Lady Brighton told them. "Any later and your opportunity will most certainly have passed."

Crispin elbowed Audra for drawing attention to the weather as the group prepared to leave. With an exchange of parting glances, Rhianna accepted she and Thayne must renew their dialogue at a future time. Moments later, Thayne was handing Rhianna into a carriage, with nothing but a squeeze of the hand to express herself.

*

Thayne was miserable. Anyone who saw him would've had to have been very hard-hearted not to feel for him. Hours passed and he did not leave his library, the east windows of which faced the white, icy land that met with Kingsley property. Throughout the night the snow had fallen heavily; no soul in Thornton dared leave his house. For Thayne, this more specifically meant no visiting Kingsley Manor, no Rhianna.

All afternoon, he could be found sitting in a brown leather armchair. The now-dying fire providing him no warmth, the glass of brandy on his desk no comfort, and the book on his lap, upon whose cover his eyes had not glanced, no diversion. The young lord laid his head against the chair back, one hand dangling over the armrest to stroke his dog, Ranger. With absent eyes he gazed forward, not seeing the wall clock upon which they rested. Rather, he saw only Philippe Vallière, snowed in also, but at Kingsley Manor.

Snowed in with *her*.

He moaned. The visions he conjured in his mind had not only brought on a headache, but also worsened it with each passing minute. That hint of a returned French accent in Rhianna's voice rang in his ears. The last vision of her in the carriage departing from Ravensleigh replayed continuously in his mind's eye. *Damned Frenchman*, he thought. *Why could he not stay from whence he came?* Undoubtedly, Thayne imagined, he would have Rhianna for himself before the snow thawed.

He heard a knock at the door. Lady Brighton entered, partially awakening him from his disquieting thoughts.

"Wondering if I am still here, Mother?" He smiled weakly, and she closed the door behind her. "My body is, but my mind is not."

The lady's face held a look of tender pity that only a mother can feel.

"I know, Thayne," she said gently. Pressing her lips to his

forehead before taking a seat brought a sigh from him. "Must you do this to yourself? The snow may last for days or weeks . . ."

"Please, I beg you, do not speak to me of the snow continuing. I have nothing if I cannot be optimistic there," he told her.

"Then of what shall I speak?"

"Talk only of springtime, and of horses. Of Frenchmen who return to their homes with their sisters *only,*" he cried, in his worsening state of affliction.

Rising to his feet, Thayne took his stand beside one of the east windows. He beheld the dismal scene before him with chagrin and his person grew more somber still.

"You come in hopes of bringing me solace, and I am grateful. Only you come in vain. Forget optimism! There is neither solace, nor hope."

A moment of silence ensued and Lady Brighton, having tried several times throughout the day to comfort him, must now be convinced that nothing but time could do so.

"I only wish I knew, one way or the other," he said suddenly. "If she is to go with him, then let it be done with. But the torment of standing here helplessly as the wretched plans are made is insufferable!" In his moment of insanity, Thayne grabbed for his coat, saying ardently, "I can bear it no longer. I will make my way there before it is too late!"

Leaping from her chair, Lady Brighton hurried to calm him. "Do not be unreasonable. It is impossible to leave now. Only let the snow melt . . ."

"I very well can't stand by and let it happen!" he cried, as she took him lovingly by the arms and gently moved his dark hair away from his eyes.

"Look at me, Thayne," she insisted. "You mustn't let your imagination run away with you. You are wild, my love. Are you sincerely going to ride there, unshaven as you are and half-intoxicated? You wish her to see you like this?"

"I wish to see her. That is all I know."

"Yes, and you shall. But, I declare, if you have this much doubt of a return in her affections for you, then perhaps your own feelings are severely misplaced."

This last stopped him. What if Rhianna did not care for him as he had thought? Philippe Vallière would not have much difficulty in winning her heart. It would be foolishness to risk all health to reach her, only to find himself in time for the announcement of their engagement.

Further downhearted, he agreed to forego his trip and stay home, but he could stay no longer in the library.

"As there is nothing to be done at present," Lady Brighton suggested, "Crispin has been having difficulties with his arithmetic. I'm sure he would be glad of any assistance you might be able to offer."

Thayne hung his head low and returned to his desk to finish his brandy.

"Tell Crispin I shall be there in a moment."

*

Guilford Kingsley's health worsened dramatically within a few days and soon he was confined to his bed. The weather would not permit even the doctor to be called and the entire household was consumed with his condition. His cough was frequent and his appetite was lost. Audra often insisted Rhianna accompany her to visit with him and he was so very lethargic Rhianna began to lie awake at night, considering what Kingsley Manor might be like without Lord Kingsley.

It was not a happy vision.

Days passed and he did not improve. Ought she to leave with Philippe and Soleil and return to France? How could she leave Audra at such a time? What was there to hope for between her and Thayne Brighton? After one particularly unsettling night, rather than spend her early morning overlooking the rotunda from her bedroom window, as usual, Rhianna decided to make her way to the morning room in hopes of some distraction.

There, she found Philippe, standing by the windows, overlooking the approach.

"Good morning," he greeted her. "You are up early."

Rhianna met him at the window. "I haven't been sleeping well. How is the weather?"

"It has abated," he told her, holding back the curtain and allowing her to take a peek for herself.

Though uncomfortable in its own way, Rhianna was grateful to find Philippe alone in the morning room, as opposed to Desmond.

"Soon, Soleil and I will have to begin our trip back to France," he told her, demurely. "What with the weather being so uncertain and Soleil's wedding . . ."

Rhianna reached for a scone and broke off a piece. She chewed it gingerly before realizing she did not have much of an appetite. She quickly placed it down on a small round plate on the table.

"I should have expected it," she replied, "but I've been so happy to have you both here, I couldn't bring myself to think of the day you would leave."

"We don't have to leave without you," he told her.

Oh, that she had stayed in her room that morning! Rhianna fully knew what he was leading up to and she trembled with the idea of it. She sorely wished that things could have remained as they had been, as when they were children together. But children they could not stay. *That* relationship was something lost forever.

"It is unthinkable that I should come all the way to England, all this way to see you," Philippe continued, "and return to France without addressing a very particular subject." Philippe gently slid his hand down her arm and took her hand in his. "Let us conclude the conversation we were unable to finish one year ago."

The idea of marrying Philippe had not been dismissed from her without careful consideration. In fact, it had not yet been dismissed at all. To agree would promise a life of comfort among people she knew and cared for. In addition, it would bring her into a higher position in society than she ever imagined possible—*Countess* Rhianna Vallière!

Now, a decision must be made.

"I have no secrets," he told her. "My feelings are unchanged. You know what they are and, yet, I do not know what yours have been, either then, nor now."

His voice was deep and affectionate; it helped Rhianna to meet his gaze. For a moment, she imagined that she *could* love him in such a way, and perhaps she already did.

"Everything was so sudden. I left almost immediately," she evaded.

"Dreadful day," recalled Philippe. "When you left, no one felt it so much as I. Since then, it has pained me every day thereafter. I was never one for change, but a separation between ourselves was more than I was prepared to endure."

"Philippe, I needed to come," she reminded him, gently. "You must remember the circumstances . . ."

"Yes," he said. "If I seem unmindful, forgive me. I do remember."

Here, he paused with respect for her late parents and Rhianna took advantage of the moment to breathe. Each coming sentence brought forth new dread, for she knew to what end he was leading and there was no way of avoiding it.

"Why did you not return?" he asked at last.

"I was . . . not ready," she confessed. "When Lord Kingsley offered me the opportunity to live at Kingsley Manor, it was a chance to fulfill my childhood dream. Everything was new and exciting . . ."

"You wanted a change?"

"Yes."

"Did you want also to move on?"

At this moment, a particular lord from a certain house called Ravensleigh entered her thoughts. The image filled her with strength.

"I was not sure *then* of what I wanted," she told Philippe. "But I believe I now know what that is."

"You do?" he asked eagerly. "You have captured all my attention."

"I wish to stay in England."

With this sentence came a hideous pause. Without Thayne's image still before her she could never have endured it.

"Well, I could spend half the year in England, half in France. It is a small thing and will not . . ."

"I wish to stay in England," she repeated, adding, "as Audra's governess."

"Let us be direct, can we not? I ask you, please, be clear in your meaning. If you do not love me, then say so."

Such cruel, painful words! It was not the case with Rhianna, but her love held a different form.

"Philippe, you are so very dear to me. Indeed, you will never fully know what it has meant to me to know you. I hope that I shall always know you and call you my friend because with all of my heart, I love you—only not in the way you want me to."

In Rhianna's heartfelt anguish of telling him this, her tears would not be restrained and they fell one by one over their clasped hands. Philippe, who had in the past proven his extraordinary ability to control himself, must have thought little of his own sadness as he tried to comfort her.

"Do not cry, Rhianna. The truth is painful, but I was not altogether unprepared. I saw the future," he proclaimed, with effort. "Did I not tell you on the day you left us? 'You will go, and you will meet an Englishman, and you will fall in love.' I believe those were my exact words."

Rhianna started at this, and replied, "Philippe, I said nothing of the sort . . ."

"You didn't have to," he said gently. "I could see it in the way you looked at him, the way you smiled at him, how you addressed him. It put a glow about you . . ."

"Who, Philippe?" she implored, never imagining she might hear from his lips the very name of the man who held her thoughts captive.

"Lord Brighton," he told her, with an accepting tone. "Your feelings might not have been obvious to the rest of the world, but to myself, who knows you so intimately, it was as if you *had* said that you loved him. And that he returns your affection is the only thing that comforts me, because I know you will be happy in your life with him. Rhianna," he promised, "I so want you to be happy."

"Philippe! If I *did* have such feelings . . . I . . ."

"Do you deny that you love him?"

She hesitated. A declaration such as this was not something she was prepared to admit to herself, much less to a man who had, only moments ago, proposed to her for the second time. His perception in this matter astonished her, but to confirm it would only injure him more.

"I cannot say exactly what my feelings are for him, for I do not know myself," she declared to him. "Never mind our positions in society . . ."

He stopped her at once. "What are positions in society but manmade barriers among people who are in God's eyes all equal? True love is pure, as God is pure, and it will allow no culture to stand in its way."

"Philippe, I want to be sensible and content with my life as it is, and I am. Let us leave it at that."

"Well," he submitted, "as you wish. If ever you become discontent with anything at all, remember you can still have a life with me. Until the day I hear of your marriage, I shall wait for you."

At this, Rhianna would have begged otherwise, but Philippe restrained her lips with his own. It was not the enthusiastic, passionate kiss that likely would have occasioned had she accepted his proposal, but rather, it was sweet and tender. He lingered just long enough, before allowing the moment to become the precious memory she would unceasingly keep close to her heart.

Alas, Rhianna was aware that any attempt to persuade him differently would be ineffectual. Philippe meant every word of what he said and would go back on not a word of it. She removed her hand from his grip and held him as she had many times before, overcome by a sadness that would not soon diminish. Their brother and sister relationship was gone for all time, and Rhianna felt the pangs of loss deeply.

Chapter Eight

All was dreadfully quiet—even the house itself seemed to sleep—but Rhianna lay awake in her bed, never expecting rest to come. Her mind raced and thoughts of the morning's conversation with Philippe tormented her. The hour struck midnight as she was hoping he would recover quickly, but she knew he would not.

Hushed voices in the hall suddenly broke her thoughts. It seemed odd that someone should be traveling these halls at this hour. Even the servants, if up and about, had better places to be and—was that a lady's voice? Rhianna snuffed out her candle and listened. It was, and the voice was a distinctly familiar one. Indeed, Lydia Kingsley was most certainly walking past her door, and she was not alone. Though she could not make out what was said, Rhianna was sure that Lydia was speaking to at least one or two more persons.

As the voices faded down the hall, Rhianna closed her robe around herself, determined to investigate what she deemed too curious to ignore. Besides this, it was too welcomed a diversion for her afflicted mind to pass up.

A tremble ran through her as the excitement of exploration heightened and she tiptoed through her own room so the house would not tell on her. Reaching for the door handle, she turned it ever so gently. With a moment's pause to listen for activity in the hallway, and hearing none, she opened the door.

It creaked.

Rhianna looked at it accusingly. Under any other circumstances, she was certain it would not have made any sound at all, but this night it *would* do its part to reveal her intentions. She began to imagine the house was as much a conspirator in Lydia's affair as its mistress.

Rhianna ventured down the hall, her eyes adjusting gradually to the darkness. A few scattered windows allowed enough moonlight to guide her, for she dared not bring a candle. Vaguely, she could still hear them as she approached the staircase where they had descended. Desmond, too, was with her, and a second man, but their words could not be made out.

Cautiously, she took one step at a time, all the while straining to hear them. She made out a few words, here and there. It quickly became clear that the voice of the second man was the dreaded Cousin Pierson. Rhianna embraced her inner sleuth, determined to know their purpose. After all, why would Desmond be sneaking around with them in the middle of the night? It would have been one thing, certainly, to hear Pierson with Lydia alone, but the three of them together screamed of conspiracy.

Soon, the threesome halted in the Great Hall. Rhianna dared not go as far as the landing, as the stairs beyond turned to face their small group, and she opted to wait only a few steps back.

Suddenly, an eruption of raised voices made their words audible.

"It has been nothing but excuses from you since the beginning! Only a year and a half ago, we were so close—but then *she* arrived and everything we worked so hard for was undone!"

Rhianna started at Pierson's outburst and her hands twisted around the stairway banisters. Her pulse raced as she wondered to what—and to whom—he referred.

He continued, "I have long begun to think she is not so in the way as you say, but just another excuse of yours."

"No, my love," Lydia took pains to convince him. "I have long been devoted to this course, and to you. It shall be done in no time at all."

"I can see why he would doubt your words, Mother," Desmond injected.

"What a notion! Besides, we are back on track, but these things must run their course. Only exercise patience . . ."

A few muffled syllables followed this, while Rhianna considered moving another step or two down the stairway.

Finally, just before they parted, an upset Pierson cried, "This has dragged on for too long!"

Lydia attempted to hush him, mumbling something about the servants, and Desmond anticipated something "by the end of the week." Moments later, they were parting, but no one exited the front door. Rhianna hurried back to her room as quickly as she quietly could.

Pierson was staying at the manor—of that one thing she was certain. Not only had the door not opened, but no one had traveled in or out of the house for days due to the snow. As Rhianna closed and locked her bedroom door, her mind continued to race. Had Lydia buried Lord Kingsley already by moving her lover in? Her memory of Pierson meeting Lydia in the courtyard on the night of the ball added to this idea. Rhianna could not but wonder if he had been at Kingsley Manor for some time, hidden from Lord Kingsley's knowledge. And what could be the nature of this scheme that Lydia may or may not have doubts regarding? Worse still, who was this "she" that interrupted said plan around the time Rhianna came to Kingsley Manor? Rhianna tried to prevent her mind from wandering unrestrained, but it fought her otherwise. The feeling that they perhaps referred to *her* was disturbing.

Thus, with an array of new thoughts to consider, she lay back in bed with any and all possibilities of sleep now irrevocably gone.

*

"It makes sense for us to go now, before winter really begins." Soleil sounded as if she was trying to comfort herself, just as much as Rhianna. "I hope you will come to France for the wedding," she wished, as the tears continued.

"I should like nothing more!" Rhianna exclaimed, embracing

her as tightly as her arms would allow.

"You could bring Audra, if the Kingsleys are agreeable," Soleil added. "I can see why you enjoy her so much. She is so very likeable."

The carriage door was open to her and Soleil sighed at the sight of it.

"This is *not* goodbye," Rhianna reminded her. "I shall see you in the spring."

"And we shall write often!"

Philippe assisted his sister in. As Audra had stayed at her father's bedside and Lydia and Desmond had said their goodbyes in the foyer, Rhianna drew a short breath as she turned to face Philippe alone.

He put forth a worthy effort in his attempt at a positive demeanor, but the sadness in Philippe's eyes as he turned to Rhianna exposed his true feelings.

"I cannot pretend I do not wish you were coming with us," he told her, at last, "but I hope you know, Rhianna, that I wish you every happiness."

At that moment, Rhianna's heart burned as she felt his devastation. Embracing him, she reminded Philippe of how much she truly loved him. He stoked her hair and when she pulled back, kissed her forehead.

"I forever remain your devoted admirer," he promised.

Hardly could she see through the tears as Philippe lifted himself into the carriage and they drove away.

*

Rhianna stared blankly at the paperwork before her. Tapping her pencil absentmindedly against her schoolroom desk, she replayed Soleil and Philippe's parting moments in her mind. It had been some hours since, but still the memory consumed her. She wondered how far they had traveled and how different her life would have been had she joined them.

Envisioning herself as Philippe's wife, she knew she could never feel for him as a woman ought to love her husband, but still, she hoped she had not made a mistake. As Audra continued at Lord Kingsley's side, Rhianna had time to consider her life as an employed woman, a governess, as the years went by, with no family and no permanent home. Her heart felt heavy and tears bubbled forth again.

Suddenly, the door burst open.

"Hello, my dear Miss Rhianna Braden, owner of the loveliest name in all of England. Behold! She possesses, indeed, the loveliest of many things."

Rhianna arose from her seat in the schoolroom and wiped her eyes quickly as Desmond approached her. Abruptly awakened from her meditative state, it took her a moment to feel fully alert. In that time, Desmond was before her, the smell of alcohol strong on his breath. He stretched out his hand, intending to intertwine a lock of her hair within his fingers.

Defensively removing herself from his reach with a large step back, Rhianna held her nerve and suppressed her dismay.

"I think you had better leave, Lord Kingsley," she told him firmly, hoping to hide her alarm.

Shamelessly, he stepped forward and placed his hands on her shoulders, seizing her where she stood.

"Preparations for Audra's lessons can wait. I have something to say which I imagine shall be of great interest to you." He paused, his potent exhalations resting upon her neck and his grasp tightening. "I have been hoping for an opportunity to again see you privately."

Forcefully, she told him, "I have no wish of seeing you privately, Lord Kingsley."

"Oh?" Desmond replied. "You resist me without knowing what I offer?"

She held her chin high. "There is nothing you could offer me that I could be interested in."

"I see," he continued, his voice lowering to a deep, harsh whisper, a hint of agitation in his bearing. "I daresay Lord Brighton has got to you before I did."

With her heart pounding in her chest, a cold shiver ran up and down her spine. Rhianna felt trapped. Hopelessly, vulnerably trapped.

"Unhand me," she demanded, as calmly as she could.

What seemed a long moment passed until Desmond did as she requested.

"Of course, I expected to find competition. Such a lovely creature as yourself—and you are more extremely so than most—with all the accomplishments of a well-bred lady, mingling in our society, teasing us with your charm and innocence . . ." He trailed off for a moment and smiled to himself, before continuing, "Naturally, it was only a matter of time before one of us desperate blokes came crawling to you with our secret admiration and desires, our pledges of gifts in exchange for clandestine pleasures."

His manner of informality was on its own enough to make her quite ill, but his words still more so. Desmond paralyzed her with his proposal and appalled her beyond hope of future recovery. Left with no avenue of escape, she went on listening in disgust.

"I realize the delicacy of the matter. Such a strict, impossible world we live in! The beauty of an arrangement between you and me is, we already live under the same roof—none of this sneaking out of the manor in the middle of the night business. No one will ever know. What say you? Keep in mind, that whatever *he's* promised you, I can do better."

Rhianna shook her head. "You have made a mistake coming here," she said, her voice shaking. "You have proven yourself vulgar and ill-bred, and your suggestions are crude, your behavior improper. How dare you compare yourself to Lord Brighton, or any other gentleman? It is offensive!"

He laughed. An abhorrent, vile laugh.

"And what knowledge have *you* of men? You think other

gentlemen are any different, do you? A pity it must come to you this way, but take a good look at me. You will find nothing different in any other man." Leaning toward her, with an air of domination, he added, "Not even your precious Lord Brighton."

Rhianna took a step back away from him, but he restrained her again. Pulling her roughly against him, he grew fierce. Desmond Kingsley's severe temper manifested itself.

"I suppose you fancy he likes you. Loves, even. Yes, I see that you do. Look at me! Do you also imagine yourself one day as mistress of Ravensleigh? What a child you are! Surely by now you know that you are not the sort of girl men marry," he sneered. "You are good only as a lover, Rhianna!"

"Do not be so familiar with me, Lord Kingsley! Never did I imagine you would so far overstep this boundary. I insist you leave at once!"

"Insist, do you?" he returned wildly. "Do you forget to whom you are speaking? My dear Rhianna, you may not *like* me, but do you honestly dare dream of more than being the paramour of Lord Desmond Kingsley, owner of this great house who, influential in society, can provide you materially with all your heart's desires?"

His eyes blazed, his veins swelled in his face, his teeth clenched. Then, in an ill attempt to appeal to her once more, he softened his voice, to say, "This I will do for you, and more . . ."

"Stop this!" she cried. "Stop, I tell you! You are *not* lord of Kingsley Manor. You ought not rush your father's death!"

"And what if I was?" he demanded furiously. "My father is very sick, you know."

"Let go of me! I would sooner die than consider such an indecent offer as the sin against God that you propose!"

He threw her body violently to the floor of the schoolroom. Rhianna grasped at the air for support, but found nothing to break her fall. She lay beneath the chalkboard and stared up at Desmond, stunned.

"Damn you, foolish girl! I would have filled your life with riches that you cannot imagine!" he proclaimed, stiffening his frame and tightening his fists. "Just as well! What do I want with the daughter of a curate? I should have known better when I thought of you. I curse the day you entered into this house! But it is no matter. I shall soon have you gone. You will see the folly of your decision and live to regret it all the days of your unfortunate life."

With that, Desmond Kingsley stormed out of the schoolroom, slamming the door behind him.

*

The horse galloped through the field west of Kingsley Manor. The farther she rode from the house, the more dreamlike the encounter with Desmond became. Only, the fear remained and the tears continued. The force of the wind carried them away from her cheeks only to make room for others. It seemed hours since she had left that schoolroom.

Days.

Years.

The scenery around her blurred, the trees, the sky, all of it had a far off feeling, as though she were not riding through the field at all, but only imagining it. The sound of birds chirping, of her horse's hooves beating against the ground, even her own, labored breathing all seemed so distant.

For how long she had traveled when it appeared, she could only guess. A Roman temple, with its front stairs, surrounding columns, and round dome, not unlike the Kingsley's rotunda, came upon *her* it seemed, rather than her coming upon *it*. It was breathtaking, wildly impressive, and not a building she had ever seen before. She was momentarily stunned and looked at it in wonder. Had she wandered into Thornton Gardens? She did not think she had gone so far south, yet found nothing she recognized in what surrounded her. The trees ahead offered little visibility as to what lay beyond them, but she felt sure Kingsley Manor was yet behind her.

So captivating was the temple, and so welcome a relief to her mental distress, that when *he* appeared, she hardly knew. Until Rhianna recognized the person riding toward her, dread overtook her and she recognized it as the only thing that felt real in the nightmare she struggled to outrun. Squinting into the distance, which came quickly upon her, and was, perhaps, not so distant at all, she saw a man on a horse approaching.

A chocolate-brown-and-white, spotted horse. She recognized d'Artagnan before even its rider.

"Good heavens, what has happened?" Thayne asked, with alarm. "Miss Braden, what is the matter?"

He motioned his horse up to hers and took the reins, which had slipped from her feeble hands.

"I did not expect to meet anyone out here," she told him. "In fact, I hardly know where I am."

"You are almost to Ravensleigh," he told her.

"Ravensleigh?" she repeated, her mind slowly returning. "I am so sorry. I thought this was still part of the Kingsleys' land."

Sensing Thayne's eyes, as they examined her with troubled concern, Rhianna kept hers on the pommel of her saddle, inwardly struggling to awaken from the horror that had earlier met her. If only she never had to return, if only she never had to see Desmond again and his words could be erased from her memory! Until that wish was a reality, she could not find relief.

"Are we not friends?" Thayne appealed. "You need not apologize for being in a place in which you are always welcome. Now, I entreat you, please, to waste not a minute more. Whatever it is, let me help you."

"There is nothing you can do to help," she declared, despairingly. "Please understand. There is only one thing to be done."

"And what is that?" he encouraged her.

"I am leaving," she told him. "I am returning to France."

"God help me!" cried Thayne. "Then you have agreed to marry the Frenchman after all?"

Rhianna observed his panicked semblance with surprise. "No," she answered. "No, it has nothing to do with him."

"Then you have *not* given him your hand?" he asked, for absolute clarification.

"No," she returned.

Thayne breathed an audible sigh of relief and attempted not to hide it.

"Then, pray, what are you running from?" he pressed. "Surely, whatever it is, it cannot be so bad that you must flee to another country. Think of how miserable it shall make everyone who knows you."

Rhianna knew not what to tell him. "You do not understand . . ."

"I do not understand because you have not told me," he declared, his voice sick with worry. "*Help* me to understand. I want so desperately to comfort you."

As he offered her the reins of her horse, she took them, saying, "Your motives are gallant, Lord Brighton, but I'm afraid what I most need is time alone with my thoughts."

Thayne considered her desire momentarily, but Rhianna sensed he was not going to leave her without receiving something of an explanation. She wondered if even a complete explanation would do much to encourage Thayne to leave her side.

"You've certainly come to the right place," he replied, at last. "There's no escaping your thoughts here. But in good conscience, I cannot leave you. I can promise only to be a silent companion."

It was not until this moment that Rhianna perceived a sense of relief at his presence and argued no further. She quickly wondered that she had asked him to leave at all, as the idea of his departure, had he heeded her request, was all it took to renew her feelings of dread. Yes, with Thayne Brighton, Rhianna felt safe.

She made known to him her wish of exploring the temple and Thayne was quick to assist Rhianna from her horse. Soon, both she and her princely escort were climbing the stone steps of the structure, but she could form no words of admiration or questions regarding its construction. As they entered its circular corridor, the wind a bit stronger there as it danced between the columns, Rhianna was glad Thayne did not demand the release of his proffered arm and found pleasure in walking quietly with him for a time.

In keeping with his promise, Thayne said very little, but hoped with each insignificant comment he might encourage her to speak her mind.

"I always enjoy my ride to Kingsley Manor," he offered, several moments after a remark on the temple's architecture had proven unsuccessful. "Plenty of time to think."

She halted. The unexpected movement separated their arms as Thayne continued forward, but he soon turned to face her. Rhianna's eyes focused on the view between two columns that faced a faraway, but visible Kingsley Manor.

Her beautiful, tainted Kingsley Manor.

"What were you thinking about?" she asked him, distantly.

That Thayne did not immediately respond did not seem odd to her at first, as their walk had offered a great deal of silences, though such a question should have compelled him to give an instant response. It happened at this moment that a particular gust of wind blew upward, tossing Rhianna's cloak over her shoulder and revealing, not only a large tear in the skirt of her peach dress, but also a rip in her sleeve, exposing a long, dark bruise down her left arm, accompanied by bloody scratch marks. Rhianna herself had been unaware of these products of her fall in the schoolroom, seeing them only as she noted Thayne's frightened expression and followed his eyes to them.

It was there his eyes remained, as he asked, "Has someone . . . violated you?"

"No," she hurried, feeling an urge to return her cloak to its place and following the impulse.

"Are you further hurt?"

She shook her head. "No."

"Who has done this to you?"

It was here she hesitated. Thayne's voice, while calm, exuded retaliation and vengeance and she feared the consequences of his learning the source.

"Miss Braden," he urged, "*who . . .*"

His own words seemed to choke him. He met her gaze.

"*Rhianna,*" he begged, "please."

She melted at the sound of her name from his lips and knew if there was anyone to trust, it was Thayne.

"Please don't do anything rash," she prefaced. "He was intoxicated and . . ."

"Desmond?"

Reluctantly, she nodded. "Yes."

His nostrils flared. His eyes glowed with fiery rage. His hands clenched into fists. Thayne drew a deep breath.

"Soleil and Philippe left this morning for France. I should have gone with them!" she regretted.

"Absolutely you should *not* have gone with them," he told her, maintaining a control Rhianna found impressive considering the emotions he could not hide. "Let us tell Lord Kingsley what has happened at once."

Rhianna protested, "No, indeed. Even were I inclined to speak with Lord Kingsley on the subject, he is far too ill. It does not appear he has many days left."

"Lord Kingsley is dying?" he asked, another facet of misery in his voice.

"He has been bedridden for days. Any moment may be his last."

Thayne thought for a moment. "Come, let us go there together."

Her eyes widened with fright. "I cannot."

"You have my word," he swore, "no one will harm you from this moment forward. I must see Lord Kingsley and you must get a change of clothes. After, I hope you will stay at Ravensleigh."

Having previously felt there was no escape but to return to Kingsley Manor come what may, the prospect of staying in the safe arms of Ravensleigh was an overwhelming relief.

"What of Audra? I cannot leave her," she told him, suddenly. "Not now. She is so afraid."

"Your safety must come first," Thayne insisted. "Perhaps," he added, "she will come with us."

Rhianna considered this. Perhaps Lord Kingsley himself would prefer that Audra not be around for his final moment. And Crispin would be an excellent distraction for her. Thayne's generosity was the ultimate solution.

The idea was settled upon and Rhianna consented to go with Thayne to Kingsley Manor.

"Thank you," she whispered, hardly knowing how Thayne's hands had found themselves clasped around her own. "Although you are undoubtedly wishing you had never run into me, I do not know what I would have done, had I not run into you."

"You would have found yourself at Ravensleigh, undoubtedly," he told her. "You would have been safe. And," he added, "I wouldn't want you anywhere else."

As he urged her toward the stairs, Rhianna hesitated.

"Lord Brighton," she said, "you have been so kind, and your offer to stay at Ravensleigh is very generous. However, I hope you will do me one more favor."

All attention, he quickly closed the gap that had threatened to grow between them.

"Name it."

"Before ever I mount my horse, I beg you will promise to distract me from my thoughts on this ride of ours. I cannot be allowed to think of what has happened or I may just turn around and ride as far from Kingsley Manor as ever."

Thayne's urgent wish to depart was quickly abandoned and a softness of manner replaced the intensity that preceded it.

"Of course, I would be happy to be of such service," he told her gently. "Now, let's see," he wondered aloud, "with what story or manner of speech shall I distract you?"

"Why do you not tell me," she suggested, "what you were thinking of before you met me today and all the unpleasantness associated with me?"

"There is no unpleasantness associated with you," he insisted.

This forced a faint smile from her lips. "Very well, that *accompanied* me," she corrected.

This being more acceptable, he was able to reply without further hesitation. "I shall gladly tell you what I was thinking. I was thinking of the woman who has run away with my heart."

This answer was not what she anticipated, and she found herself quite startled. If this was his way of distracting her from Desmond, then he had picked an excellent subject. *He could not mean you*, Rhianna told herself. Desmond's words rang in her ears: *You are not the sort of girl men marry.*

"Miss Leighart has a great deal to offer," she stumbled, wishing she had somewhere to run and suspecting she had quite lived the worst day of her life—and it was just barely noon.

Thayne looked at her curiously before letting out a chuckle. "I was not thinking of *her*," he replied.

"But you will marry her," she said impulsively.

Rhianna regretted her words, but more than this, she regretted the truth of them. Even if she were the woman to run away with Thayne's heart, she was certain Austine would be the woman to wear his name.

"Do you seriously think that?" he asked her.

Rhianna felt him looking upon her, but could not meet his eyes. The desire to flee to the temple's stairs to end their conversation was overwhelming.

"I have no plans of marrying Miss Leighart, nor shall I ever," he pledged. "I despise everything about the woman, her vanity firstly, not to mention her lack of every other feeling. Rhianna, you know as much. I'd sooner agree to burn in hell than marry Austine Leighart."

With that, he put his arms about her waist and his black hair rested on her forehead as he gazed at her.

"Lord Brighton!"

"I am in love with *you*, Rhianna," he told her, passionately. "I know this is not at all the right time to tell you, but you must know it and I can hold it back not a moment longer."

Did she understand him correctly? Or, had the day so overwhelmed her she was now hallucinating?

"How can you? I have no title, no inheritance to speak of . . . I have . . . nothing . . ."

He covered her lips lightly with the tips of his fingers.

"If I was going to pursue such things, I would have done so by now," he told her. "What I want in a wife is you."

A wife.

"With the greatest of selfishness I have wanted you for myself, from the day you lay unconscious in my arms. From the moment I beheld you, I have loved you, with feelings acute and whole, feelings that have overtaken my every breath and thought and action. Every part of me, you have consumed." He stroked her chin, as he continued, "I have suffered indescribably since that snowy night you left Ravensleigh, torn from me as flesh from bone. How I ached at the loss of you, Rhianna! If you could but know the half! The days, the hours, the minutes, all of them tormented me without mercy, to the end that I hardly believe I at last have you before me. And you speak of inheritance and titles? What is fortune and position in this world to the hope of gaining your affection?"

Rhianna searched his face—dare she absorb the sincerity in his eyes and the forthrightness in the contours of his brow? Even as he spoke each word, his honesty issued forth naturally, so much so, that despite being inclined to believe otherwise, she could have no doubt that his love for her was genuine.

"Your affection," he continued, "is all I ask for in this world."

"You have it," she breathed.

Thayne's lips exposed his white teeth in a beaming smile that matched her own.

"Will you marry me, Rhianna Braden?"

"I will," she answered, elated. "Yes!"

Overjoyed, Thayne wasted no time in expressing his happiness. He leaned down and kissed his future bride with earnestness. Hardly could he contain his joy when at last he looked at her.

"Can this be real? Can I be so fortunate?" he asked blissfully. "Can this divine creature I see before me, in all her angelic glory, love this foolish, contemptible boy, who proved himself unworthy of her from the start?"

"With all my heart," she confessed.

It was all she could say before Thayne's lips silenced her from further exclamations. They moved against hers with passion and, taking her by the arms, he pulled Rhianna to him.

She winced.

It took everything he had to pull away from her. Thayne looked down at her torn sleeve and quickly eased his grip on her wounded flesh. Rhianna could see in his expression that Desmond had flashed through his mind and the fire returned to his eyes.

"It's all right," she told him gently.

He examined the marks on her arm closely before covering the open tear with his large, warm hand.

"Come," he said, "let us go and get you changed."

She nodded and, after Thayne stole a final, quick kiss, they descended the steps of the Roman temple and rode their horses to Kingsley Manor.

Chapter Nine

Kingsley Manor felt different to Rhianna as they approached. Once the home of her happiest thoughts, it stood brooding on the English countryside, a certain inhabitant poisoning it from the inside out. Her eyes darted from window to window, searching for Desmond. Would he be watching for her return?

Thayne and Rhianna moved toward the manor together, leaving their horses to the servants. Henry hurried to the door to greet them.

"Lord Brighton, Miss Braden," he welcomed. "How fortunate you have arrived."

"Hello, Henry," Thayne returned, as they entered. Rhianna watched his eyes search the doorways, the staircase. "The house is awfully quiet this afternoon."

"It is, sir, yes," he acknowledged. Turning to Rhianna, he said, "Lord Kingsley has been especially anxious to speak with *you*, Miss Braden. There is no time to waste."

"Anxious to speak with *me*?" she repeated.

"Yes, Miss. He has been asking for you vehemently this last hour. Very ill, I might add. Very ill."

"Good heavens," she cried. "I shall go at once."

"Shall I fetch a doctor?" insisted Thayne.

Henry thanked him. "Dr. Logan, as well as Mr. Weathersby and Miss Kingsley, are at his bedside as we speak."

"Are Lady Kingsley and Lord Desmond Kingsley not also with him?" he pressed, slyly.

Henry shook his head and appeared to glance around him before speaking further. When he did, his voice was low and guarded.

"Lord Desmond Kingsley has gone out and Lady Kingsley was

. . . er . . . dismissed from him."

With this last, Henry rendered their small circle speechless. The Kingsleys' marriage was not a close one, to be sure, but would Guilford dismiss his wife from his bedside at such an hour?

Looking as if he had said too much, Henry immediately invited Rhianna to follow him directly to Guilford Kingsley.

"Lord Brighton, may I offer you the comfort of the drawing room? Undoubtedly, Dr. Logan, Mr. Weathersby, and Miss Kingsley will join you there momentarily."

"Not at all, Henry. I will have to insist on joining you in escorting my fiancée to Lord Kingsley's chambers. If it is his desire to speak privately with Miss Braden at that point, he may do so."

Henry's eyebrows rose infinitesimally, but he said nothing. He nodded his assent and hastily led them upstairs. There, a group of servants were gathered in the hall outside Guilford's bedroom, whispering and waiting for news. Undeniably, they were aware he was asking for Rhianna and they eyed her curiously.

Henry knocked on the door and entered. "Miss Braden and Lord Brighton," he announced.

Henry stepped to the side and Thayne followed Rhianna into the room. The door was closed behind them.

The atmosphere was grim. Guilford lay in a large, white bed that made him look small in comparison, pillows propping his shoulders at a slight incline. His face was ashen and his body frail. Beside him, Dr. Logan and Weathersby spoke in hushed, somber tones.

Audra, kneeling beside the bed, raised her red, swollen eyes to them, leaving a stain of tears on her father's sheets. At the sight of Rhianna, she ran to her and buried her face in the folds of her governess's skirt, her sobs so weakened from the extended strain she made no sound. Rhianna's arms swiftly enfolded her, her fingers stroking the girl's tousled blond hair, and she wondered how long Audra had been stationed here without rest or refreshment.

Rhianna then met Guilford's gaze. "Lord Kingsley," she called sadly, his feeble condition cutting her to the core, "I'm so sorry I was not here sooner."

"Rhianna." He smiled wider and drew a long, deep breath. "Please."

Perhaps it was the circumstances, but that he called her thus did not give her any pause. In fact, it seemed the most natural thing in the world.

He gestured to a seat beside him that only moments previous had belonged to Dr. Logan. Thayne was already beside him, on bended knee.

"What can we get you?" he asked Guilford, attentively.

"A moment with Miss Braden, if you please," he answered, patting Thayne's hand that had found its resting place upon his shoulder.

Lord Kingsley's gaze was yet upon her and would not be diverted. Thayne looked to Dr. Logan, who read the question in his eyes.

"There is no immediate danger in removing the child," the doctor answered.

Thayne nodded dutifully and rose to his feet as Dr. Logan and Weathersby retreated to the hall.

"I shall be just outside this door," he told Rhianna. Then, leaning toward Audra, he petitioned, "Why do we not see if Katie can get you something to eat?"

Her head turned to him slowly, her lips quivering. Audra involuntarily tightened her hands around the strands of material she held in her grip. Thayne gently brushed his fingers against her wet eyelashes and patted her damp cheek compassionately.

"At least to drink, Audra," Rhianna supplicated. "You can come right back."

Thayne held out his hand to her. She accepted it and silently allowed him to lead her out the door. He closed it quietly behind them.

Rhianna quickly took her seat at Guilford's side. Lord Kingsley in the last few weeks was reduced to nearly half the physical man he had been. She had put on a brave face with Audra nearby, but the tears welled up in her absence. Leaning toward him sorrowfully, a flood of memories flashed through her mind of happier times: when he met her in France to escort her to England, when he offered her a position as Audra's governess, when he insisted she attend the ball, and when he prepared to host a visit from the Vallières . . .

"I was wondering how I would ever put what I have to say to you on paper," he told her, pushing himself up on his pillows.

He coughed.

"I'm so sorry, Lord Kingsley," she expressed, regretfully. "I should have been here."

"No apologies," he insisted, with a slight wave of the hand. "I'm surprised you returned at all, after Desmond frightened you out of the house."

Suddenly, she remembered the state of her appearance, her torn dress and disheveled hair. Yet, this alone would not have told her story.

"How did you know?"

He drew another deep breath. "It was the only time Audra left my side," he answered. "She went to look for you. When she overheard what happened, she told me." She saw a spark of anger in his eyes. "I banned him from the manor. He will not return as long as I am still living."

"Lord Kingsley, I would never ask that of you."

"It will not be for long, I assure you. Afterward, Lydia will do as she pleases. I only wish I could have done more. And I wish there was a way for you to care for Audra in my absence . . ."

Guilford's last words struck a chord with her. "Do not say such things . . ."

"Oh, but I must! My situation cannot be ignored and there is much to be done before my time is up."

Greatly distressed, Rhianna could not respond. The thought of separating from Audra crushed her under the best of circumstances, but this, the thought of separating from Audra as she lost her beloved father, was devastating. Rhianna pressed her hand to the side of the bed for support.

"Not to worry," he assured her. "I have made arrangements for you both. All will be well . . ." She looked at him in amazement, as he added, ". . . but first . . ." Guilford Kingsley raised himself up further in his bed and cleared his throat. "I am sorry for the tale I have to tell you, and I hope you can forgive me."

He drew as deep a breath as he was able and begged her to hear him out fully. "Thirty years ago, I came into contact with a family by the name of Rotherhithe," he began. "The Rotherhithes were a prominent family, with a solid reputation and significant wealth—at least, such was the pretense. They were the talk of London at the time and my father soon arranged for my marriage to their eldest daughter. I had hardly known her two months when we were wed. You know her today as Lydia Kingsley.

"Unbeknownst to all, the Rotherhithes had lost their fortune to dishonest and self-indulgent lifestyles. When Lydia and I were united, it became clear the connection worked only as a political advantage. Financially, it benefitted only Lydia. It was a difficult lie to surmount and it was not the only obstacle to a successful union. As is the case with most arranged marriages, Lydia and I had no attachment to each other. Try as I would to make our family work, her heart lay with her cousin, Pierson."

Lord Kingsley paused. It was more speaking than he had done recently and he took a moment to catch his breath. Rhianna, offered him a drink of water and he accepted with her assistance.

"Lord Kingsley," she said delicately, "with all due respect, I cannot fathom what your purpose can be in telling me such intimate details . . ."

"Time passed," he continued with effort. "Lydia and I were strangers living under the same roof when Desmond was born. A horrific child, mind you, that went through one governess after another. There was only one who really tried to work with him, shortly before he was old enough to send away to Oxford. Her name was Haldana Greenhalgh; I called her Hallie."

Rhianna froze in her seat, suddenly terrified that with one small movement she might miss a word of what he had to say. This was an unexpected turn in the conversation and she was inwardly thrilled that she would finally know something about Hallie.

"The Greenhalghs, like the Rotherhithes, had at one time been extremely wealthy. Unlike them, however, they did not lose their wealth to corruption and decadence. Rather, an unfortunate accident, a fire, claimed not only their home and land, but the lives of Hallie's parents and siblings. Hallie alone survived.

"Forced with the reality that she would need to provide for herself, she knew what her options were. She did the only thing that is open to a woman who falls into such a situation. Hallie became a governess. She was eighteen years old when she found a position here at Kingsley Manor." Guilford pressed his lips together and his eyes watered. With the tears that followed, he added, "It was then, for the first time in my life, that I fell in love."

This tale did little to assist Rhianna, who continued to fight her own tears, as she had from the moment she sat beside him.

"She was the most beautiful of women," he went on, his breathing labored more from emotion than illness, "an angel of heaven. Kind, compassionate, loving—everything that Lydia was not. There was not to be found a gentler soul on all the Earth, and what was more, she returned my affections. I was the happiest of men, then. Lydia and Pierson could have taken all of my possessions—and mind you, they tried—but so long as I had Hallie, it mattered not. With her, I felt true happiness."

Guilford paused again and cleared his throat. At the same time, he examined Rhianna's face and she wondered if it appeared to him more emotional or captivated. He proceeded.

"Not many months passed when Hallie became pregnant with my child," he told her, quickly, as if he had never before said it aloud. "I knew Hallie could not stay in the house once her condition became obvious, but I was determined to provide for her. Around her fourth month, she resigned as governess. My hope was to bring her with me to my Irish estate, Wyndgate, but my business at the time would not allow me to leave England. Neither of us was keen on being separated, so I moved her to my hunting lodge. It was intended to be a temporary solution, while she waited out the pregnancy.

"Of course, someone would need to care for her. At Hallie's request, a letter was sent to her old nanny, the woman who had brought her up as a child. They were very close. I believe you know her," he smiled, and the blood drained from Rhianna's face as she guessed whom he meant. "Mauvreen came to live with her as a caretaker and, ultimately, served as her midwife. Hallie carried the baby to term, and gave birth to a daughter." He paused. "For the second time in my life, I fell in love."

Rhianna's heart moved for him. In such an unfair world, she was glad there was some happiness to be had for him, however sinful. She offered Guilford another glass of water. Rhianna found just enough time to wipe away a tear without his noticing, as he sipped.

"To my greatest devastation," he went on, after a heartfelt moment of silence, "Hallie did not survive. As you may be aware, *My Dearest Haldana* is buried in the garden behind the lodge."

"I've been there," Rhianna confessed. She surprised herself when she spoke. "Surrounded by roses."

"They were her favorite." Speaking with impressive honesty, he told her, "It was there that my life would have ended, as well, but for the baby that lived."

"Please go on," Rhianna encouraged, as he hesitated.

Lord Kingsley nodded, as if gaining courage. "By the mercy of God, Hallie was blessed with seeing and naming her child before her death. But the miserable question arose as to what to do with the baby. I could not bring her to Kingsley Manor and she could not be raised by Mauvreen in the lodge. It was sheer coincidence that, at around that same time, Mrs. Braden also had been pregnant and was due to give birth."

At hearing this, a short gasp escaped Rhianna's lips. "Are you speaking of myself?"

Guilford shook his head. "Actually, I am not. Mrs. Braden gave birth to a stillborn. You can see its unmarked grave in the churchyard, next to the Bradens' graves today."

Rhianna's spirits fell at hearing this. She had never known of her mother's loss, and she inwardly mourned the death of what she imagined would have been an older brother or sister to herself.

"Mr. Braden was one of the few who were aware of my situation and I turned to him for help. Offering to provide financial support, I begged that he would take my child and raise it as his own."

Rhianna's brows furrowed as she considered this. Suddenly, her heart was racing. She had no siblings. Her father must have declined his request.

"What did . . . *my father* . . . say?" she asked, choking on her own words.

Guilford's eyes were pained as he looked at her. "He said that he would."

All at once, his words rushed in at her. The room was void of air. Her limbs went numb. The fibers of her very being felt disjointed and an internal struggle to remain whole—to remain *her*—ensued.

"Rhianna," he told her, gently, "you *are* my daughter. I only pray that you understand why I had no choice but to do what I did and can forgive me for letting you go."

She knew not when her free hand covered her mouth, but she was grateful the other still supported her against the bed. Rhianna felt the pressure of emotion building within her and she feared its release.

"I want you to know how very much I have loved you from the beginning," he added, "and how very much I love you now."

Rhianna stood and faced away from him, her every extremity entirely without sensation. She was conscious only of the fierce pounding of her heart as it pumped her blood wildly through her veins. The back of the chair she had been seated in became her new source of physical stability while her entire life began to flash before her eyes. The emotional distance displayed by her parents during her young years with them. How very much she did not *look* like them. Their lack of communication during her years in France. It was little wonder that when Lord Kingsley arrived to tell her of their funeral arrangements, that she felt little other than obligation to return to England . . .

When Lord Kingsley arrived.

At that moment, the pieces began to fall into place for her. His traveling to France was not, at least solely, out of gratitude to Mr. Braden. He traveled to France for *her*. His devotion to her comfort, his kindness, his familial manner, and . . .

And then something else occurred to her, and she turned back to him. She began to feel one all-encompassing emotion at a time, starting with hope.

"Audra?" she asked.

Guilford seemed relieved to see her face him again, and nodded. "Your half-sister."

Euphoria.

And then . . .

"Desmond?" she breathed, sickly.

He shook his head. "Lydia and Pierson's child."

Shock.

Relief.

Rhianna shivered, as if her body required it to expel any other possibility of a relation to him. A moment later, she asked Lord Kingsley the only full-length question she could articulate.

"Why are you telling me now?"

Guilford sighed. The impression was in relief. There was no doubt he had been anticipating a release from this secret for some time.

"There are several reasons," he confessed, "some of them purely selfish on my part. I want you to know how much you were loved by your mother, who in only a few hours loved you enough for your entire lifetime. You deserve to know that you sing with her voice—the voice of an angel, truly."

Rhianna recalled how Guilford excused himself from the drawing room the night she performed for the Kingsleys and Brightons.

"I want you to know how much you have been loved by me, from the moment I knew that you were coming into the world," he continued. "I want you . . . I want you to know how very much you look like your grandmother, Catherine Kingsley." He smiled. "You know, Dowager Lady Whitehall may not have seen a ghost that night at the ball, but I couldn't blame her for thinking it."

As he spoke, the strength in her legs began to fail her and she reclaimed her seat beside him. So much for single, identifiable emotions—she no longer knew how to feel. It was all too much. Rhianna recalled the moment during the ball when everything stopped. The old woman's loud cry, her frightened face, her *certainty* that Rhianna was "Catherine."

"Fortunately," he continued, "there is no one else still living who knew my mother in her youth to recognize you. But those are the selfish reasons for telling you the truth, Rhianna. There are some practical reasons, as well."

Rhianna was certain she could not speak for some time, but she took his hand in hers. It was all she could offer for the moment. Guilford beamed. She felt him squeeze her hand, but his grip was weak.

"Kingsley Manor," he told her, his voice a raspy whisper, "unfortunately, is entailed to Desmond. As much as I wish I could do something about that, I cannot. However, Wyndgate is unentailed."

"Wyndgate," she repeated. "The Irish estate you spoke of?"

He nodded. "It is more desirable to Desmond than even this house and the title that comes with it because of the debt that he and Pierson have incurred through their compulsive gambling. Pierson has no rank in the peerage and is very likely to end up in debtor's prison. But Wyndgate could be sold and the debts absolved. That is, if Desmond were to inherit it, which Lydia has always assumed. The fact is, Rhianna, it is the one aspect of my wealth that I can control. It also happens that I care very little for Pierson's debts when I have two daughters to care for. The will I have drawn up leaves Wyndgate to you and Audra, fifty-fifty."

Rhianna's mouth fell, but he left her little time to absorb his words.

"Of course, Lydia and Desmond still have no idea I deeded the benefice to Mr. Braden some twenty years back in exchange for taking you. At the time I had done so, I stipulated it not become public knowledge. Mr. Braden, of course, had no objection so long as he was receiving all the tithes and revenue from the glebe. You can have no idea of my relief when you readily agreed to my request for discretion on the matter. Lydia and Desmond will not be happy when they find out," he warned her. "You will have friends on your side, though. Weathersby can be trusted, as well as my lawyer, Mr. Brown. Of course, I will let Brighton know my wishes . . ."

Brighton.

Thayne.

A hazy idea passed through her mind that this would affect her future with him, but she pushed it quickly away. There were other things to take over her thoughts.

"I don't know what to say," she told him honestly. "This is so inconceivable . . ."

"Not at all," he assured her. "I may leave unentailed property to whomever I choose, male or not, relation or not."

She shook her head slowly. "No . . . everything . . . it is all so . . ." Rhianna choked on her own voice. "Who else . . . knows . . . about me?"

Guilford wet his dry lips. "Besides your mother and me, Mr. and Mrs. Braden, and Mauvreen, obviously, Weathersby is the only other person who knows all. In fact, he is the one who delivered you as a baby to the Bradens one windy night." He sighed. "I wish I could tell the world you are Rhianna Kingsley, my eldest daughter, but to the world you must remain Rhianna Braden," he lamented. "I am sure you can never forgive me, but there are no options for illegitimate children."

Suddenly, Rhianna's heart stopped. She could never keep this from Thayne, and once he knew the truth he would never marry her. Marrying a governess was beneath him as it was, but a bastard was something else altogether. Devastation was slowly creeping up on her.

"I realize it will be impossible for you to continue here once my will is read," he acknowledged, "not to mention what Desmond has done. I have contacted a family—friends of mine—named Bridgeford. Lord Bridgeford and his wife live about thirty miles or so northwest of here and their daughter Emily is in need of a governess. They are hoping to hear you are available."

Lord Kingsley, in this one action, showed more affection toward her than the curate had in nearly a decade. All this, arranged for her in advance! It helped to push aside her other thoughts, that just when she believed her days as a governess were behind her, she would be off to live with another family, working with a new child, one that was not . . .

Her half-sister Audra.

"Lord Kingsley," she began, "*Father* . . ." The word sounded strange in her mouth. "I want you to know how much I truly appreciate . . . everything. I have no doubt that you love me. You have not neglected me, all these years, making sure I was cared for, that I received education, that I had a home. I can see that."

For the first time since the room had cleared of all other persons, Guilford Kingsley was silent. Rhianna's small speech was not delivered without emotion, and that she did not reject him seemed to ease him.

"That is all I could ever hope for."

"I understand perfectly," she finished, exhaling as she spoke the words. "And . . . I harbor no resentment. In fact, I feel . . . *happy.*" The surprise of this revelation reflected in her voice. "I always felt I belonged here. It all makes sense."

"I expect nothing from you, Rhianna," he assured her quickly. "I forgive you."

A peaceful look fell upon his face and, in that moment, Rhianna was sure she would have nothing to regret upon Guilford Kingsley's passing.

"My mother, Catherine, lived here at Kingsley Manor during her later years," he struggled. Rhianna could see his energy was failing him. "I have stored some of my personal items in her old bedroom and keep it locked at all times." Rhianna knew the room at once, the only locked door in the house. "Weathersby has a key," he told her. "I have instructed him to give it only to you."

"To me?"

"In the upper drawer of the corner dresser you will find the address of the Bridgefords."

She nodded, as if accepting her fate.

"And Rhianna . . ." he smiled, ". . . uncover the portrait over the fireplace."

A knock rapped on the door and Henry entered. "Lord Brighton," he announced, and Thayne stepped around him.

"Forgive me, am I intruding?" Thayne asked.

"No, no," Guilford assured him.

Rhianna was expecting Audra to rush in behind him, but she did not appear.

Thayne must have read her thoughts, for he answered them, saying, "Audra fell asleep."

Rhianna suddenly remembered there was a world outside of Lord Kingsley's bedroom. "I'll go check on her," she told him, rising. "It is only fair that you have your time with Lord Kingsley."

Thayne shot her a worried glance. "Why do we not go together?

I won't be long."

"Desmond Kingsley is not returning to the manor for the time being," she assured him.

With a look at her father, she smiled and took leave before Thayne could object further.

*

With the door to Guilford's bedroom closed behind her, Rhianna noted that the servants had been shooed away. Only Weathersby remained, and she turned to him.

"Mr. Weathersby, I . . ."

"*Miss Braden.*"

He held out his clenched hand to her. Her eyes lowered to the fingers that held the key to Catherine Kingsley's room and the hallway around her began to swirl. She blinked, held out her own hand, and felt the key drop into it. She closed her fingers quickly around it.

"Thank you."

His thin lips pulled a little to the sides, but his expression was stiff. It was clear he cared for Guilford deeply and the worry that consumed him could be read on every part of his face.

Rhianna looked beyond him to the hallway, knowing exactly where to find Catherine Kingsley's room. The thought of unveiling its contents sent a mild thrill up her spine and, suddenly, she was torn. She wanted to look into Audra's eyes with the knowledge she now had of their true relationship. Indeed, it overcame almost every emotion in her.

On the other hand, once Thayne left Guilford's room, he would likely not leave her side and she so wanted Catherine's room to herself . . .

She followed the L-shaped hall down to the end, made the right turn and, passing door after door, followed it to the northeast side of the manor. Hardly had the door to Catherine's room appeared than she pushed the key into the lock and turned.

The *click* as it unlocked pierced her and Rhianna's fingers trembled as she mustered up the courage to turn the handle. So many secrets, so much of the past lay behind that door. Instinctively, she glanced over her shoulder before entering. The thought of Lydia Kingsley happening upon her crossed her mind and Rhianna imagined her response to the truth of her identity and inheritance. Indubitably, she thought, Lydia would lock her in the room with the ghosts of the past and take the key away with her.

With a burst of energy, she walked through the open door and closed it behind her. She coughed. A thin ray of sunlight shone through the thin, white sheets that covered the windows. Rainbow-colored dust particles sparkled in the air, revealing a thick cloud that enveloped the room. It was clear no one had been here for some time. Rhianna knocked a spider from her wrist and watched as it scurried away under the high bed before her, also covered in white sheets, as was the rest of the furniture. A long rectangular dresser stood silently to her right and the chest of drawers in the far corner. The fireplace, long without warmth, its embers black and cold, watched her as if surprised to see a living, breathing human being again. The room as a whole did not seem indifferent to her being there; rather, despite its cold, dusty appearance, Rhianna felt welcomed.

She walked a few more steps into the room, which was not unlike her own rose bedroom. The same high ceiling, the same tall windows, the same creaky wood floor gave it a familiar feel. She peeked under the white sheet of the long dresser. Beneath it, golden handles could be lifted to open mahogany drawers. She imagined the gowns that might still exist there, the berets Catherine would have clipped in her hair, the gloves that would have decorated her hands . . .

Rhianna couldn't resist pulling the top middle drawer toward her, but *The Last Will and Testament of Guilford Kingsley* met her as the only item. Disappointed not to find some exquisite article of silk, she began to shut the drawer, but stopped midway. She examined the cover for some time, before lifting the will from its resting place and considering whether she would review its contents. She carried it with her as she continued to walk toward the center of the room. Distracted, Rhianna allowed her fingers to run along the edge of the bed and she imagined the indistinct image of a woman lying there . . .

Guilford's mother.

Her grandmother.

"*. . . uncover the painting over the fireplace . . .*"

Guilford's instructions resounded so clearly in her mind, it seemed as if he spoke them aloud to her at that very moment. Reflectively, she obeyed, dropping the will to the bed and moving spellbound toward the fireplace. Brushing away the spider webs that had woven their way between the sheet and the mantel, she took the corner of the fabric and tugged. It fluttered to the corner of the fireplace.

And there she was.

Herself.

The room around her disappeared. Rhianna stumbled back. She looked upon the old portrait, her breath stolen from her. The green eyes, the red hair, the fair skin, and the same peach dress that now rested upon Rhianna's shoulders—the bottom inscription read *Catherine Kingsley*, but it might as well have read *Rhianna*. The likeness between them was astonishing, almost as if it were a mirror's reflection.

Her thoughts raced as she fingered the tear in the fabric of her sleeve. For the first time since Guilford had explained everything to her, it suddenly felt *real*. Nothing in her life was what it had seemed. Those she thought were her family were not. Who she believed she was, she was not. No longer was she the daughter of a curate with parents who did not love her, and no longer was she governess to the daughter of a wealthy family. She was Rhianna

Kingsley, a stranger, an heiress, with a father and a sister she hardly knew, and a fiancé she could not marry. She could not but brace herself against the bedpost for support, as her knees grew unsteady beneath her.

Then, vaguely she became aware of someone standing in the doorway. "Rhianna?"

The tone was warm, gentle, and crushing all at once. Rhianna's eyes and mind were locked on the portrait, but she managed to wonder how many more times she would hear Thayne's voice.

She heard him begin to approach. Then, he stopped. Surely, he had seen the portrait and she was grateful not to have to explain. Now, he knew.

"How did you know where I was?" she asked in a whisper.

He explained quickly, sounding a bit out of breath. "Weathersby pointed me in the right direction. There was a Desmond sighting in the manor. I have been searching all the rooms of this hallway for you, nearly frantic." He added, "I was close to this room when I heard you gasp. I would ask why, but it seems unnecessary."

She hadn't remembered gasping audibly. Rhianna turned to him; Thayne's hand that had gestured toward the portrait fell to his side.

"I didn't know," she told him. "Until today, I had no idea."

Rhianna folded her arms around herself, as if holding her body together. It seemed it might fall apart at any moment. Thayne looked at her, but she watched as his eyes rose to the portrait. He took a few steps forward, until he was beside her.

"Catherine Kingsley?" he read.

His voice was inflectionless, his words just barely a question. It sounded more as if he were stating a fact.

She nodded.

Thayne gently reached his hand under her chin and examined her features, then the portrait, and back again. "Lydia?"

This is it, she thought. *I shall never see him again after this day.*

"No," she mouthed.

Illegitimate.

The word sounded in her mind, over and over again. She thought she read it in his eyes as he did the calculations. Guilford, after all, had been married to Lydia for thirty years. Rhianna came from no previous, legal union.

Quickly, she drank in his features, burning them vividly into her memory. His dark hair and lashes. His blue eyes. His straight nose. His square jaw. His full lips. His broad shoulders. His soft fingers that brushed suddenly against her cheek, catching a tear in their wake.

"Desmond?" he asked, his face at once contorted.

She hesitated to speak, knowing every word drew them closer to their last exchange.

Finally, bowing her head, she resigned. "He is Pierson's."

Without warning, Thayne looked relieved and wrapped his arms around her waist. "Well, thank God for that! I cannot imagine having *him* as a brother-in-law, even a halfblooded one."

Then, he smiled.

"How can you even jest?" she cried with a weak voice, easing him away from her. "I did not think you capable of cruelty, but you clearly wish to torment me!"

Thayne frowned. "I'm sorry. This is rather incredible, isn't it? I should have been more sensitive. Are you all right?"

"No, I'm not all right!" she returned, watching her hopes of not explaining fly out the tall, sheet-covered windows. "I don't know who I am anymore and everything has fallen apart."

Her last several words were barely audible, and although Thayne did not seem to grasp her meaning, he was quick to comfort her.

"You are my soon-to-be Rhianna Brighton," he answered, his voice calm and reassuring, "and whatever you think is going to fall apart, we will figure out together."

He took her hands in his and she rejected them.

"As if we could still be married!"

Rhianna nearly choked on the words as she spoke them. Her heart, no longer racing, ached with every beat. Her involuntary movements of breathing and blinking were a chore she had no power for. Standing took all her strength.

"Well, why on Earth wouldn't we be?" he returned at once. This time, Thayne was taken aback. The alarm finally inflected in his voice.

"I hardly have to spell it out for you. Illegitimate children cannot be legally married. It is impossible!"

At this, he pulled her to his chest and held her tightly, rocking gently from side to side. A rush of his scent and the warmth of his body engulfed her. Swallowed by grief, she ceased to resist him.

"Rhianna," he soothed, "my dear, sweet, lovely Rhianna. Listen to me." She felt his hand wrap around her head, his cheek pressed against her hair. "There is not a man or woman in England who suspects this. The parish register has a Miss *Braden* listed as the very *legitimate* child of a respectable family. *That* is the woman I fell in love with and *that* is the woman I am going to marry."

As she registered this, she said nothing.

"Do you still wish to marry me?" he asked her, easing back and looking into her eyes.

"That should be my question to you."

"Nothing has changed for me, Rhianna. Do you still wish to marry *me*?" he repeated.

"Yes."

Thayne's lips at once besieged hers, finalizing the matter. Rhianna's fears began to melt slowly away. The emotions swirling within her were powerful and would not easily abate, but that she had nothing to worry about Thayne was fully convincing. His passionate kiss quickly persuaded her to believe he not only still wanted her, but that nothing could change his mind.

For some time, Rhianna allowed him to continue to persuade her thus, partly for the reassurance of his affection, partly for the lack of energy to refuse, and mostly for the desire that he awakened in her. Thayne made little effort to hide his own longings, and excepting a single pause to meet her gaze, he showed himself in no particular rush to convince her of his unending love.

*

Rhianna recognized the voices in the hallway at once.

"Is he not *mortal?* I do not understand!"

Pierson's frustration was evident, as Lydia tried to satisfy him. "He is strong, cousin. He survives what no other man would."

Pierson tapped his foot anxiously against the floor. "Neither you nor Desmond have been able to get to him to give him the final dose."

Persuading him to calm himself, and persuasion was her greatest skill, Lydia said, "You cannot hurry these things. Everything will end perfectly. You can be sure I'll see to that myself."

It had little effect on him. "*Hurry?* This should have been finished a year and a half ago!"

Rhianna covered her own mouth and looked at Thayne, who himself looked intently toward the door of Catherine Kingsley's room, his arms still wrapped tightly around her.

"Time is running out for me, Lydia," Pierson continued. "If you cannot get this done tonight, I will have to leave England . . . *and you.*"

"My love, if you can but give me a few days . . ."

"You have had your time! You are not able to do it," he accused.

"I want nothing but for it to be done," she assured him. "Is not everyone convinced he has been ill for some time of natural causes? They are all expecting his death at any moment."

"You think me a fool! Prove your commitment. If Guilford Kingsley is not dead by midnight, you and I are through."

Pierson could be heard walking around the corner and down the east hall. Lydia appeared to chase after him.

"I will find a way . . ." her voice faded.

Rhianna was shaking her head. "The final dose? They are

poisoning him? They are poisoning Lord Kingsley!"

"I have to admit," Thayne told her, "I did not think them capable of this."

"Thayne," she hurried, a wave of revulsion shooting through her, "they are after the money from the Irish estate. They do not realize Lord Kingsley has left it to Audra and myself. Who is to say when they find out that they will not attempt to kill us, as well?"

Suddenly, she recalled a certain late night meeting between Pierson, Lydia, and Desmond and she knew a murder had already been attempted, and not against Lord Kingsley only.

"What if they have tried this before?" she told him, as her thoughts raced from one to another. "I have heard Lord Kingsley was sick before I arrived. What if they were poisoning him then? I overheard Pierson say that 'when *she* arrived, everything was undone.' Oh, Thayne! What if he was referring to me? He accused Lydia of having doubts and giving excuses not to follow through on some scheme. Only now, I think he must have been referring to this—killing Lord Kingsley! Imagine, Thayne, if Pierson thought me interfering in some way, a man already with murderous intent. Perhaps he and Desmond were the persons in the woods that day at Ravensleigh. Perhaps Pierson *did* have something to do with my accident. Why wouldn't he try to get rid of me? If Lydia truly has had doubts about the murder and used me as an excuse to delay this terrible scheme, Pierson might have been quite determined." Thayne stood stiff, as she concluded, "Now, time has run out. Lydia must choose between Lord Kingsley and Pierson, and it appears she has made her decision."

Thayne looked at her anxiously, his grip tightening around her. "We must hurry back. Lydia will be a desperate woman tonight."

He took her hand and they hurried out of the room. Rhianna dared not think of the outcome. One thing was certain: If Lydia and Desmond were determined to kill Guilford Kingsley, they would not hesitate to kill *anyone* who stood in their way.

*

It was a room Lydia had never entered and little thought of. Though a gray-haired woman by the time she came to live with them, Catherine Kingsley added to the difficulty of her sneaking Pierson to and from the house. Anything remindful of her was disagreeable to Lydia and she had, in fact, so far removed the memory of her stay from her mind that the very existence of the bedroom was forgotten—and so it would have remained had the door not been left ajar. On the way back to her own bedroom, Lydia halted before the open door and peeked into the sheet-covered room, wondering who would have had any interest in entering it.

On the bed, a document caught her eye and curiosity immediately took over. Seeing that no one else was around, she entered, despite a distinct feeling of being unwelcome and out of place. She approached and snatched the document that was Guilford's will and examined its contents, her eyes focused on finding the one bequest that mattered . . .

Her hands quaked so violently, she could no longer read the words on the printed page. Soon, her entire body convulsed with fury. The blue veins of her forehead popped and bloodspots scattered around her eyes, while despite the cold in the air she began to sweat with hate. Lydia found herself clenching her teeth, her mouth at once dehydrated, as she realized the document had been executed twenty years previous.

It would have been one thing to leave Wyndgate to Audra, but the curate's daughter? A mere baby at the time, what could sway him to steal from his own family in such a loathsome manner? Lydia, yet convinced of an affair between them, wondered at his clear fixation on Rhianna Braden from the beginning of her existence and was all but baffled—until she looked up and her eyes fell upon a portrait . . .

Catherine Kingsley.

Lydia was taken aback. She stared at the unveiled painting, the shocking resemblance between Catherine and Rhianna turning her white with rage. The portrait's eyes in turn met hers with a disapproving gaze and Lydia recognized the feeling. For some time, she had attempted to dismiss sensations that the dead woman was watching her from every corner of the manor. Indeed, though, she was. *Rhianna* was watching her—Guilford's bastard child. Lydia wondered little who the mother was. And now the girl lived under the same roof, with no future purpose but to torment her, just as Catherine had, watching her with accusing eyes while stealing her family's fortune.

With these thoughts, Lydia escaped the room as fast as she could, leaving behind her a quiet, empty room, a sliver of sun shining favorably on the unveiled portrait of Catherine Kingsley, the white sheet that had before covered it hanging loosely down the side of the fireplace.

Chapter Ten

"Lord Kingsley told me we could trust Mr. Weathersby," Rhianna told Thayne. "What of Dr. Logan? Ought he to have discovered the poison in his system? Do you imagine he could be conspiring with them?"

With his hand on the doorknob to Lord Kingsley's bedroom, Thayne paused. All the servants had left. The hallway was empty but for the two of them.

"Pierson was specific that neither Lydia nor Desmond was able to get to Lord Kingsley to give him the final dose. If such is the case, it would seem they are working alone," he thought aloud. "Not to mention Dr. Logan has had full access to Lord Kingsley, and if all that was required was a final dose, he certainly hasn't administered it."

"Yes, but Mr. Weathersby has been consistently at his side. Perhaps even Dr. Logan's full access is not opportunity enough under watchful eyes."

At last, he shook his head. "There is nothing to be gained for the doctor by the death of Lord Kingsley," Thayne said, resolutely. "Nothing is impossible, but we are going to have to take the chance and hope the doctor is on our side."

Rhianna nodded, her hands wrung anxiously together. Thayne kissed her forehead and opened the door.

Guilford lay in bed sleeping, his previous confession having pressed his strength to the limit. Weathersby and Dr. Logan stood nearby, their faces grave, as they had been all along.

"Gentlemen," called Thayne.

"Lord Brighton," they greeted. "Miss Braden."

Rhianna half curtseyed, eyeing both men suspiciously. She

didn't want to, but she couldn't help it.

"Dr. Logan," Thayne addressed, in a no-holds-barred manner, "I have a very serious question to ask of you, and I beg you will excuse my directness."

Dr. Logan appeared at once concerned. "Of course."

"Have you ruled out the possibility that Lord Kingsley has been poisoned?"

"Poisoned?" echoed Weathersby.

Dr. Logan appeared equally aghast. "Sir?"

Thayne watched his reaction closely. "Something that could have been administered over a period of time to make it appear he was ill of natural causes?"

The doctor's brows furrowed together, his mouth parted. He looked at Guilford with what appeared heavy concern.

"Arsenic," he answered, his voice monotone. "It would be nearly undetectable. Lord Brighton," he glared at him, "what exactly are you suggesting?"

"A very serious allegation against Lydia Kingsley, Desmond Kingsley, and her cousin, Mr. Pierson, Doctor. Miss Braden and I are, in fact, witnesses to a conversation between two of them on this very subject."

Weathersby's mouth opened as if to gasp, but no sound was heard. Dr. Logan rushed to Guilford's side and examined him.

"It would explain his symptoms," the doctor said, his voice hurried, panicked.

"Dr. Logan," Rhianna asked, hesitantly, "if such is the case, could he be saved?"

Her eyes were wide, pleading. For a moment, she forgot he did not know he was her father.

Dr. Logan seemed to consider the likelihood. "It is possible," he told her, cautiously. Then he shook his head. "Could Lady Kingsley be capable of this?"

The room fell silent.

"Rhianna, may I speak with you outside?" Thayne asked. She silently agreed. "I will return, gentlemen."

They seemed not even to hear him and he exited with Rhianna.

In the hallway, Thayne's hands enclosed her face, his hold gentle yet tense. "I want you and Audra to leave this place. It is not safe."

"Where shall we . . . ?"

"Ravensleigh."

Rhianna's eyes turned toward Lord Kingsley's bedroom door. Thayne was not unaware of her concern and his thumbs softly stroked her cheeks.

"There is nothing you can do here, Rhianna," he told her delicately.

"What will you do?"

"I will call on some friends. Some live close and can be here in a matter of hours. In the meantime, I will personally watch over Lord Kingsley. The guilty parties are not aware of our knowledge. It will buy us some time." She allowed him to accept her silence as agreement. "Let us speak with Henry. I will have him call my carriage and we will get you a change of clothes."

*

Thayne carried a sleepy Audra to the carriage in front of Kingsley Manor, seeing for the first time the sisterly resemblances between her and Rhianna in their pale skin and large eyes. His driver, Barton, stood at the ready.

"But I don't want to leave . . ." The emotional exhaustion had taken its toll on Audra; her words were mumbled and weak, her eyes closing.

"It is only for a little while. I will watch over your father while you keep my mum and Crispin company. Crispin is already waiting for you."

She sighed, surrendering to the physical limits of her body. Thayne gently placed her down beside the maid and manservant

Lady Brighton had sent to accompany them on their short journey to Ravensleigh. They tossed a blanket over her as Thayne tipped his hat to them both.

Rhianna was speaking with Henry at the front door, each nodding to the other, when Thayne turned to her. Then, she made her way toward her fiancé. Despite the circumstances, Thayne allowed himself a moment to admire the woman he adored, her red hair as it sparkled in the mid-afternoon sun, her green, almond-shaped eyes that lit up when they met his, and even her long, hooded cloak as it twisted around her in the wind. He cherished the moment, knowing the time to appreciate it was now, for who could say how the hours ahead would pass?

Her gloved hands reached out to his.

"I do not know how soon it will be before we are together again," Thayne told her.

There was so much more to say, but he hesitated. Thayne's intention had been to prepare Rhianna for a long absence, but as those few words passed his lips he realized *himself* what that would mean—a pain acute and severe. Instantly recalling the snowstorm that had all too recently kept them apart, this too would keep them at a distance for an unknown, excruciating period.

But there was no time to consider that. Besides, there was no alternative. At least this time he could remind himself she was promised to him.

"I love you," he concluded.

Her worried expression softened, and her cheeks grew rosy with her faint smile. "I love you, Thayne Brighton."

He allowed the sound of his name from her lips to echo in his ears.

"Whatever damage has been done," he at last promised her, "I will not let any further harm come to Lord Kingsley."

She nodded. "I know. Please be careful."

He promised with an abrupt kiss and assisted her into the carriage. They exchanged anxious glances before the door closed between them.

"Barton," Thayne instructed, "go *directly* to Ravensleigh. Stop for no one, do you understand?"

"Certainly, sir."

Thayne knocked his hand against the side of the carriage as Barton lifted himself up to the driver's seat and urged the horses forward. He watched for a moment as the coach carried his beloved toward safety, and then reentered Kingsley Manor.

*

They had not traveled far down the approach when Rhianna watched Thayne enter the manor. Then, as instructed, Henry gave her the signal she was hoping for: the coast was clear.

"Mr. Barton! Mr. Barton!" she cried to the coachman. "Please stop the coach!"

"I beg your pardon?" he called, slowing the horses.

"Please stop!" she called again.

Rhianna was on her feet, her hands on the door. She leaned over to give Audra a kiss on the forehead.

"Where are you going?" she asked Rhianna, groggily.

"I promise I'll meet you at Ravensleigh in no time at all."

"Miss Braden," Mr. Barton called, "Lord Brighton instructed me not to stop."

"Yes, absolutely, once you are on your way you must not stop for anything at all," she agreed. "Only, we have not yet left Kingsley Manor and I really must go back." The coach came to a halt and Rhianna helped herself down. "Thank you, Mr. Barton. Please continue without me. Miss Kingsley must be at Ravensleigh as soon as possible."

Barton appeared very confused as she secured the door, and then shrugged before continuing on.

She nearly ran back to the manor. She had always liked Henry, and he had always liked her. She knew she could ask him the favor of providing her a horse. A servant was already bringing it around.

"Thank you, Henry," she said, out of breath and smiling. "He would have never let me go."

"Keep a sharp eye out, miss," he told Rhianna. "There are some unsavory characters in our midst."

"Yes." The stable boy handed her the reins of her favorite steed. "I will, Henry. Thank you again."

She galloped down the Kingsley approach, gone as quickly as she had escaped the Brighton carriage that traveled yet within sight before her.

*

Thayne's elbow rested in his hand, his fist supporting his chin, as he stood beside the window of Guilford's room, his back to the scene outside. Dr. Logan leaned over Guilford with his stethoscope, the latter having awoken since Thayne's return. Weathersby continued to stand gravely in the corner, pacing occasionally.

Servants had been sent out to various households, bearing Thayne's handwritten notes to each male of age, requesting they come at once to Kingsley Manor. He expected they all would come. He expected three to arrive relatively quickly.

"Gentlemen, may I have a word with Lord Kingsley?" he requested, suddenly.

Each was happy to oblige. Time was passing slowly as they waited and a change of scenery was welcome. Dr. Logan rose from beside the bed and followed Weathersby quietly into the hall.

Thayne took a seat beside Guilford and smiled. "I want to thank you, Lord Kingsley."

Guilford examined him curiously. "Ought not I be thanking you, who willingly remains in such circumstances, away from his family, under this disgraceful roof?"

Thayne shook his head. "No. It is a small thing compared with what you have done for me."

"Pray, tell."

Thayne drew a deep breath and smiled. "You have given me a family. A future. Happiness that I never imagined possible," he told him. "And I hope you will forgive me, for had I known sooner, I would have asked your permission for her hand *before* she said yes."

His face smoothed, his brows raised, his lips spread wide across his face. "Indeed!" Through all the illness and exhaustion, energy issued from his core. "Rhianna? The future Mistress of Ravensleigh?"

"Yes." He grinned at the merriment in his voice. "And I can only hope you will still give your blessing."

"Thayne," he called him, tenderly, "you are one of the most honorable men I have ever known. It is exactly the happiness that I wish for you both. Nothing should please me more."

Thayne took his hand in a firm grip, grinning from ear to ear. "I will always take care of her. You don't have to worry."

Guilford struggled to place one of his hands over Thayne's arm. "You have given me *peace* that I never imagined. Thank you." Then he jested, "Well, it looks like my good friend Bridgeford is still going to need a governess."

Thayne looked at him curiously, but Guilford had no time to explain. There was a quick rap at the door and Henry entered.

"I beg your pardon," Henry breathed, as if he had run up the two flights of stairs from his post. "Miss Braden . . ."

It was if he could hardly get the words out for lack of air. At the name, adrenaline shot through both men. Thayne jumped to his feet.

"Henry, speak!"

"She took a horse," he hurried. "She said she was going to visit a friend . . ."

"Miss Braden left in a carriage to Ravensleigh," Thayne told him tensely. "I watched her drive off with my own eyes."

"That you did, sir. But after you returned to the manor, she exited the coach and took a horse. I'm so sorry to have helped her. I should be relieved of my duties at once. But Mr. Pierson and Lord Desmond Kingsley also happened to be on horseback and, at once appearing from the side of the manor, followed after her!"

"Henry, is this true?" Guilford asked him.

"My lord," he bowed quickly.

Thayne rushed at the window and saw the distant outline of two riders on horseback, both of them men. "Good God—we never closed the door!"

"Thayne?"

In this one word, Guilford's voice held all the strength of the previous words spoken together.

"We never closed the door to Catherine's bedroom," he told him. "They must know." He turned to Henry. "Where did you say she was going?"

"A friend's house, sir. It is all she told me."

"Lord Kingsley? Can you have any idea?"

"Yes." His voice was confident. "There is only one place it could be."

"There is more thing, my lord," Henry added, uneasily. "One of the stable boys claims to have seen something dreadful. It was after Miss Braden's horse accident . . . Forgive me, Lord Kingsley, but he alleges he saw Lord Desmond Kingsley remove a dart from the leg of her horse."

"Why did he not say so before?" cried Guilford.

"My lord, he tells me that Lord Desmond Kingsley saw him. That he threatened his position if he ever spoke a word of the matter. The boy was apparently afraid."

Thayne addressed Henry again. "My horse—quickly! I leave at once."

*

The trip to Mauvreen's felt elongated, nearly unending, and Rhianna knew it was not because it had been several weeks since she had been there. Her heart raced well ahead of her and she felt as if she could not catch up to it. One central thought consumed her, namely, if she could not be beside her father as he lay dying, she could at least be beside her mother. Not only, but Mauvreen was at last free to tell her everything and Rhianna's thoughts flew as she considered all the details she could provide, from what her mother was like as a child, to her relationship with Guilford Kingsley, to her final hours.

If only this trail would end!

The air was cold, but she hardly felt it. The woods seemed to watch her more closely than usual, but it did not frighten her. Even her horse seemed agitated, but it gave her no cause for concern. Rhianna's mind had so overtaken her that she noticed little of the physical world around her.

At last, the lodge came into view. She tied her horse and knocked earnestly on the wood door. Mauvreen answered almost immediately, as if she had been expecting her.

And with just one look, Mauvreen knew that Rhianna knew the truth.

Mauvreen smiled, her wrinkles setting deeply into the curvatures of her face. "Well! I suppose you are not here to see *me*," she said, her eyes sparkling.

"I am here to see both of you," Rhianna said, confirming her presumption.

"That's more than your father would say." Rhianna stepped forward and Mauvreen took her in her arms. "Come inside."

As Rhianna entered, there was something different about the lodge. It felt familial, homey.

"This lodge holds so many memories," recalled Mauvreen, as if she could look about the rooms and see the past as clearly as the present. "All the years I've imagined this moment, having wanted for so long to share my memories with you," she told her, "and I still do not know where to begin."

Rhianna agreed. "There is so much I want to know and I don't know what to ask."

Mauvreen raised her hand, as if she suddenly knew exactly which direction to take. "There is something I want you to see."

Rhianna followed her upstairs, where she was led to a bedroom at the end of the hall. Mauvreen allowed her a moment to silently examine it. It was a modest room, plainly decorated, with a window to the garden in the back. She looked down at the roses and the white fence, but the gravestone itself was not within view. Rhianna returned her attention to the room and wondered who in times past had come and gone from it.

"This is where you were born," Mauvreen explained. "It was in this bed that you spent your one and only day with your mother."

Her eyes fell upon the bed. Rhianna made her way to it and laid her hand upon the sheets. If only she could remember. Kneeling beside the mattress, she closed her eyes and almost imagined she could.

"When you first looked up into her eyes, Guilford was exactly where you are now. *'I have a name for her,'* she said to him. *'She must be called Rhianna.'* I'll never forget how she looked at you."

The scene played out in her mind. She imagined her mother, worn out from childbirth, using all her strength just to hold her, at once knowing her intimately and bonding with her for all eternity.

"Her heart," Mauvreen told her, "was yours and no one else's, from the first moment she saw you, to its last beat."

Searching her soul for what she most wanted to know, Rhianna discovered that if nothing was answered but *one* question, she could be at peace.

She examined the bedsheets as she spoke. "Was my mother happy, Mauvreen?"

"My child?"

"It just seems that life was not very fair to her," she confessed.

"I cannot help but wonder if, in the end, could she have been content, so secluded from society, her family, her prospects, her hopes all gone . . ."

Mauvreen took a seat on the bed beside Rhianna. Holding one hand in her own and patting it tenderly, Mauvreen smiled broadly, her glassy eyes distant with pleasant memories.

"By no means was she unhappy, Rhianna," she assured her. "I can promise you. In fact, she was quite the contrary—especially those last five months of her pregnancy. Though she was so secluded from the rest of the world, I daresay those were the happiest days of Hallie's life. She was madly in love with your father. He was all she needed in the world. And then she had you."

"Did Lord Kingsley truly love her, as he told me?"

She nodded. "He adored her the way she adored him. You can see in the devotion he displays to this day, visiting her regularly these twenty some years later, how he loved her then, and loves her still."

"I wish I could have seen them together," she mused.

"You have seen the way he smiled at her," Mauvreen told her. "It is the same way he smiles at *you*."

She envisioned it, but the image was fleeting. Rhianna's thoughts quickly reverted back to present day and she rose.

"My father is dying, Mauvreen. Lydia has poisoned him."

"I should have known!" declared Mauvreen. "She has been a frantic woman since Pierson was threatened with prison. I did not expect that she would go to such lengths to get Guilford's money."

"Except Lord Kingsley has left all his unentailed property to Audra and me. If she succeeds in killing him, it will be all for naught."

"I doubt she will stop there. You must prove she was behind the poisoning or she will surely come after you both."

As she was speaking, Mauvreen seemed detached. Her expression was concerned, her eyes squinting and her head tilted. She appeared to focus on a distant sound.

"Do you hear that?"

Rhianna felt inclined to listen. As the room around them fell silent, both clearly heard the sound of horse hooves beating against the ground.

Mauvreen's eyes bulged and she squeezed Rhianna's hand tighter than before. "Can Lydia have any idea of what you have just told me?"

Rhianna was shaking her head no when she recalled her hasty exit from Catherine Kingsley's room. Had she and Thayne locked the door behind them? Had they even closed it?

"Is it possible that someone has followed you here?" Mauvreen added.

"I was supposed to go to Ravensleigh," Rhianna confessed, her thoughts racing. "Thayne did not think it was safe for me and Audra to remain at Kingsley Manor. If anyone were to follow me . . . if Thayne had any idea . . ."

"Thayne?" she repeated.

"Oh," she blushed, "well, Lord Brighton, rather. He has proposed, Mauvreen. I was going to tell you . . ."

Both gasped at the sound of a shattered window followed by a *thud*. No sooner had they heard it than they were on their feet. Exchanging fearful glances, each knew someone other than Thayne Brighton was circling the lodge. The front door was unlocked and there was no time to waste.

Fire greeted them at the bottom of the stairs. An enflamed rag lay a few feet from the rock that had carried it into the lodge, flames flickering along the curtain of the window it had crashed through. Mauvreen quickly reached for a nearby broom and attempted to smother the blaze, while Rhianna locked the front door.

Another window was broken. Mauvreen pointed Rhianna to a closet that held another broom and she grabbed it on her way to the kitchen. Shattered glass lay strewn across the floor and flames engulfed an oval rug. Rhianna beat her broom wildly against them, afraid to think beyond her current task. Only one thought was inescapable: *She should not have come here.*

The kitchen fire was conquered when Rhianna looked up and saw what she feared most. There, through the broken window of the back door, she made eye contact with the one man she'd hoped never to see again. From atop her father's horse, Aramis, Desmond Kingsley glared at her, his bloodshot eyes exuding malice. The intoxication of the morning had worn off, but the memory of her rejection had not vanished with it and Desmond was in no mood to forgive.

Rhianna fell to the floor as he aimed his pistol.

"Mauvreen, get down!" she cried, as a bullet whizzed over her head.

She could hear Mauvreen as she, too, dropped to the ground in the other room. More bullets sounded above them as Rhianna crawled over to her friend, pushing aside shards of broken glass along the way. As they sought shelter together behind the stairs, she paid little mind to the broken skin left in its wake or the red fluid that oozed steadily down her forearm.

So much for my change of clothes, she could not help but think.

"Desmond," said Rhianna.

Mauvreen nodded. "Pierson is in front."

The hopelessness of their situation was soon apparent. Flames licked the remaining, jagged glass of the front window—fire had been set to the outside of the lodge and the conflagration was climbing from the ground up. It was only a matter of time before the entire lodge was swallowed by it.

As the temperature rose, the two women refused to allow panic to overtake them as they considered in silence their grim options. To remain inside the lodge offered no hope. Outside the lodge, bullets at a minimum awaited them.

"Mauvreen, I'm so sorry. I never thought I would be putting you in any danger by coming here."

Mauvreen waved her hand. "None of that," she insisted. "It is not your fault that those are evil men out there. Know that you made an old woman happy by coming to visit her today."

Shots sounded through the air again, and though this round did not penetrate the lodge, the women felt the horror they tried so hard to suppress.

"Mauvreen," cried Rhianna suddenly, "does Lord Kingsley keep any rifles here? After all, it is a hunting lodge . . ."

"Yes, but I have no idea how to use them," she returned. "Do you?"

"We must try, or else there is no escape!"

Another shot was heard hissing through the forest, but this came not from the pistol of either Desmond or Pierson. One of the horses neighed and went galloping away from the lodge. Then another shot was heard, and then another.

"Rhianna!" a voice called.

"Oh, Mauvreen, it's Thayne!" Her hopes picked up at once. "Yes, we're here!" Rhianna answered.

They heard d'Artagnan's whinny over the crackling of flames and Mauvreen tugged in vain at Rhianna to stay down, but she was determined to look around the steps, through the window.

Through the crawling blaze, Pierson could be seen, wounded and horseless, victim to one of the bullets fired only moments ago. He gripped his shoulder tightly and winced in pain. With his pistol empty, he screeched in defeat before tossing it aside and running away into the woods.

"You weak, useless coward!" Desmond shouted after him.

Unwilling to flee himself, Desmond sat atop Aramis, his pride no doubt intact, and faced Thayne defiantly.

"Brighton!" he called. "Wonderful to see you! It really has been too long."

Thayne's own checkered walnut and foliate engraved musket glared at him threateningly in the forest light.

"You won't be getting away with a cuff to your jaw this time, Desmond."

"Oh, come now," he said, his face turning red with the rage he tried to conceal. "Still defending the governess?"

Thayne aimed his musket toward his head—a clear shot. "Go, before I shoot!"

As long as Thayne had a loaded musket there was nothing more he could do at present, but Rhianna suspected Desmond's intentions would not easily be put aside. With his pride so deeply wounded by the woman who was due to inherit *his* money, Rhianna was afraid to consider how this would end.

"Would you shoot an unarmed man?" Desmond hurried. "Let us be gentlemen about this, shall we? Meet me on the Thornton Cliffs."

"A duel? I accept!" Both grinned. "Seeing as you have no bullets, my sword and I will see you there. Now *go*!"

"I shall be waiting!"

With that, Desmond kicked his horse in a fury and rode off to the north.

Meanwhile, the heat in the lodge was reaching unbearable levels. Smoke covered the ceiling. A weakened beam above the doorframe began to crack. Rhianna and Mauvreen were covering their noses and mouths with fabric from their sleeves when Thayne leapt from d'Artagnan and kicked in the front door.

"Come!" he cried.

No sooner had he spoken the word than he was beside the stairs, offering his hands to them. Scrambling to their feet, Rhianna and Mauvreen accepted and he ran with them toward the door at a speed they could not attain on their own.

"Wait!" cried Rhianna, pulling her hand from Thayne's grasp and turning back.

"No, Rhianna!"

Nearly thrusting Mauvreen out the front door, he ran after her. Taking her by the shoulders, he pulled her back.

"We have to get out of here!"

"My mother's picture!" she insisted. "I cannot leave it!"

He looked quickly about him. "Where is it?"

"The table, by the sofa!"

The familiar drawing of a young woman encased in an elegant, silver frame held extra meaning for her now. This young woman, lovely in every respect and holding a bouquet of roses was more than the mysterious Hallie, her gown of lace and ribbons more than just a pretty dress . . .

"Get out of here!"

Mauvreen stood with open arms on the other side of the door. "Come quickly, Rhianna!"

Flaming tapestries surrounded her; crackling sounds echoed throughout the lodge. Splinters of glass sparkled in the fabric of her skirt and her bloody arm throbbed at her side. Still, she stood frozen, her eyes on Thayne as he ran for the drawing.

"Thayne!" she called suddenly. Although her mother may be gone, she intended to keep Thayne. "Never mind it! Let us go!"

Mauvreen reentered the lodge to lock Rhianna's arm in hers and urge her desperately out of the building. Rhianna turned to face her, unable to think clearly, unable to move. Only with a glance back, seeing Thayne close behind, she at last conceded. She ran with Mauvreen to the horse still tied to a tree some ways away from the lodge, before turning back again.

A moment after, the doorway poised to collapse above him, the young lord emerged and leapt to safety. The lodge would not stand for long and the drawing of Hallie was not to be seen, but they had escaped. She embraced Thayne as he approached.

"I'll remember," she said, with great strength. "I don't need it, Thayne. I *will* remember and redraw it myself."

Stroking her hair comfortingly, he caught his breath, and replied, "You don't have to."

Thayne pulled the image from inside his jacket pocket and handed it to her. Pressing it to her chest, she bowed her head to his shoulder.

In gratitude she would have remained there, but for the horse that trotted toward them. Thayne quickly raised his pistol toward the visitor, but relaxed his arm when Weathersby came into view. The man riding beside him was also familiar to him.

"Weathersby! Thorngate!"

Both men looked in horror at the fiery scene before them.

"Good God, Thayne," cried the man, Thorngate, "what has happened here? Is everyone all right?"

"We are," he replied. "Pierson took off toward town. We need men to try and track him."

"Pierson has been captured," Thorngate told him.

"What of Desmond?" asked Weathersby.

"I know where he is headed," Thayne told them. "I need someone to take Miss Braden and her friend to safety."

Weathersby volunteered.

"No," cried Rhianna to Thayne, "you mustn't follow him!"

He took her shoulders in his hands. "I will meet you at Ravensleigh."

"We will come with you," she hurried.

Mauvreen laid an understanding hand upon her arm, urging her to reason.

"No," Rhianna cried again. "Someone *must* go with you," she insisted to Thayne.

"I will go with him," Thorngate stated, urging his horse forward.

More men approached who had followed the lead of Thorngate and Weathersby. Many had come in response to Thayne's call for assistance—not his friends only, but friends of friends, as well as servants.

Thayne kissed Rhianna, briefly, but emotionally. "We will be together again before this night is out. I swear to you."

Without a word further, he mounted his horse, and he and Thorngate took off into the woods.

Even as Thayne disappeared, Rhianna's eyes lingered on the spot where she had last seen him. She was hardly aware as Weathersby was soon beside them, ready to assist Rhianna onto her horse and Mauvreen onto his own. Rhianna was grateful he did not hurry her too much, and allowed Mauvreen a moment to put her loving arms around her.

At last, with a final glance at the burning lodge, Rhianna consented to follow Weathersby and Mauvreen toward Ravensleigh.

*

Thayne galloped purposefully toward the cliffs, daylight fading into the west. The colder air that accompanied the twilight and the approaching North Sea was exhilarating. Thayne felt alert, ready. The mental image of the fiery lodge, the woman he loved within, kept his thoughts focused, determined.

Desmond waited plainly in the clearing. He sat tall on his horse, his sword drawn.

"Stay back," Thayne instructed his friend.

"If you need me, I will not be far behind," said Thorngate.

Thayne advanced, his cloak riding the wind that rolled over the cliffs. At their base, tumultuous waves could be heard crashing against the rocks. All at once, salt and smoke filled his senses, a mixture of the sea air and the smoldering fumes of his jacket. The latter became a focus—a steady reminder of why he was here.

Stopping halfway to tie d'Artagnan to a tree, he watched from the corner of his eye as Desmond leapt from his horse, carelessly releasing it. It appeared Thayne was not the only one who imagined that, of the two of them, only one would need a horse to return home.

"You brought a *second* to our unconventional duel?" mocked Desmond, as Thayne removed his cloak, stripping down to his white shirt and cravat.

"I won't be needing him."

"Are you sure?"

"Quite."

"Ought he not to inspect our field of honor or the equality of our weapons?" he jeered.

"I am satisfied on both counts."

Desmond nodded. "And here I expected you to object to the time of day simply to prevent our continuing. Good form, Brighton. I thought I would find you more fearful of your own demise."

Thayne held a firm grip on the handle of his sword as he stood before Desmond Kingsley. "You have insulted my fiancée, you have frightened her, you have injured her, you have attempted to violate and murder her. Not only, but you have conspired to kill Lord Kingsley. Today, Desmond, it will be *your* demise I will be reporting."

Desmond smiled. "To the death then?"

"To the death."

Their blades clashed, the tips rattled, and the physical fight quickly met the intensity of emotions behind it. One man's force matched synchronously with the other, Desmond's ferociousness and Thayne's fervor, every collision, every clank bringing them to new heights of aggressiveness. With the sun slipping quickly away from them, their swords grinding together, the fierceness in Desmond's eyes turning to madness.

Suddenly, Rhianna appeared at left. The frenzy broke as each caught sight of her, but the break was momentary. Desmond recovered the quickest, forcing Thayne's sword, while still in hand, to the ground, and caught him with a left hook blow to the face.

"She is a pretty little whore," Desmond taunted.

The strike had little effect and Thayne was quickly recovered. The words, however, had more of an impact. He shoved Desmond back and his sword was pointed toward him once more.

*

Rhianna thought little of leaving Weathersby and Mauvreen at the edge of the woods. Her heart would not allow her to be separated from Thayne, knowing to what he had agreed. Despite knowing there was nothing she could do to help, waiting and wondering at Ravensleigh was no option to her.

Little did she know how very helpless she was, as Lydia's pistol pointed directly toward her.

"Miss Braden."

Rhianna's stomach sank at the sound of her voice and, though she did not need to turn to know to whom it belonged, she met Lydia's gaze.

"I knew there was something about you the moment you arrived," Lydia told her, disdainfully. "At first, I thought you were my husband's mistress—I even had you followed for a time—but instead you are worse! A bastard, long-lost daughter! I wonder, did you imagine you could swoop in at the last moment and steal the fortunes from his rightful and lawful family?"

"Lord Kingsley would not be facing his last moment had it not been for you," Rhianna said. "But you didn't really want it to come to that, did you? Somewhere in that black heart of yours, you care for him."

"Seems he is not the only one facing his last moment now, doesn't it? Although, this time around I have more reason to have you dead than before."

"Before?" Rhianna repeated.

"Oh, I was more than willing to see you suffer a tragic riding accident after I discovered you were in possession of the benefice. But *Wyndgate*—"

"What are you saying?"

Lydia sneered at her. "Oh, I suppose I shouldn't say 'accident'. Horses are not generally fond of being shot with a dart. My Pierson may have a knack for using a blowgun, but seeing as how that was unsuccessful, Desmond is far more skilled with a sword. Perhaps I'll let him show you just how very skilled he is when he has finished with Lord Brighton."

"Pierson used a blowgun on my horse?" Rhianna cried.

"And to think there was no evidence whatsoever after Desmond removed the dart. It would have been a very simple, unsuspecting death, had you not walked away from it."

"Why did you not try again?" Rhianna asked, hoping that in keeping Lydia talking she might find an escape.

"Desmond wanted you for himself, to put it simply."

Now, she had heard enough. "Even if you succeed in killing all of us," Rhianna told her, "*your Pierson* has been captured and is off to prison for attempted murder. No inheritance of Lord Kingsley's will release him."

Lydia's nostrils flared and her bloodshot eyes widened. "Liar!"

"I am not."

Thorngate, who had not been at an angle to see them, now heard Lydia's voice. He stepped forward, his pistol aimed at Lydia.

"Drop your pistol, Lady Kingsley!"

Addressing Thorngate and Thayne, Lydia demanded, "Drop your weapons or I will shoot her!"

Thorngate hesitated. Thayne and Desmond stood very close together, their bodies almost one in the dim light. Their struggle appeared motionless, as it in fact was.

Thayne stepped away from Desmond, pulling his sword from where he had pierced his chest. Desmond fell to the ground.

"*Desmond!*"

Lydia ran wildly toward him, her pistol firing a single shot before she dropped it to the ground. Clutching his upper arm where the bullet had grazed it, Thayne backed away as Lydia threw herself over her son's body.

Rhianna raced to Thayne's side, quickly tearing off a piece of her skirt and tying it tightly around his wounded arm. Thorngate advanced, his pistol pointed toward Lydia.

The latter shook visibly as she examined Desmond. Allowed a moment, Lydia was rapidly assured of Desmond's death and she turned first to Thayne. Then, Lydia's eyes met Rhianna's. They were as lifeless as the man who lay beneath her. The exchange was silent, but the evil emitting from Lydia was terrifying.

"Lydia Kingsley," said Thorngate, "please rise. You are hereby arrested for the attempted murders of Guilford Kingsley, Thayne Brighton, and Rhianna Braden."

Lydia's eyes last turned to Thorngate.

Expressionless.

Dead.

She rose slowly. At last, fully erect, Thorngate approached her, but she stepped back. When he started toward her again, she took another few steps back. She raised her hand at him, urging him to keep his distance. Thorngate waited, his pistol still aimed. All eyes watched as Lydia continued to back slowly toward the cliffs.

Her intentions at once obvious, Thayne ran toward her, his cry cutting through the evening air. "Lydia, no!"

He was followed quickly by Thorngate, but neither was in time. Lydia jumped.

Rhianna screamed, but she heard the cry as if it came from someone else. Then, she recognized her scream as combined with Lydia's. She clutched her chest with terror as Thayne and Thorngate fell on the ground, their arms outstretched over the ledge, grasping for Lydia Kingsley.

When Rhianna's voice silenced, there was no echo of it. All that could be heard were the wind and the waves.

Numbness set in. Even as Thayne's fingers tangled through her hair and his uninjured arm embraced her, she felt nothing. Pressing her head to his chest, Thayne shielded her from the sight of Desmond's body. And there, in the blackness, her face hidden against Thayne's breast, Rhianna kept her eyes tightly shut, gasping for air that would satisfy her lungs.

*

The blood that soaked through the arm of Brighton's white shirt caught Lord Kingsley's eye as Thayne and Rhianna entered his bedroom. Mauvreen, who had insisted that Weathersby take her to Kingsley Manor after Rhianna left, sat next to him, a basin of water beside her as she pressed a wet cloth to his forehead. Guilford had not rested since Thayne departed Kingsley Manor. Word reached him quickly as to where the night had led, and Desmond's request for a duel. Any and all hopes of keeping the concluding events from him for the night were dashed.

"Oh, my dear child!" Mauvreen laid down the cloth and ran to embrace Rhianna, as if she were truly her own child.

Rhianna, using her last ounce of energy to bring Mauvreen into her arms, pressed her body tightly against her own.

"We are well," Rhianna managed, answering the question that was foremost in the minds of all.

Weathersby sighed with relief; Mauvreen wiped away tears. Dr. Logan attempted to remove Rhianna's makeshift bandage from Thayne's upper arm, anxious to see the damage himself.

Lord Kingsley, his breathing slow and steady, but deep, and his manner bracing, patiently awaited the answers to his other questions. After Thayne appealed for the doctor to wait outside, he and Rhianna both made their way to Lord Kingsley's bedside, she on his left and he on his right. His suspicions were evident; Rhianna preferred to imagine him prepared for news of Desmond's death. Thayne's eyes confirmed thus and a deeper breath followed, as Lord Kingsley's head fell against his pillow.

"Did you kill him quickly?" he asked Thayne.

"I did," he said, his voice feeling, yet final.

Guilford nodded, his eyes low, accepting. When they rose again, he knew there was more.

"Lydia appeared," Thayne proceeded.

Lord Kingsley was at once alert. He clearly did not anticipate this.

"It was nearly that very moment," Thayne continued. "She had discovered your will and aimed her pistol at Rhianna—"

"Lord Kingsley," Rhianna interrupted, seeing this was too long a recount for him, "she jumped from the cliffs. Lord Brighton and Lord Thorngate tried to stop her. They fell to their breasts on the ground to reach out for her, but she was too quick."

She took his hand in her own and his fingers closed around hers. Visibly shocked, he hardly flinched as Mauvreen approached and again applied the cold cloth to his neck and forehead.

"I'm so very sorry," Rhianna expressed.

Silence overtook the room as Lord Kingsley contemplated this report. Some minutes went by as Rhianna watched him struggle to come to terms with the deaths of Lydia and Desmond who, no matter how wicked, were still his wife of thirty years and the boy he raised from birth.

"Let us discuss details at another time," he said at last, taking Rhianna's face in his hand. "My girls are safe. That is all that matters to me now."

Thorngate entered. Seeing the news had been given, he removed his hat and quickly offered his condolences.

"Lord Kingsley, I understand the doctor expects your health will improve," Thorngate remarked hopefully.

"There is no reason to suspect otherwise," Lord Kingsley verified. "It will be a long road, undoubtedly, but in some months' time, I expect to be back to my old self."

"Throwing dinners and balls," Mauvreen positively assured him.

"Preferably," Guilford replied, "a wedding."

Epilogue

Dearest Countess Soleil Deveraux,

It seems but yesterday that we were children together, mere acquaintances at Madame Chandelle's—how different things are! We are grown and you are a married woman. I admit that I envy you tremendously. Thayne and I still have some weeks to go. I know I have said it before, but I must say it again—I am so sorry I could not be there for your ceremony. I appreciate your understanding I could not leave Audra at such a time.

Happily, I can report that Lord Kingsley's health is vastly improved and he has only this morning told me he will allow Audra to join us on our trip to France. Audra was beside herself with delight at news of said permission, and I shall be delighted to have her with me, as well. I think it shall be an excellent distraction for her, although she is doing very well, considering her loss. Mauvreen, my childhood neighbor, as you know, has been a great source of comfort to her and will prove to be an excellent governess, I am sure of it. Since she moved into the manor they have gotten along famously, and as I prepare to move to Ravensleigh it relieves me to see Audra will be in such good hands. Of course, Lord Crispin Brighton has also been an infinite source of comfort to her, but that is something else entirely. I will save my stories there for when I see you.

Give all my love to your family. I am particularly glad to hear that Philippe is well. The moment I walk down the aisle I shall be at your side.

I remain & co,

Rhianna

"Come along, now, you've been at that letter all morning. Is it too much for an old woman to ask for you to try on your gown for its final fitting?"

Rhianna smiled at Mauvreen as she sealed up her letter, the blue-and-gold drawing room never before seeming so peaceful in all her days at Kingsley Manor. Audra drew quietly near the open window that overlooked the front approach and the spring air carried the tunes of baby sparrows in their nest above. The house was still and undisturbed by the evil that had plagued it for so many years.

"Lord Kingsley will be here any moment," Rhianna reminded her. "When I return, I promise."

"I just love to see it on you," Mauvreen returned, wistfully. "It's like seeing it on your mother all over again."

Rhianna's smile widened as she recalled the gown Hallie wore in the portrait Rhianna first saw in the lodge as a little girl—a portrait now kept safely beside her bed. Coincidentally, it was the same gown Rhianna would wear on her wedding day, accented by her mother's brooch.

"I didn't know you knew her mother, Miss Mauvreen," Audra interjected innocently.

"Oh yes," Mauvreen affirmed. "I used to be her governess when she was little like you."

Audra smiled. "I imagine she liked you, as I do. After all, if I can't have Miss Braden forever, I suppose you'll do very well as my governess."

"I have no doubt that she will," Rhianna declared. "And I hope you will both be at Ravensleigh every day."

"Of course!" Audra decreed. "*After* we return from France!"

Audra's enchantment with the prospect of seeing something beyond Thornton, England came through in her voice. The words danced from her lips and rang through the air like a bell.

A servant announced Lord Kingsley, and he entered.

He greeted all, adding, "My apologies, Miss Braden, for the delay. I just received a letter from a Mr. James Middleton whom I think would be an excellent curate for the Thornton Church."

"Indeed!"

"Mr. Middleton has been in need of a parish since the owner's son of his previous post was ordained. He comes very highly recommended and, not only, but his wife is originally from Thornton. Miss Braden, I would imagine you knew her. She used to live across the street from the church."

"Brenna?" Rhianna cried. "We lost touch so many years ago."

"Well, if you approve, Mr. and Mrs. Middleton are available to move in a month's time."

"Yes! I could imagine nothing better," Rhianna agreed.

"So it is settled. Good! We can finalize the paperwork this afternoon. When you return from France, you and all the Brighton family must come to Kingsley Manor to join us in having dinner with them."

Audra squealed with delight at the idea of new friends, paired with the mention of France and dinner with the Brightons.

Raising the cloak that was folded over his arm, Lord Kingsley asked, "So, shall we?"

"We shall."

"Where are you going?" Audra asked, as Rhianna followed Lord Kingsley to the door.

Maureen interposed. "Now, now, Miss Kingsley, mind your business. Don't you think they would have invited you if they could have brought you along?"

"We won't be long," Rhianna promised.

Audra nodded submissively and watched through the window as Rhianna and Guilford each mounted a horse and rode down the approach.

*

She had stood before Hallie's grave before, but now it was different. It was no longer the mysterious grave of an unknown woman, entreating the curiosity of her young mind to discover the secrets of a life gone by. No, rather, it was the grave of her mother, and she knelt before it a daughter, her father beside her. There, the three of them remained silently in each other's presence, their little family together in the only way possible.

The forest was quiet but for the shovel that struck the earth above Hallie's final resting place. Using the blackened tool from the remains of the lodge, Guilford dug a hole before the tombstone. Then, with several bare root roses from her satchel in hand, Rhianna placed them into the ground and covered them with the surrounding soil. The original garden may have burned to nothing in the fire that led to the cabin's ultimate collapse, but Rhianna and Guilford hoped to see it back to its original splendor in a few seasons' time.

The trees around them seemed, as always, to watch and to whisper. Rhianna felt them pleased, as Hallie would have been, to see her and Guilford together. And despite his grievous sickness, brought on by Lydia's greed and desperation, both knew that, without it, this moment would not be possible.

As she looked out over what remained of the lodge, Rhianna considered the possibility of moving Hallie to the churchyard. Over twenty years she had been buried in the woods; certainly, there would be no scandal in having her in the churchyard now. But turning to Lord Kingsley to suggest it, she bit her lip. Seeing the way he was curved low to the earth, his cloaked back arched, his grey head bent forward, his eyes as sad as they were those twenty years back, she realized Guilford could not grieve the way he needed to in the open, Thornton graveyard. Not only, but in such a circumstance there would be no visiting Hallie together, for the world could never know of their relationship as father and daughter. The notion of moving Hallie faded almost as quickly as it appeared.

These few moments' of silent reflection passed until, dusting as much of the dirt from her hands as possible, Rhianna took one of

Guilford's hands in her own. She smiled faintly at him, presenting him with his top hat. She was happy to see him smile in return as he received it and they rose to their feet. The expression told her what she had been hoping all along: that in a relationship with a daughter the world denied, Guilford Kingsley was at peace with the small amount of harmony that life had offered him.

*

The night before the wedding, the Brightons arrived at Kingsley Manor. It was there they would stay, before traveling together to Thornton Church for the morning ceremony. Quickly, they shuffled, one after another, into the Kingsley drawing room, excitement billowing in the air. Smiles were wide and appeared quite permanent, and there was not one who seemed willing to attempt a removal. The occasion was altogether too cheerful; the smiles would remain into the days ahead.

Only Thayne and Rhianna stayed behind. Slipping from the crowd before ever he entered, Thayne met Rhianna on the portico of Kingsley Manor.

"I wonder how long before they realize we are gone," Rhianna smirked.

"Much too quickly," Thayne assured her, raising the back of her hand to his lips.

"You are quite the gentleman tonight."

Thayne grinned mischievously. "*Tomorrow* I shall not be so content to kiss your hand."

He leaned in to kiss her properly, but movement in the window of the drawing room captured her eye and twisted her neck. Turning to the object of her attention, Thayne shook his head at the sight of Crispin and Audra as they twirled and spun, no doubt to the tune of a song only they could hear, laughing in a swell of infatuation.

"Will you tell her?" Thayne asked his bride.

Rhianna turned her eyes to him again, this time without distraction. Thayne's stubble of black beard arrested her and she wondered how she ever looked aside previously.

"When she is older," she mused. "I can't tell you how awful it is, hearing her call me 'Miss Braden.'"

"Mmm," he considered, examining her from all angles. "No, that won't do, will it, *Miss Rhianna Kingsley?*"

Rhianna laughed at the sound of her birth name, but Thayne shook his head.

"No, that won't do, either."

"Won't it?" she replied.

"No, indeed, I rather think Lady Rhianna Brighton suits you better."

He smiled at the sound of it, and she returned the gesture.

"I am beginning to wonder at my habit of changing names so frequently," she quipped.

"Well, then," he told her, leaning in for the kiss his lips demanded, "let us make this the last time."

In the mood for more Crimson Romance? Check out *The Reluctant Debutante* by Becky Lower at CrimsonRomance.com.

ABOUT THE AUTHOR

Amanda L. V. Shalaby lives just outside of New York City with her husband, Matthew, her two Shih Tzu dogs, Huntley Rochester and Isabella Jane, and a Persian cat named Sebastian. She is a member of The Romance Writers of America (RWA). *Rhianna* is her debut novel.